BEGIN, END, BEGIN

A #Love Oz YA Anthology

Amie Kaufman, Melissa Keil,
Will Kostakis, Ellie Marney,
Jaclyn Moriarty, Michael Pryor,
Alice Pung, Gabrielle Tozer,
Lili Wilkinson, Danielle Binks

EDITED BY DANIELLE BINKS

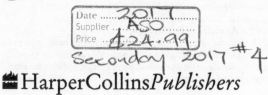 **HarperCollins**Publishers

HarperCollins_Publishers_

First published in Australia in 2017
by HarperCollins_Publishers_ Australia Pty Limited
ABN 36 009 913 517
harpercollins.com.au

HarperCollins_Publishers_
Level 13, 201 Elizabeth Street, Sydney NSW 2000, Australia
Unit D1, 63 Apollo Drive, Rosedale, Auckland 0632, New Zealand
A 53, Sector 57, Noida, UP, India
77–85 Fulham Palace Road, London W6 8JB, United Kingdom
2 Bloor Street East, 20th floor, Toronto, Ontario M4W 1A8, Canada
10 East 53rd Street, New York NY 10022, USA

A CiP record is available from the National Library of Australia.

Cover and internal illustrations by Kate Pullen of The Letterettes
Typeset in Bembo Std by Kirby Jones
Printed and bound in Australia by Griffin Press
The papers used by HarperCollins in the manufacture of this book are a natural,
recyclable product made from wood grown in sustainable plantation forests.
The fibre source and manufacturing processes meet recognised international
environmental standards, and carry certification.

Contents

Dear Reader: a note from the editor   vii

One Small Step …   1
Amie Kaufman

I Can See the Ending   25
Will Kostakis

In a Heartbeat   67
Alice Pung

First Casualty   85
Michael Pryor

Sundays   121
Melissa Keil

Missing Persons   155
Ellie Marney

Oona Underground   179
Lili Wilkinson

The Feeling From Over Here   207
Gabrielle Tozer

Last Night at the Mount Solemn Observatory   253
Danielle Binks

Competition Entry #349   279
Jaclyn Moriarty

Dear Reader,

Books are family. Books are community.

Characters come into our lives, and we're invited to walk beside them. An author welcomes us into the world they've created, a view into their mind's eye.

Any book you hold was nurtured by many hands: early readers, agents, publishers, editors, illustrators, designers, type-setters, printers, publicists, librarians, teachers … the list goes on and on.

Books create communities — bringing together characters, ideas, writers, words and readers. This book was created *by* community.

In 2015, the Australian Library and Information Association (ALIA) surveyed public libraries to find out the list of Top Ten most borrowed books. It was disappointing to find only two Australian titles featured in the young adult category, which was overwhelmed by American books, many bolstered by blockbuster film adaptations.

Our community's response was the creation of #LoveOzYA — a hashtag coined to harness the conversation, and talk about our love of Australian young adult literature, to champion our stories.

LoveOzYA was born from readers and writers and all who love Australia's national youth literature. It was not born out of patriotism or a rejection of international voices — far from it. LoveOzYA has been about the inclusion of voices. And it has been a movement, as the name suggests, about love.

This was the spur to create #LoveOzYA — not only an anthology, but an entire movement devoted to the promotion of Australian creators and their stories.

This book is a love letter to that movement, and all who got behind it.

I hope you enjoy it, as much as we loved creating it.

— Danielle Binks

Before ...

'You have a letter from Harvard,' my mum said, standing at the kitchen counter and tearing open a foil packet for lunch.

'I didn't know the postal service made it all the way to Mars,' Dad chimed in, raising his hands in pre-emptive self-defence. He's been making that joke at least since I was born, and presumably longer — so that's a minimum seventeen years in circulation, or nine, if you're counting in Martian.

'Oh,' I said, careful to keep my tone neutral. 'Usual offer?'

'Usual offer,' Mum agreed. 'They have a great medical program. And they have a really excellent student–teacher ratio. A lot of the teaching happens face-to-face, that's very rare on Earth.'

'That ...' I struggled for a response that didn't sound completely unenthusiastic. I wasn't in the mood for the usual Talk About My Future. 'That's good to know, I bet that's important.' I was already backing towards the door.

'Zaida, this can't wait any longer,' she said. 'The networks are jostling for your first interview, once you've made your decision. Harvard's the best offer yet. There really isn't much to think about.'

'I have inspection duty.' And I needed to get out of that conversation. We'd been dancing around this issue for months, and the walls were narrowing in on me. I was in a world of *hurry up*, when all I wanted to do was slow down.

Dad called after me as I grabbed my gear from the tub by the door. My pressure suit is made just for me, tight enough to stop my body wanting to explode all over the place in the lower pressure outside the habs. (I kid, I kid. I wouldn't explode. I'd just bleed from my eyes, then die, relax.)

'Don't forget you need to record your diary tonight, Zaida. We have to transmit it before bedtime.'

I couldn't help myself; I snapped back: 'Is there any chance either of you is more interested in *me* than my media appointments?'

The door hummed closed on their joint protests and I bolted to the end of the hallway, getting around the corner before they could decide on who had to follow me and deal with me this time.

Ugh. The Diary. Yet another expectation to stack up alongside all the others, of which my future university choice was not the least. I hated the fact that even as I was making my escape, I was mentally slotting in the time I'd need to do my hair and makeup before I sat down for a super-casual chat with a few billion of my besties back on Earth.

I understood why people were interested in the diary, and I didn't blame them. But even though I'd have handed off that duty in a heartbeat if I could, I can't change the way things are: I was the first person born on Mars. I'm the one they want to hear about.

Now …

Our red world spreads out before me, the smooth plain the colony's situated on giving way to gently rising ground to the north, topped off by a faraway, craggy mountain range. To the east lie vast acres of solar arrays and the tops of the water pumps, which stand up above the fields of reflective black panels like giant scarecrows. The sky's a pinkish orange, and I can see a dust cloud off to the west I don't like the look of, but for now it's far enough away that we can get to work.

I thumb the button for the communicator on my suit. 'KK, if you could go anywhere on Earth, where would it be?'

My best friend considers the question for a long moment. 'Arashiyama,' she says eventually. 'It's a bamboo grove near Kyoto. The buildings go all the way up to the edge, but they preserved it, and my Jiji says when you're inside, you can pretend there's nobody else in the world. It's fifteen metres high, twenty in some places. What about you?'

'Where wouldn't I go?' I say, jumping down from my place atop the curve of the dirt mound hiding our buildings and making my way along to the next camera I need to check. 'Ireland, because it's the greenest, wettest place I can imagine.'

'So, so yes,' she agrees. 'Green hills and mist, it doesn't even sound real.'

'And the Australian outback, definitely.'

'But that's just big and red and dry,' she points out, laughing. 'You haven't seen enough of that?'

'I bet it's different.' I go silent, because suddenly I'm wondering if I should have raised Earth at all, given her odds of making it there.

When I glance down at her, she's stopped outside Airlock 742, one up from where we exited the habs, and she's leaning in to look at it. 'Everything okay, KK?'

'The seal doesn't look right,' she says. 'I don't think —'

The next second the airlock blows, the door snapping open right into her face. She spins away from it and the door collides with her power and air at the back of her suit, a cord whipping free and snaking around like a living thing as it vents her precious oxygen.

Before ...

I made tracks for the greenhouses, keeping the speed on. The hallway to that section was long and dimly lit, the ceiling a curved arch cut into the dirt and rock above it, the lights fixed every ten metres or so, powered by the huge solar arrays above. We're underground here — almost the whole colony is underground, safely shielded because radiation is not your friend. Every angle is calculated, every line efficient.

I think my parents wish they could plan me just as carefully, no part of me without a purpose, no part of me wasted. Maximum return for their efforts.

There are plenty of structures aboveground, but if you just flew over the top of us you'd never guess there were a thousand and some people beneath it all — watching shows and school lessons sent from Earth in batches, tending greenhouses, running labs, living life. My parents and I are just three of them.

I was a total accident, obviously. A *happy accident*, my parents always correct me. I think it's kind of hilarious, to be honest. Mum was the first colony doctor. You'd think that out of everyone available, she'd be pretty clear on how birth control works, right?

She was one of the original eight on the very first settlement mission. It was a one-way trip, and though the plan was for others to follow, whether that happened was always going to depend on what they found when they got here, and how the first mission went. My mum's the kind of person who picks a course, then commits to it full tilt.

Dad came in the third wave, and by the time they got together and then *got-together-boom-chicka-wow-wow*, the colony was one hundred strong.

And baby made one hundred and one!

Congratulations, it's a girl!

Mum ended up giving instructions to Dad (who was then the colony's only nurse) through gritted teeth as they got me delivered between them, with ninety-eight adoptive uncles and aunts busy hand-sewing baby clothes and blankets and toys, because the colony supplies didn't have anything baby-sized. And here, you can't exactly order something for next-day delivery. Meanwhile, the whole of Earth held its breath as it waited for updates on a seventeen-minute time delay.

The very first Martian. That's me. Hi.

They held vigils while Mum was in labour, presidents and prime ministers made official statements, the heads of pretty much every religion prayed. Humanity didn't mean to get pregnant, but once it happened, they were all in. It wasn't your average entrance into the world — any world — is what I'm saying.

No pressure.

Everyone was so invested, after all that caring. So it turned out I didn't just have ninety-eight uncles and aunts. I had nearly nine billion. And they all still want to know what I'm doing *all of the time*. I took my first steps on camera, spoke my first words on camera, and I still make video diaries to camera, which apparently rate through the roof back on good old Earth.

My parents never meant to have a kid who was a celebrity, any more than they meant to be celebrities themselves. And I don't know if they keep it up out of some weird sense of duty, or they like it, or what it's about, really.

Just that nobody's ever asked me if I'd like to get off the ride, and my parents make sure I keep on sending back those diaries, inviting everyone out there into our lives. It's just habit now — whatever happens throughout my day, there's always a tiny part of my mind tracking whether I should snap a selfie, figuring out how I'll caption or describe this bit of news. My updates are followed by a few billion people, which is even weirder, because in all my life, I haven't met much more than a thousand.

I waved to a couple of those people with my free hand as I made my way along the hallway — Josh Ribar and Thanh Lê — and Josh made finger guns, kapowing me as we passed. Thanh was talking at top speed as usual, bouncing along beside Josh — Earth has three times our gravity, so it's much easier to bounce here — and Josh was looking at me instead of listening.

Mum's worried Josh is trying to spend too much time around me. I haven't told her she has *nothing* to worry about. If I do, she'll just find something else to fixate on, right?

Now ...

Keiko huddles on the ground as I race towards her, dropping to my knees to skid in beside her. Her lips are moving, but I can't hear anything over my headset — her power cord's severed and nothing's getting through. Her eyes are huge, mouth open as if she's already struggling for air, though I know she has a few minutes sealed inside her suit with her.

I grab at the cord, my gloved fingers fumbling as I yank it in close to my helmet, trying to see if the auto shut-off has worked. It's stopped wriggling, so I think it has — I can only hope there's enough air left in there to keep her going until we get inside. But we have more problems than the air. Without power, the heating coils in her suit will already be cooling.

I reach for her elbow to help her to her feet, and she shakes off my hand, big eyes trying silently to communicate something to me. She flicks her gaze down, and when I follow it, I realise she has her right hand clapped over her left forearm in a death grip. The door must have torn the suit.

Which means she probably doesn't have a couple of minutes worth of air at all.

And then, because we're not already having a bad enough day, the first eddies of dust start swirling in around us. The storm must have been moving a lot faster than I figured.

This is really, really bad.

Before ...

Thanh's already accepted a scholarship to Oxford, and Josh wants to study somewhere in Europe as well. All the first-gen Mars kids are getting sweet offers, and now it's time for us to decide whether we'll stick here or see the homeworld.

They all talk about it, but none of them has asked *me* what I'll be doing. I'm always slightly set apart — and I'm not even sure I realised it until recently. I have a unique place, even here on Mars, and I just felt like it was normal to be slightly on the outer. But even here, among my friends, there's a special shape

I'm meant to fit into, trimming off any parts of me that might stray outside the lines.

University's the decision that's causing all the most fun discussions at our hab lately. Mum and Dad say it's a huge opportunity for me, and we have to make the most of it.

Hear that? It's an opportunity for *me*, but *we* have a decision to make.

Only a few people have ever returned from Mars to Earth, but it's possible, just very expensive. The gravity's a problem too, of course, but my parents have had me exercising on resistance machines literally since I was a baby, building the muscle and bone density I'd need for full gravity. Theirs has long since gone, and they'll never make the return trip. For me, it would be a slightly uncomfortable transition, but an achievable one.

So now I'm seventeen, it's the question on everyone's lips. We have the money, from all the press. But I have my own money, as well — my gran left it to me. *For whatever you want*, she said in the vid.

But I've never known what that was.

I shoved university, Earth and my parents out of my mind as I turned the corner towards the greenhouse and saw Keiko waiting for me. She flashed me a quick grin, we bumped knuckles, and headed inside. Her long braid swayed as she held the door open for me with her hip, and I squeezed past her.

Keiko is my best friend. We've been that way since the second day we met.

Once I was born, the timetable on sending families to Mars changed, and Keiko was the first one up with her parents. We were both four, and apparently I screamed my head off when I saw her. I'd never seen anyone my own size before, and I didn't know what she was.

So the first day was kind of a write-off, but we've been inseparable since that second day. Keiko's the only one who doesn't care who or what I am, apart from just being me. She's been around way too long to be impressed. You'd think things would be simple around Keiko, right? They're not.

Mum worries about keeping me away from Josh, but truth be told … she'd be better off worrying about Keiko.

Problem is, Keiko has no more idea of this fact than Mum does. I've never mustered the guts to tell her.

We made our way into the long, narrow greenhouse in companionable silence, breathing in the damp air. I love the greenhouse, so different to anywhere else. Lamps hang from the ceiling, plants burst from their shelves, filling every available inch, leaving you wet where you brush past them. It's the only place inside the settlement where you can find even a little bit of chaos. You can't plan for exactly how plants will grow, after all. This place manages to break the rules, when nothing else does.

The greenhouse is underground just like the rest of the complex, but it never takes much to imagine it's a jungle somewhere on Earth. The plants aren't just for eating — they also play a part in the O_2 recyc program, and a lot of people come here simply to see some green. Turns out that's important to humans, even on the red planet.

We stopped without needing to consult, to check on a plant we've dubbed Horace. He's really a small tree now, spindly clumps of moss clinging to his trunk. In years past he served as a secret mailbox, where we'd leave each other little bits and pieces hidden among his roots. Buried treasure, we called it, because that was as close as two kids on Mars came to X marking the spot.

Now …

I flick my communicator to the broadcast channel as I wrap my arms around Keiko's waist, helping her to her feet. The airlock shouldn't have hurt her — it's a movie myth that those things blow with incredible force, usually before some poor astronaut's sucked out into space. But I can see its jagged edge where the seal broke, and that's what did the damage.

'Central, this is Zaida, we have a breach.' I can hear the high, sharp note of fear in my voice. I ignore all the formalities, don't bother hailing properly. I just want another voice down the line. I want to know I'm not alone, facing this. Forget chaos, forget colouring outside the lines. I want order and rules, a procedure to follow, a way to fix this.

Marguerite Syvertson's voice is in my ear a moment later. 'Zaida, go ahead.'

I can't see Airlock 741 through the dust cloud that's blown in — the world is red, and Keiko's shaking in my arms as I walk us slowly forward. My heart is pounding. If that rip gets any bigger, if her suit loses integrity — I push the thought out of my mind.

'Airlock 742 blew during inspection. Inner doors looked like they held. Keiko's suit's damaged. I'm walking us back to 741 right now.'

'Okay, keep breathing, Zaida,' Marguerite says, soothing and calm in my ear, though she and I both know the appropriate reaction is to freak right out. 'Remember your training. I'm mobilising a medical crew.'

But the airlock's taking forever to show up. Am I definitely walking in the right direction?

I think so.

I have to be, 742 was to my right.

But which way was I facing when I started to walk? Towards the habs, or away?

Before ...

'You have a line right between your eyebrows,' Keiko said, giving Horace a pat with one hand, and looking across at me.

I immediately pressed a finger between my brows, trying to smooth it out. 'Just Mum,' I said. 'Apparently Earth's calling again, still wants its Martian back.'

'Who this time?'

'Harvard.'

'Is that in North America?'

'I think so. Good med school, I hear.'

She didn't reply, and we fell silent. I never know how to discuss this problem with Keiko. My parents are deadset on trying to choose my future back on Earth, convinced they know what university and course will suit their idea of who I'm going to be.

But Keiko's father's pushing just as hard for her to stay on Mars with him. He says she has a family duty. Neither of us is getting what we want, and neither of us looks like we'll be getting a vote anytime soon.

We reached the small, dry platform at the end of the greenhouse where we'd change before letting ourselves into the pressurisation section. Keiko made herself smile, reaching for the good mood we'd abruptly lost. 'Did your dad make the joke about the postal service coming out all this way?'

'He'd have given that up years ago if you didn't keep on laughing at it,' I pointed out.

'Then you're stuck with it,' she informed me cheerily, peeling off her shirt over her head. I forced my eyes down and away, though I knew exactly what Keiko looked like in her underwear. I've seen her change thousands of times. Her skin's a lighter brown than mine, smooth and perfect, and she's more straight lines than curves, narrow hips and long legs. Her underwear's identical to mine, simple and grey, because it's colony issue. But since I figured out that I'd like to see her in it as often as possible, it feels kind of squicky, looking at her without her knowing that.

Once or twice I've wondered if she *does* know — she said the other day that Katie Telgar looked cute with her hair cut short, and I turned that single comment over for hours, searching for clues in it. But I don't know whether Keiko plays for my team, and I'm terrified to ask, because it's a small world up here, and she's my very best friend.

It's not like she'd care which variety of human I'd most prefer to see in their underwear, but I'm pretty sure it'd be weird around *anyone* once you'd told them you like them, and they'd told you they don't like you back, not that way.

I don't have a lot of experience with this kind of thing, but I think that's how it goes.

Now …

Keiko's shuffling in front of me, all her concentration on keeping her suit intact. This is her personal nightmare. I have the money to get to Earth because my grandmother left it to me. Keiko has it — not that she can use it — because her mother died of a suit breach on a mining expedition, and the colony paid compensation. And I can't even comfort her, not without a working radio. She's hyperventilating — I can feel her ribs heaving against my arms — and I'm not far behind her. My heart's drumming in my ears, and I try to make my movements smooth, where they want to be panicked and jerky.

Keiko's legs suddenly start to give, and she sags in my arms, head swaying from side to side. Her right hand begins to peel away from her left arm, and I clap my own left hand over it, holding her ripped suit in place like a vice. That means I have to keep her moving with just one arm wrapped around her ribs.

A moment later her foot catches on a rock, and we both stumble and fall together, landing in a tangled heap on the ground that drives the air from my lungs, sending up more dust to join the cloud all around us. My arm lands under her and pain shoots up into my shoulder, but I force myself to hold on.

I have to hold on.

I wouldn't know which way was up now, without the ground beneath me, pressing into my sore shoulder. Red dirt's scattered across it, red dust hanging in the air as the cloud moves through, every possible landmark invisible. I wriggle to get my arm out from under Keiko, keeping hold of the rip in her suit as she lolls onto her back. Her lashes are fluttering, and now she's the one with a line between her brows, looking up at me in confusion.

She pushes onto her elbows, trying to get free of me.

'Keiko, no! Hold still!' I'm shouting — as she keeps trying to wriggle free, I'm screaming — but her comms are out and she can't hear me. I'm screaming inside my own private little world, stuck inside my suit. I'm screaming on the broadcast channel, I think, but Marguerite doesn't say anything, doesn't risk my concentration.

I have my helmet pressed against Keiko's, as close as I can get. Begging her with my eyes to understand me.

She stares up at me for a long moment, then goes obediently still.

Slowly, painfully, I start to pull the two of us to our feet. Now I have no idea which direction the habs are in.

And we're running out of time.

Before ...

I wriggled into my pressure suit, yanking it up my legs by degrees and over my hips. It has heating elements woven through the inner layer to guard against the freeze-your-toes-off temperatures out there, an O_2 tank and a power unit strapped to my back in a slim casing, and a clear helmet to offer 360-degree views of the red, red world outside.

I thumbed the button on my comm, and tested the direct channel first. 'Opera is a form of music sent to torture us,' I intoned.

I saw Keiko's shoulders shake as she laughed, and she reached for her own button. 'Zaida Bedri has no culture,' she replied. 'Test complete.'

I thumbed the button in the other direction as we made our way through into the airlock. 'Central, this is Zaida Bedri, ID MCA101. I'm with Keiko Ando, ID MCA236. We're heading into Airlock 741, and then outside for visual-inspection duty. Waiting on your clearance, please.'

There was a moment's silence as the door swung closed behind us, and Keiko checked to make sure it was latched properly. Then I heard the warm tones of Marguerite Syvertson down the line. 'Afternoon, ladies. This is Central confirming clearance for MCA101 and MCA236. Keiko, just let me hear your channel, please?'

Keiko spoke — after all, if something went wrong, you wouldn't want just one person's broadcast working. 'Keiko Ando, MCA236, ready to go outside and do some A+ inspecting. Dust should fear me.'

Marguerite was laughing when she replied, 'Out you go, ladies. I have your beacons on the monitor, sing out if you need us.'

I thanked her, and switched back to private. No matter how many times we'd done this, there were some safety protocols you never missed. 'Okay for airlock, KK?'

'Okay, Zeebee,' she confirmed, giving me the thumbs-up. 'You want to selfie before we go?' Keiko's as used to my routine as I am.

'Nah, on the way in. Looks more Martian with the dust all over our suits.' I smacked the button with my open palm, and the pressure slowly changed around us, until we'd equalised with the atmosphere outside. Once the sensor gave them the all clear, the outer doors swung open of their own accord, and we made our way out.

The thing about Mars is that it's full of dust, and that stuff gets *everywhere*.

Huge areas like the solar arrays have systems to clear the dust, but when it comes to small areas, you really have to do it by hand. So, once school's done for the day, this is one of our duties. Every minute accounted for, everything on a list, every moment governed by a rule or procedure — for our own safety, of course. That's life on Mars.

Still, life's what you make of it, and I don't mind the work — mostly I can pair up with Keiko on the roster, and it makes up some cash to spend on the imports our parents don't think are necessary.

We split, working our way along the outside of the mound that covers the building in each direction, inspecting camera fittings and portals in turn, pulling brushes from our belts to sweep them clean if they needed a little TLC. When I had to get to something up high, I jumped, grabbing at the curve of the roof and scrambling up. That's one thing I think I'd never get used to on Earth — I could only jump a third as high there. Brings a new meaning to the term 'earthbound'.

We're pretty much caught up now.

I was about to ask Keiko, like the idiot I am, where she'd like to go if she was on Earth, and she was going to tell me about a bamboo grove in Kyoto.

And a minute after that, my carefully ordered life was going to turn to chaos.

Airlock 742 was going to blow.

Now, now, now …
I can't leave her, because I can't trust her to keep the pressure on her suit, so I'm forced to bring her with me, walking her in front of me like a giant puppet as I stumble along in zero visibility, searching for the buildings and safety. She's doing her best to move her arms and legs, but she's almost a dead weight, and since she doesn't know what I'm trying to do — she's only half conscious — most of the time she's more harm than help.

I walk us in each direction in turn, because I know we can't be more than fifteen paces from the curve of the buildings. Once I've done my fifteen, I swivel what I desperately hope is a hundred and eighty degrees, then return and try the next direction.

I do this six times, over and over, forcing myself to stay calm, ignoring the fact that I'm crying now, that my nose is running, not that there's a thing I can do about it inside my helmet. It's starting to fog up because of all the moisture, a drop of water running down the centre of my vision.

And finally, *finally*, the most beautiful thing I've ever seen in my life looms up ahead of me. A big, rectangular sign: AIRLOCK 741.

I pound the release button with my fist, and we stumble in together, the doors taking an eternity to close behind us. I feel the pressure shift, and I'm sobbing inside my helmet, turning Keiko in my arms so I can check her face. Tears stream down her cheeks too, and she's heaving for breath, her brown skin turning slowly grey.

Abruptly the doors through to the greenhouse swing open, and the lush, green plants are right there in front of us, Horace swaying slightly from the breeze of the doors. I grab for the release on my helmet and yank it off, dropping it to the ground, the headset going with it. I unlatch Keiko's for her with shaking hands.

She's still breathing. She's still breathing. She's still breathing.

The words echo around my head like a train on a circular track, rattling the same message over and over. *Still alive, still alive, still alive.*

My legs fold, and the pair of us sink down to the floor. The medics are coming. My parents are coming. All I can do now is wait, let her breathe.

Then the doors at the far end fly open, and both my parents — the medics — come pounding in, followed by a sea of adult legs. I don't bother looking up to check who they belong to.

Big hands lift me away from Keiko, and my mother kneels to lean over her, pressing an oxygen mask to her lips.

It's hours later when I'm allowed into the infirmary. 'Allowed' is a stretch, in fact. My mum's gone home to eat, and her relief, Dr Lu, is busy enough that I can sneak on by. They let me wait outside, and they did tell me she was okay, but until I see her, *I* won't be okay.

I scuttle into Keiko's room and the door hums closed behind me, and when I turn to look at her, she's horribly pale under the bright lights, but she's *looking at me*, and she's smiling, and my heart wants to beat straight out of my chest in relief.

'Hey,' she whispers.

'Hey.' I'm suddenly not sure what to say, weirdly shy. I go for safe territory — teasing. 'Look, I don't know how to tell you this, but Horace saw you making a scene in the greenhouse before, and I think he's a little taken aback. He thought you were tough, you know?'

She laughs, a proper laugh, and I sag back against the door. Now it's my legs' turn to stop working.

'If you take a selfie with me right now, I'll kill you,' she says, still smiling, though her voice is weak.

'Are you okay?' I whisper.

'I am,' she says. 'I promise, I'm fine. Maybe not if it'd been much longer, but you did it, Zee.' Her voice drops lower. 'Come over here.'

I close the distance between us, sitting on the edge of the bed, and I reach for her hands, taking them in mine. She feels so warm, so alive. With a tug she brings me nearer, and I curl down to frame her face with my hands, press my forehead against hers, soak in the fact that she's *here*, that she's okay.

And a moment later, I don't know how, my lips are on hers.

Lightning surges through me, and my brain fries, and it's like every atom of me is on fire, tugging towards her. It's the most dizzying sensation I've ever had, and her hands are on my shoulders, mine still cupping her face, and this is everything I've imagined, over and over.

But then she makes a soft sound, and I realise this is *Keiko*, and everything screeches to a halt.

What am I doing?

I sit up straight, jumping back like she's red hot, and for a long, silent moment we stare at each other. 'Um,' I say, my cheeks burning, always at my most eloquent in moments of total, horrifying disaster.

'Oh,' she says, not much better. But she sounds more surprised than anything else.

'Do you think you can just stop existing if you wish really, really hard?' I murmur, desperately wanting to look away from her, but finding I can't.

Her reply is gentle. 'Zaida, is this what you want?'

The words echo in the silence between us.

Yes, this is what I really want.

And in this moment, I realise this might be the first time I've ever really thought about that. I'm just so used to thinking about what everyone else wants, and how I'm going to handle it, how I'm going to make it work.

I know what my parents want. What the colony wants. What billions of people on Earth want. I know what everyone who has a stake in my life wants. When the freaking *Pope* prays at your birth, you feel a responsibility to get it right for people.

But what *I* want? Separate from all those other people, outside the mix of obligation and opinion and expectation?

Zaida, is this what you want?

'Yes,' I say.

'Okay then,' she replies, her lips curving to a slow smile.

And then we kiss again. And it's amazing.

Thankfully, we've stopped by the time Dr Lu sticks her head in the door to check on Keiko, her brows lifting at the sight of me sitting on the bed with Keiko's hand folded in mine. 'I didn't know I had an extra patient,' she says. 'She needs sleep tonight, Zaida. Five more minutes, then home you go.'

The door hums, and suddenly I'm a little shy about looking back at Keiko.

The real world just showed up. We both just remembered we have to decide what to do with this thing that was born between us only a few minutes ago. I can't think what to say, so I kiss her again, real quick, just because I want to one more time.

She's smiling when our lips part. 'So, Harvard, huh?'

My brain's still on kissing, and I don't understand what she means.

'I think that's what we were talking about, right?' she says, still smiling. 'Before we went outside?'

I don't know why we're talking about it again now, but I answer anyway. I'll talk about whatever she wants, really. It's Keiko. 'It's what Mum wants. It'll be so much worse than here. You think the media's bad now, it'll be beyond bad there. But I can't see how to get out of it.' Getting out of it matters a whole lot more, suddenly. Because now I have something that's all my own, a part of myself I want to protect.

'It doesn't have to be so bad,' she says quietly. 'They can only chase you if they can recognise you.'

'Is there anyone alive who doesn't know my face?' I ask. 'And I'm going to stand out anyway. I'm Martian tall, that makes me distinctive.'

'So you're tall,' she replies. 'Me too. We could cut our hair. Dye it green, get contacts, get some mods. There are ways.'

'We?' I echo, and she smiles, and lifts our joined hands so she can kiss my knuckles. A shiver races up my arm, straight to a place between my shoulder blades. 'But what about your dad?'

She doesn't answer the question. 'Who would you be,' she says, 'if you weren't going to be Zaida Bedri, future doctor, future spokesperson for Mars, future saviour of humanity?'

'I'm beginning to realise I have no idea,' I admit. 'I never thought about just *not* being any of those things. But I think I need to find out.'

We kiss again. She has really soft lips. 'How do you want to find out?' she asks.

'Well,' I say. 'I'm noticing that when I just stop worrying about everyone else, stop thinking so hard and do what seems right, it goes pretty well.'

'If this is an example of that, I like how it's going,' she says.

'Could you …' I hardly want to ask it. 'Would you want to go to Earth? Would he let you?'

'You know,' she says slowly. 'I love my dad. Love him to pieces. But I think this is my decision. Maybe I don't want to go to Earth forever, but I want to see what it's like.'

'Who knows what we want to do forever,' I say. 'Everyone wants us to decide what to be right now, to know what path we want to start down, what path we'll stick to for the rest of our lives. But we're *seventeen*.'

'So maybe we don't pick a path just yet,' she suggests.

'That's what I'm thinking,' I say slowly.

For whatever you want, my grandmother insisted, when she sent the money. And maybe this is what she meant. For what *I* want. Not what everybody else wants for me.

'So what do we do instead?' she asks.

'Perhaps we do dye our hair green,' I say. 'Disappear for a while. Take a year off. Travel. Figure out who we are when we're not being told who to be.'

'Where would we go?' Keiko asks, twining her fingers through mine.

'We could start with a bamboo forest,' I say.

And she smiles.

I Can See the Ending

WILL KOSTAKIS

It's different, when you know it's ending. You have the chance to look at it properly, really study it. Whatever was weird at first that became normal becomes weird again. You start to miss it when you haven't quite lost it yet. And you have to work hard to stay present, really appreciate it, which only leads to more proper looking, more studying and more weirdness …

Sunday mornings, the centre plays classical music for the shoppers who aren't here yet. Workers wear baggy jumpers over their uniforms as they rearrange displays behind shuttered shopfronts. Some talk to themselves, some dance.

Nina doesn't dance. She doesn't work retail either, she says she's allergic. She leans against a tall fridge and sips her smoothie. She has a navy-blue streak dyed into her hair. It's nothing new — she's cycled through coloured streaks for as long as I've known her — I'm just noticing it again. Along with the name badge that reads *Damien*, and the scar on her cheek she calls Foreboding Backstory, but really, the doctor just nicked her during the C-section.

When the centre closed the food court to make way for some European clothing chain, we were banished to the basement with homewares and electronics everyone can buy cheaper online. Nina and I are from two different worlds. I work the register at Phat Buns, a twelve-year-old's greasy fever dream, and she's the teen queen of the juice-bar island HealthiU. Their smoothies come with activated almonds, standard. For an extra three dollars at Phats, we substitute our signature phat buns for deep-fried crumbed chicken fillets. But that said, for six hellish hours every Sunday, we're unlikely allies, trading fries for smoothies, triple cheeseburgers for fruit salads. And today, we're over.

Phat Buns has been flirting with the idea that I'm too expensive to work weekends, and like the person who unfriends you on Facebook when a birthday notification reminds them they don't really like you, Tilly called on my eighteenth last week to let me know she was yanking me from the Sunday roster. She offered me Thursdays after school, which I refused because one, a six-hour shift after a six-period day sounded like hell, and two, it wouldn't be the same. I could forget casually eating fistfuls of nuggets at the counter and taking extra-long breaks in the walk-in with free soft-serves — weekday managers lack all chill. And Nina wouldn't be there.

She squints over at me. 'Adam, you look bored,' she says.

'I am.'

She sighs like I've just revealed some heavy truth, then she pushes off the fridge, discards her drink and reaches for a rag. She wipes down the bench with all the enthusiasm of, well, an eighteen-year-old wiping down a bench. She gets me. We get each other. I wonder if we'd be friends if we met in any other place, if we went to the same school or were invited to the same birthday party. Are we friends because we're trapped together, or is there more to us than fries and smoothies?

Will we be friends after I'm gone? Can we? I mean, is it possible that our friendship could extend beyond short bursts of conversation, metres apart? Or even further, to maybe ...

'How's your girlfriend?' Karl asks from the back.

I don't bother looking at him. 'Shut up, Karl.'

Everyone who works Sundays acts like Nina and I are inevitable, like a guy and a chick can't have solid banter that builds for years and goes nowhere. I guess part of me must have believed them, because now it feels so ... unfinished. Even though it never actually started.

'You hungry?'

I turn. Karl is hunched over the grill, checking the temperature of various breakfast meats with a needled instrument. When he's done, he stacks them on an opened muffin to make one of his towering breakfast monstrosities. My stomach churns.

'I'm good.'

He's not fazed, more for him. He's been back crew for the two years I've worked at Phats. Recently promoted, he's exercising his managerial right to grow a beard. *Beard* is probably too strong a word. There are patches.

'You ready to open?' Karl asks.

'I'm sure we'll survive,' I say.

He chews with his mouth open. A bit of meat almost escapes, and he guides it back with a light touch. I tear my eyes away, back to the front, to Nina. What if she was my girlfriend? I wonder what shape dating her might take. Without meaning to, I live it: the two of us sitting against the concrete brick wall of the service passageway, shoulders touching and ...

I fall back into my body, and Nina feels too far away.

'Oi,' I call.

She stops wiping down the bench. 'What?'

I ask her when she finishes work.

'Quarter past two.'

I finish at two. That gives me enough time to run some water through my hair.

I ask if she has plans.

The service passageway is her idea. She says it's like seeing the world's seams. The shopping centre's glossy white walls and faux-marble trimmings vanish. The passageway's just concrete bricks and exposed piping. We find a spot far enough from the bin that it doesn't smell like garbage. She brings the smoothies, I bring the burgers and chips. I sit and she sits close. Our shoulders touch.

It's like that jarring moment when you see a scene from the trailer in the actual film, and you're pulled out of the action for a sec. It's enough for me to lose grip on the conversation. She finishes her anecdote — someone called Ed found the goose behind the woodshed — and she makes a face like she's expecting a laugh. I laugh.

'So, Adam,' she says, tilting the remaining half of her burger away from her mouth, 'what's the deal with this?'

I search her eyes. She can probably tell my hair's wet. Shit.

'What? I just wanted to hang. We hardly ever talk, y'know? Like properly sit down and talk.'

'True.' She stares harder. 'But nah, that's not it.'

'Are you saying you don't want to hang? 'Cause I can leave if you —'

'Shut up.'

'Can't. It's not in my nature.' I push on. 'Who do you live with?'

'A talking squirrel and a cat that solves crimes.'

'Be serious.'

One eyebrow arches in delicate condescension. 'Whatever you're doing, it's not subtle.'

I shrug. 'Go with it.'

Nina relaxes. 'My dads and my brother, Declan.'

It's a detail I can't believe she's gone this long without mentioning, and the only follow-up I can think of is, 'Oh, gay dads?'

'Dad doesn't say they're gay. He just says they really like having sex with each other, which is gross when he says it so I don't know why I'm repeating it to you.' Her words run together like she's eager for the sentence to stop. 'How about you?'

'Just Mum, no dads.'

'Oh, now I feel selfish.'

She doesn't show much remorse. She polishes off her burger and moves on to the chips we're meant to be sharing. She has the bag in her lap. I don't mind. I still have the melted cheese on the inside of the burger wrapper. There is nothing in the world that will ever come close to melted burger-wrapper cheese. I peel it off the paper and drop it into my mouth. I food moan. Heaven. I'm going to miss it.

'Get a room,' she says.

I'm going to miss *this*.

'I wanted to hang because today's my last shift.'

She drops a handful of chips back into the bag. 'What? Why?'

'They're replacing me with Dimitri.'

'Who the fuck's Dimitri?'

'He's fifteen.'

'So?'

'He's cheaper.'

'That's bullshit.'

'Look, I'm not the first guy to be aged out of a fast-food job.'

'But Dimitri isn't gonna smuggle me chips ...'

'Nice to know that's what you'll miss the most.'

She's unapologetic. 'They're really good chips.' She holds a few up as evidence and halves them with a single bite. 'Y'know, Gloria always gave me grief that we were gonna pair off.' She clicks her tongue and eats the rest. 'Guess we proved her wrong.'

I don't trust myself to look at her, in case I give myself away. 'Yeah.' I sigh.

I want a diversion, and I get one in the form of Dan, in his oversized Phats uniform, wheeling a bin down the service passageway. I pull my legs in and we nod at each other. Nina's quiet, contemplating something.

When Dan's far enough away, she asks, 'Why didn't we, though?'

'Huh?'

'You don't have a girlfriend, do you?'

'No.'

'Boyfriend?'

'No.'

'Then why haven't we gone out?' She sits up a little straighter. 'Invite me to the movies.'

'What?'

She doesn't blink. Her gaze cuts through me. 'Invite me to the movies.'

'Um ... Do you want to go to the movies with me?'

'No, jeez, pick a more creative date idea.' She barely gets through the joke before she laughs. She tries to compose herself, but the laughter escapes her closed-lip smile in bursts.

My heart pangs. Her brow twitches. I lean in and —

— hesitate for a fraction of —

Our lips touch. We kiss. Time slows. Her chest rises into mine. I reach for her cheek. I feel her scar beneath my palm. Our bodies shift closer. The bag in her lap crumples.

Time bends. I feel the hot rage before I see her. We're standing on some street. She's shouting, spitting, all rage, too. She's older, we both are. I can tell without a mirror. I know the difference in my joints, my body seems less cooperative as I amble towards her. She raises a hand and throws something at my chest. I catch it, almost fumble. She leaves. I hold a ring.

I crash back into my eighteen-year-old body, and Nina feels too close. I pull away. I've never seen that far before. Twenty, thirty years? My breaths are shallow, pointless. She asks if I'm all right.

I've got to go. I've got to …

'Wait.'

I'm on my feet.

Her lips have left a mark on mine. Beneath the taste of the Double Pattie Heart Clog, there's the hint of strawberry. She put on lip gloss especially for me. And I'm walking, almost running down the service passageway.

It's different, when you know its ending.

My life as I know it is scrawled on yellow notes and stuck in vague chronological order to the timber floor under my bed. I take a pen and record the details — the rage, the ring — and peel the note off the stack. I clear a patch of dust below the others and stick it down. There's a rough sequence that traces my path through high school, uni, to full-time work and now … a marriage?

'How exciting.' This is Sophia Tan, confidante and cat lover. She sits on the single bed we've pushed flush against the wall, casually stroking a Bengal cat. Sophia has been around long enough that me seeing the future is as regular as me breathing. I usually mention the details of a future in a text and she usually replies with an over-dramatic GIF from a Spanish soap opera. But this future, it isn't usual. It's worth more than a GIF. It's worth coming over for. 'It's your first love affair.'

'Can you please stop calling it that?'

Lara Bengal fidgets in Sophia's lap. Sophia tightens her loving vice grip, knowing Mum doesn't like a loose Bengal in the house.

'What else do you want me to call it?' she asks. 'You kissed a chick and flashed forward to —'

'Her throwing a ring at me.'

Sophia's looking down at Lara when she corrects me. 'A *wedding* ring.'

'We don't know that for sure.'

'I don't throw my dollar-shop ring at people when we're fighting, I'm not gonna do it when I'm old enough to afford some seriously expensive bling,' Sophia says. 'No, it only makes sense as a wedding ring. You're definitely getting future divorced. I'm so happy for you.' She hears it. 'For the stuff before that, I mean.'

I sigh. 'Thanks.'

My eyes drift from the note (*Angry, oldish Nina throws ring during fight*) to the one above it (*Me in office elevator. Suit pants, white shirt, tie*). I remember that future, saw it at the Year 10 Careers

Expo when I leaned against an investment bank's stand. I'd seen myself reflected in the mirrored back of the elevator. I'd looked older, but in the kid-playing-grown-up way twenty-somethings do when they wear adult clothes. There's so much time between that future and this latest one. I need more to go on.

'Did you see kids?'

'No.'

'Kitties?'

'No.'

'How old did she look?'

'I'm guessing forty? Fifty? Can't say for sure.'

'Well, you're fucking useless.'

'Cheers.'

Sophia has been aware of and frustrated by the limitations of my ability since day dot. In Year 5, when the futures started, she was irritated that I couldn't conjure the answers to Dr K's next pop quiz, or confirm a boy band would re-form after her favourite member quit. To be fair, I tried to control it once. She asked me what she'd get for Christmas, so to coax a future out of hiding, I tipped Mum's stash of wrapping paper and ribbons into an empty bath and sat in it. I thought of Sophia's Christmas and instead, I got my own: a tiny present with a card from *Mum*, not *Mum and Dad*. I was too scared to ever try again, so I just told her it was impossible.

In an ideal world, I wouldn't have told anyone. It's just kind of hard to keep an ability like mine secret at the start. Seeing the future isn't like it is on TV, where some wizened psychic touches something, gasps and *sees* it. Nah, it's like you're ripped out of yourself and injected into your future self. You're a stranger in your older body, seeing, smelling, hearing, touching, tasting. Then you snap back into yourself. It's enough to make you sick.

In Year 5, it made me spew a lot. I shared a desk with Sophia, and after the third incident involving her favourite cat-themed pencil case and chunks of my breakfast, I felt I owed her an explanation. She was just young enough to believe me without much evidence. She kept a stash of old lunch-order bags, and an eye out for when I seemed out of it. She became a pretty decent catch.

Short-term pain for long-term gain. She figured being best friends with a psychic would have its perks ...

There haven't been many, though. But at least the projectile vomiting's stopped.

I bend over and peel off the note closest to the skirting board (*Fired from Phats*). I scrunch it into a ball, and the other futures feel that little bit closer. Time marches on, one inevitable little yellow sticky note at a time. I take a deep, deep breath.

'So,' Sophia asks, 'when's your next date?'

'I'm not going to date her. How can I?' I'm asking myself as much as I'm asking her. 'I can see the ending.'

Sophia's supportive in her own special way. 'It's a teenage love affair. They're not made to last forever.' She lowers her head and starts cat-speaking. 'Uncle Adam is going to piss away his one chance at love, isn't he, Lara Bengal? Yes, he will. Oh, you're so pretty.'

Whatever magnetic field Lara has that attracts Sophia, has zero effect on me. She's the scratcher of forearms and the source of the putrid smell in Sophia's laundry, but for as long as I've known Sophia, she's been scarily attached to her — so much so that she rarely walks the two blocks to my place without cradling Lara.

The thought of Lara sends me flying. I collide with a self that doesn't feel that different. Sophia sits beside me, a tiny kitten in her lap. She calls her Laura, and me her new uncle. Her voice wavers when she tells Laura about her older sister. She wishes they could've met. Her eyes are red raw. She's been crying. I'm flung back into my present self and my heart hurts. The feeling lingers. Sophia doesn't notice anything's up. Her face is level with Lara's. 'So pretty,' she coos.

The cat doesn't give a toss. Sophia pays some attention to the gap between her shoulder blades, and Lara lifts her head, satisfied.

'Have you done the modern history essay yet?' Sophia asks me.

I tell her I'm too busy worrying about the future to think about the past.

'Oh, how long have you wanted to use that line?'

'A couple of weeks.'

She looks up. Her forehead creases. 'You all good?' she asks.

I clear my throat and make an effort to stand straighter. 'Yeah.'

'Trying to think of a line that doesn't suck?'

Sure, I'll let her think that. 'Pretty much.'

'Do you want to go outside and poop?'

'Wha—?' Oh, she's talking to the cat.

Lara doesn't even flinch, but Sophia reads it as a, 'Yes.' Part of me thinks she only brings her over to make it easier to leave. It's hard to argue with, 'I think my cat's about to shit on your hardwood floors.'

Sophia puts her hand on my back on her way out. 'Support,' she says.

When she's gone, I write another note. I peel it off the stack and stick it somewhere close to the skirting board.

Something happens to Lara. New cat, Laura.

Shit, indeed.

I remember the *future* of my childhood. It was all hope and optimism, my kindergarten teacher squeaking there was no life that was out of my reach. Absolutely anything was possible. But now the meaning of the word has changed. The *future* is static, a dark, inescapable thing.

Every yellow sticky note is a trap.

I hope I'm wrong. I hope I've misremembered the futures, or misinterpreted what they mean. Is it possible they're warnings more than solid truths, affected by diverging paths and missed trains?

I need a manual. I need a mentor. I … have a mother. By the time she gets home after 'long brunch', it's dark out. I've pulled the bed back over the sticky notes and any courage I may have had to broach the subject with her is gone.

It's not that she's difficult to talk to. She's never had a problem fielding questions about anything — drugs, sex, the psychic abilities that run in her family. We can talk about that joint she tried at uni, and that guy Alek from work who doesn't come by anymore, but we hit a snag when it comes to the future. I guess any conversation about it shines a spotlight on the elephant in the room: she's a fucking psychic. She has dirt on me before I'm dirty.

I can ask her any question about my ability, and she'll make some general comment about knowing a lot, and I'll start unpacking it like, *Hang on, what does she mean by that? Does she know I lied to her about LJ's? Crap, she knows it wasn't really a movie night. It was a house party. Somebody called the police. We bailed and spent the night in the park freezing our arses off, spewing vodka. Why won't she just say it? Maybe she doesn't know. Maybe I got away with it. Or is she just letting me think I did?* Then she'll smile and I'll be like, *Shit, can she read minds now?*

It's not worth the anxiety.

I have books open on the dining table while I smash out my modern history essay. She steps out of her shoes and instantly shortens. She approaches cautiously, like she's afraid to disturb me.

'Don't worry, Mr Ferguson isn't marking it.'

She exhales. 'Good. How was your day?'

'Fine.'

She reminds me it was my last day at Phats. I tell her I know.

'No big emotions?' she prompts.

'Nope.' I'm already up to unload the fridge. Reheating all the week's takeaway leftovers is a crucial part of our Sunday-night ritual. 'Big whoop, it's the last time I'll ever serve somebody fast food.'

'That you know of,' she says, and I start unpacking it like —

'No, don't do that,' I tell her.

She cackles. 'Honestly, I see no more fast food in your future.'

'Stop.' I think about it. 'And obviously. I'm too expensive.'

'Exactly.'

I get to work microwaving one ethnic dish at a time, and Mum parks herself on the couch. The other crucial element of our Sunday-night ritual is judging the contestants of whichever talent show is currently on the air. It's an escape, an opportunity to crawl out of my own head.

And it is until a teary piece to camera, in which Janelle from Narrabeen shares her struggle to be taken seriously as a spoken-word poet slash popstar. She's all hope and optimism.

'No-one can tell me there's no future in this,' Janelle says.

The judges have just told her exactly that.

'Anything is possible.'

I want to ask someone if she's right. I turn to Mum and hesitate.

✿

When I walk to school with Sophia, it's a given we won't take the direct route. Some mornings, we have to drop off her dad's dry-cleaning, others, like this morning, we have to quest ten minutes out of the way so she can visit the cheaper convenience store, because a dollar difference overall really matters.

'Yes.' She's indignant. 'It really does.'

When we get there, we immediately take different aisles. She lingers by the confectionary, and I head for the magazines. I ignore the bulky tomes to women's fashion and male body dysmorphia, and start flicking through the thin gossip rags to the ads near the back.

'You sure you don't want anything?' Sophia asks.

I want a mentor. Somebody who knows what it's like to be psychic, but who isn't going to ground me for anything in my past or future. Mum used to scoff at the flashy psychic hotline ads in the magazines she nicked from work. She said they felt too razzle-dazzle to be legit, but I dunno, I'm willing to give them a shot.

Except the ads with mysterious, glammed-up psychics are gone, replaced with dating-show recap columns written by psychics who just look like normal journalists. No fancy jewellery. No starry-night banners across the top. They don't even list their toll numbers.

Sophia heaps her selections on the counter. 'You done?'

'No.' I put the magazine back on the rack and head over. 'I can just search online like a normal person anyway.'

Sophia taps her card and runs her arm through the plastic bag before the payment clears. The moment the register chimes, she drags the bag off the counter. I follow her out and we're absorbed by the amorphous blob of corporate suits ambling towards the train-station underpass.

'It can't be that hard to find a psychic who isn't your mum or a charlatan,' she says as we descend the stairs. There's a lady sitting on an upended milk crate at the other end of the tunnel. 'What about her?'

The woman is spruiking palm readings and evil-eye necklaces to morning commuters. She is very much a charlatan.

'Yeah, no.'

'Yeah, yes. Besides, what's the worst that'll happen? She'll con you into buying a necklace.'

'But, I …' We're too close to keep talking about her.

According to the cardboard sign leaning against the wall, she's the Astounding Anne-Marie. We stop near her and she motions to her spare milk crate. It really doesn't look comfortable, but Sophia pushes on the small of my back until I step forward. I drop my bag by my feet and sit down. It feels like I've taken an oversized cheese grater to the arse.

'Hello, my child.'

Ugh. I was worried that was how she was going to play it.

I look to Sophia, but she's already out of the tunnel.

'How may I help you?' Anne-Marie asks. There's a cardboard sign at her feet that lists her services and prices.

I'm here now. I might as well …

'I actually …' My eyes drift back to the cardboard sign and the texta'd prices. I take out my wallet to mitigate the guilt. I fish out a gold coin. 'I wanted some advice.'

She licks her bottom lip. 'There is not much Anne-Marie does not see and cannot help with.'

Ugh. Third person.

She accepts the coin. 'What is it, child?'

I readjust myself on the crate. It makes it worse. 'I was wondering, is it possible to change the future? Or are you stuck with a bad one?'

'Oh.' She smiles warmly. 'If you are afraid, Anne-Marie can make sure she only tells you the good things.'

'I … meant, for me.' I check over my shoulder for guys from school. The tunnel's practically deserted. I lean in. 'I'm a psychic.' It never really stops sounding stupid when I say it out loud.

She makes a face and I think the discomfort of the seat is getting to her, too.

'There's this girl. We've been … I don't know if it's flirting, but we've been close for ages, and yesterday I kissed her.' Anne-Marie nods and her eyes dart to my palms as if they hold the answer. 'I know our future, it doesn't end well. But is it definite? Can I change it? Is that ethical? Are there cosmic repercussions? Would I be creating an alternate timeline, and in avoiding one future, does that mean the other futures I'm aware of but haven't lived won't happen?'

Anne-Marie laughs. 'Oh, darling, you read too many books. Give me your hand. Palm reading is ten dollars.'

'Honestly, I —'

She takes my forearm and pulls my palm closer to her. I gasp and it's a roller-coaster dip out of myself and into … her. There's a hospital bed, a young girl and a stern-faced doctor. The doctor's talking. He calls the girl Bridget. I feel a faint sensation on my palm. I focus on it. The details blur, the doctor's voice muffles, but the sensation becomes a touch. I collide with myself, and the Astounding Anne-Marie is tracing the lines of my palm with her thumb.

'Bridget,' I gasp.

Anne-Marie is too involved explaining the different lines to me and what they mean.

'Bridget,' I repeat. 'Who is she?'

Her thumb eases off my skin. She blinks at me.

'Is she in hospital?' I ask.

'You *see*.' Her eyes are wide. Her grip on me tightens. 'What have you seen? Tell me.'

I stammer. I didn't see much and I'm still getting over *being in somebody else's future*. I offer her something. 'I saw a doctor.'

It isn't enough.

'What did he look like?'

The more I try to recall details, the hazier my recollection. The future isn't mine and it's like my body is rejecting it.

Anne-Marie pulls on me harder. 'Is my baby going to be all right?' Her voice cracks.

I snatch myself out of her hands. I don't know how to answer her.

'Tell me. Tell me, please.' Her purple shawl rises and falls with every short, shallow breath. Whatever gift I have, she doesn't. 'Do you want money? I do not have much, I ...' She's fishing in her bum bag, plucking out shrapnel.

People invade the underpass with heavy steps and loud conversations. A train must've just arrived. Anne-Marie's eyes are locked on me, and mine, on everyone passing. Randoms. School kids. Matt and Aidan from geography. They snigger on the way past. I'm gonna cop it in class.

'Look, I … have to go to school.'

I stand and scoop up my bag. Anne-Marie pleads for me to stay. I almost run.

I don't usually consider my abject failure as a human being during geography (that's what maths is for), but this morning, it's weighing on my mind. Mostly because Matt doesn't let me forget it. At regular intervals, he leans his chair back into my desk, rubs his temple with the fingers of one hand, twinkles the fingers of the other and reels off a psychic prediction. They get less and less funny, and they weren't exactly side-splitting to begin with. Each one reminds me of Anne-Marie, how desperately she needed comfort, and how I let her down.

Matt leans back. He does the stupid thing with his fingers again. He's going for psychic, but his delivery reads more like ghost. 'In your future, I see … you being pathetic and visiting an old lady psychic in the underpass.'

Okay, so he's not wrong. I jump the fence at recess. I have fifteen minutes, thirty-five if I skip pastoral care. I take the back streets so there's less chance of somebody spotting me going AWOL. I jog as fast as I can, for as long as I can, which is not very fast, or very long, but I get to the underpass quicker than I thought was possible. Not quickly enough, though. Anne-Marie and her milk crates are gone.

Sophia saves my seat in modern history with an empty chocolate wrapper. I dust it onto the floor and she asks where I was at recess. Before I can answer, she supersedes it with a more urgent question. 'How did this morning go?'

'I got nothing. She's a fake.'

'Damn.'

I only feel half-bad because it's only a half-lie. I didn't get a solution to my Nina problem, which is what Sophia means, but I did get *something*: I'm shocking at using my gift to help others. Worse still, I know something bad happens to Lara. If Sophia comes to me for help, and I fuck it up ... I don't know what I'll do.

'Chocolate?' she offers.

I have homework, but I fire up the TV instead. I've spent so much of the past twenty-four hours worrying about futures that I feel depleted. I need to veg out and channel-surf and watch dumb game shows and forget about everything.

Mum gets in around six. She hangs her keys on the hook by the door, peels off her heels and death stares. 'What's wrong with you?'

I've sunken so deep into the couch that I'm practically horizontal. It's hard to speak. 'Nothing's wrong. What would make you think that something's wrong?'

'Besides the body language?' She walks through to the kitchen. 'Russia.'

'Huh?'

Mum remains silent until the game-show host asks the next question. 'Which country is home to one-quarter of the world's fresh water?'

I wait for it. The contestant answers, 'Iceland,' and the buzzer sounds. The game-show host is sorry, the correct answer is …

Mum cackles. I sit up and look over the back of the couch. 'Mum!'

'What?' She's biting back a smirk. 'It's not as if I asked about Nina.'

She consults the menus stuck to the fridge and I wonder what she knows and how long she's known it. She eliminates one of the menus, glances at the two remaining, and then at me. 'Don't do that with your face. If you just told me about your life, I wouldn't have to look ahead.'

'You don't have to look ahead, period. It's like reading a diary I haven't written yet.'

'But she's so lovely. We get on well. We *will* get on well, once you sort out your little dramas.' She consults the menus again. 'Chinese for dinner?'

Mum already knows. I don't know why she bothers asking. 'Whatever.'

'Attitude!' she warns. She opens the fridge and plucks out a container of chopped celery. 'And don't swear.'

I stammer. 'What? I didn't …'

'Not yet.'

'Oh, come on. This isn't fair. Nobody else has fights with their parents in four dimensions.'

She chews on a stick of celery. 'We're not fighting. You want to see fights with kids? Just you wait. Brandy is a piece of work.'

'Ah!' I cover my ears. 'Fuck, Mum. Spoilers.'

She threatens me with what's left of the celery stick.

'Sorry.' I drop my hands.

'Forgiven. Mongolian lamb, lemon chicken and mixed vegetables?'

I nod.

She dials the restaurant and even with the phone to her ear, she won't drop the subject of my unborn daughter. 'How can you not know about Brandy?' she asks. 'Haven't you had a peek?'

I can't control it. I'm too scared to try, and I'm too chickenshit to admit it. I deflect. 'Why would I name my daughter after alcohol?'

'The singer,' Mum corrects.

I'm blanking.

'You don't know Brandy? R&B, voice like silk.'

'I've got nothing.'

'She was the soundtrack to my uni years.'

'You do realise I was not alive for them, right?'

Mum sighs and someone answers on the other end. 'Jake, hello!' She laughs. 'Yes, it's Sarah.' She laughs again. We really order too much takeaway. 'We're after dinner ... Well, what would you recommend?'

I roll my eyes. I hate this shtick.

Cue the shit-eating grin. 'Mongolian lamb, lemon chicken and mixed vegetables?' she repeats back at him. 'Sounds perfect. I'll send Adam up in twenty? Wonderful.' She ends the call. 'Have a shower before you go, will you? I can smell the hormones on you.'

'Thanks.'

I'm almost out of the room when she stops me. 'You know, I saw your father when I was about your age. My friends and I were at the corner shop buying snacks for a sleepover. I grabbed the buttered popcorn and your dad just popped right into my head.'

She taps it, as if to clarify which head. 'He swept me off my feet. I didn't actually meet him until my last year of uni. By the end of our first date, I knew we weren't going to last.'

'Well, you weren't wrong there.'

'No, I was not.'

It makes me think of the Nina and Sophia futures. I wonder if it's possible. 'Mum?'

'Yes, hon?'

'Can we be wrong?'

She takes the last of the celery and tosses the container in the sink. 'I've never been.'

'I just really don't buy that I'm going to name a kid after some retro R&B singer.'

'Well, I'd tell you, but what is it you say?' She screws up her face. 'Rah, spoilers!'

'I sound nothing like that.'

She shrugs and lets the tap run. She tips the accumulated plates and containers into the sink and adds a liberal amount of detergent. Watching her, the thoughts and futures swim around in my head, they mingle and knot and I remember what she said about Dad.

I mightn't have a manual or a mentor, but I have a mother.

'Hey, question.'

She looks back at me. 'Mm?'

'If you knew it wasn't going to work with Dad, why would you even go there?' It's the most direct question about living with our ability I think I've ever asked her.

She tilts her head to one side. 'Oh, bless.'

The Chinese restaurant at the end of our street is steeped in our history. When the three of us moved west, it was the Oh Yum Bistro. We would order from images on an illuminated menu board, and sit at the round tables meant for larger families. I would play Wheel of Fortune with the lazy Susan, spin and eat and spin and eat until Mum would still the wooden disc with one hand and tell me to stop playing with my food. She and Dad would be having one of their *conversations*. She saw his mistakes before he'd even made them, and he said she didn't have any faith in him. She didn't, no. When Dad moved out, and more people moved west, Oh Yum became The Bistro. It was dark and dramatic, with home-brew beer options written on the wall in chalk. Mum was halfway through the list the night she gave me the, 'Yer a wizard, Harry,' talk in Year 7. She did it just like that, too, thought I'd appreciate the intertextuality. We quickly realised it wasn't the kind of chat we could have in public, so we became takeaway customers exclusively.

Whenever I come to collect, the smell and sound of sizzling meat makes me miss the old days when Mum knew everything and I didn't know how. When we didn't have to hide in case someone overheard.

There are three customers in the waiting area, but my eyes are drawn to one. She has a navy-blue streak dyed into her hair. Mum's insistence that I shower before grabbing dinner suddenly makes sense.

Nina flicks through a magazine too quickly to absorb any details. My heart knots itself. I want to shout her name and exchange stupid jokes, but the air between us is thick with what happened, and what will happen. I don't want to wade through it to get to the vacant seat beside her. I want to linger by the door, hope my order is called before hers, and hide my face if it isn't. But can I avoid her that easily? Our futures are entwined.

I exhale.

I wade through it, the giddy awkwardness of our first kiss, the clumsiness of my escape, and the blinding rage of our breakup. I sink into the seat beside her.

I have to say something.

'Hey.' It will go down in history as one of the greatest ever icebreakers.

Nina looks up. She's startled, but she recovers. Her face hardens. 'Hello, Adam.' There are icicles hanging from her words and I'm seriously wondering whether it's poor form to run away from two out of two encounters.

Yes? Yes. Of course it is.

Jake approaches the counter with two loaded plastic bags and I hope they're mine. He calls for a Josh. Not mine. Damn.

'You know,' Nina says, 'most people who don't want to kiss someone just don't kiss them. They don't kiss them, freak out and then piss-bolt.'

It's hard to wrap words around these feelings. It's not something I'm used to talking about. 'I wanted to.'

'Am I a dud kisser?' she asks.

'No, I —'

'Were you about to shit yourself? Because, fair warning, no excuse less than imminent diarrhoea will help you recover from this,' she says.

Josh only walks off with one bag. Jake checks the ticket taped to the remaining one. 'Gower?' he calls.

Nina stands.

'That's not your name.' I don't know why I say it out loud.

'Um, yeah, it is. Surname.'

'Oh.'

'Dickhead.'

She walks over to Jake and becomes a different, warmer Nina. Their banter is light and fun. I tilt my head back against the shopfront window. This is messed up. I want her to like me, I want to go out with her, even though I know it won't last. I'm defeated. I slide my hands into the pockets of my trackies, and there's … I pull out a pen. I turn it over. *Izzy Bella Cosmetics* is printed in pink cursive down the side. It's from Mum's work. She must've slipped it in while I was in the shower.

Nina's leaving. I look to her seat and tear a corner off the magazine. I write my number on it and follow her out the door. She's almost around the corner.

'Nina Gower!' I call.

She stops and turns. 'Just because you know it doesn't mean you have to say it all the time.'

I clear the rest of the distance between us and hold out the glossy corner with my number on it. 'Adam Thomas.'

Her brow creases.

'Please?'

She takes my number. 'I'll think about it.' She turns back and swings her dinner as she walks away. She raises her free hand. 'Notice how I'm not trying to break a world record here?'

My phone vibrates on the table during dinner. It's from a number I don't recognise. The body of the text reads, *Nina Gower.*

'You're welcome,' Mum says.

I text back a string of random emoji she'll appreciate and bite back a smile. Her response is instant: love-heart emoji, engagement-ring emoji.

I feel the future, the ring in my hand, the hot rage.

Sarcastic obvi, Nina adds.

I fight against the future, push it down and hold it there. I am here, now. The hot rage festers. I reply, *Hahaha*, but I don't even smile.

I want to ask Mum about the future, but I want her to answer like she doesn't know mine. 'There's this girl,' I explain. 'We've worked Sundays for ages, and yesterday, we kissed.'

'Yeah, I …' Something clicks and she understands what I'm doing. 'Oh, really? What's her name?'

A bit much, but I appreciate the effort. 'Nina. I kissed her and I saw our future, her breaking up with me.'

Mum nods. 'That is … surprising.'

'It wasn't just the breakup though. I felt the anger, like, I really hated her in that moment, and I think she hated me.'

Her eyes narrow. 'Fascinating.'

'My question is, I've lived us breaking up, how does that not taint everything before it?'

'Mm.' Mum straightens up and she chews on her bottom lip. She's thinking. Eventually, she settles on, 'Think of it a lot like driving off a cliff.'

'That's not reassuring.'

She points her fork at me. 'You can't see the future and be blissfully unaware, they're mutually exclusive,' she says. 'Everybody has their share of cliffs, we just have the pleasure of knowing that they're coming. We have to work extra hard to enjoy speeding towards them as best we can, teach ourselves to appreciate the wind in our hair. Life will break your heart, and if you don't learn how to live with that, you won't have much of a life.'

I'm quiet. I don't quite know what to say.

'That would be my advice to you if I had no idea what happens next, which I absolutely do not.'

I meet Nina after school. We walk home together. I focus on the wind in my hair. Not literally, there's not much hair and the breeze is piss-weak. I mean, I focus on the build-up. Easing back into our friendship, trading barbs and anecdotes until it feels more like it was before the kiss, and then nervously stretching past it, our fingers edging closer, our knuckles grazing, and then, me finding the courage to hold her hand in mine.

She doesn't look at me when she says, 'We're doing this.'

'We are, yeah.'

'If you feel the urge to bolt, make sure you let go, yeah? I'm not adequately warmed up for a sprint.'

She works it into conversation every time I see her. She has every intention of running it into the ground.

'Get it?' she asks over Macca's breakfast the next day. '*Running it into the ground?*'

'I saw it coming, yeah.'

Her navy-blue streak is now lime green. I ask what the deal is with the colours.

'This is going to sound weird and you're not gonna believe me, but I actually have supernatural abilities.'

My heart skips a beat, an excited nervousness spreads across my chest and … then I realise she's kidding. The supernatural is fiction in her world. I play it straight. 'Oh, really?'

'Totally.' She nods. 'Some people wear mood rings, I have mood streaks.'

'And what does lime green mean?'

She cocks her eyebrow. 'Wouldn't *you* like to know?'

'So long as it doesn't mean you hate the guy you're eating breakfast with.'

'No, it does not mean that.' She says it like it does. 'You are not completely insufferable.'

'I don't like you.'

'I don't like you either.'

We smile at each other. It's funny, how loud the present is when you force yourself to really listen. I don't have a future for weeks. I have Nina. We waste weekends on my bed, my body pressed into the back of hers, it's the only way we fit. We binge TV on my laptop, our fingers interlocked, and I lose myself in her. I watch her, the scar on her cheek, the freckle on her neck, the streak through her hair. It's bright pink. I run my hand through it.

'When I was a kid, I was at my aunt's house,' Nina says, talking over the video. 'She had this flight of stairs from the second-storey balcony down to the yard, and I fell from the top and hit my head on a step. I got up and walked to her. She thought I was fine. She didn't realise I had fallen from so high. I collapsed and I was in a coma for five days.'

'You were in a coma?'

'Yep. The doctors couldn't do anything. They didn't know if I'd ever wake up, and if I did, whether I'd have brain damage or not. I didn't, but … Yeah, ever since, that patch has grown white.

I was a bit depresso about it when I went back to school, so my teacher dyed it with me one lunchtime. I haven't stopped.'

My fingers trace a line up to the streak's grey-white roots. I wonder how many people she's told that story to, and how many others she's let believe her streaks are just some colourful rebellion. She twists her body to face me, and the roots are out of reach.

'Hi,' I whisper.

She smiles. 'Hi.'

We are drawn into each other and the whole pretence of watching TV is lost. There is just us, now. A frantic mess of limbs and movements. An awkward kiss, teeth click, clothes peel off and the doorbell rings.

'Was that ...?' Nina asks.

I'm off the bed and hurriedly turning my shirt right side out. 'Mum's probably forgotten her keys,' I say. 'One sec.'

Nina has perfected the art of We Weren't About To Do What You're Thinking. She's already scrolling through notifications on her phone.

I rush down the hall. The hook Mum hangs her keys on is bare. I open the door and Sophia is standing on the porch. It's a sledgehammer. She's upset and Lara's empty lead is in her hands.

'Tell me she doesn't ...' There's a sharp intake of breath and my heart cracks. 'Tell me she's going to be okay.'

I have nothing. She steps forward and collapses into me. I wrap my arms around her and hold her close.

I want to say something perfect. I should have something comforting ready to go, I mean, I knew this was coming. All I have is, 'Soph ...' It's useless.

She sniffs, and after a few false starts, she struggles through an explanation. Lara wandered the neighbourhood in the early hours of the morning, and a car hit her in the low light.

'I've been with her at the vet. I tried texting, but you didn't answer.' Sophia pulls away. 'Do you know?'

I can't lie to her. I hesitate and her face twists anew.

'Really?'

I remember Anne-Marie and how spectacularly I had failed. I don't want to do that to someone else. Especially not Sophia. I treat it as my do-over. I lead her inside and offer her some water. She declines. That was my attempt to stall. I had hoped that by the time I'd filled the glass, I'd have an inkling of what to do. I can't tell her it's going to be all right. I mean, it is. There'll be a new kitten, and Sophia will love her every bit as much as Lara, but …

Nina emerges from the bedroom, hands in her jeans pockets.

'Oh. Hi.' Sophia wipes her eyes and tries to make herself seem presentable. 'Nina, right?'

'Yeah.'

Sophia sniffs. 'Sophia.'

'Hi.' Nina smiles faintly. 'Is everything okay?'

'Not really, but yeah.'

'Did you want something to eat? I have chocolate in my bag.'

Sophia sniffs again. 'What kind?' She stops Nina halfway through the brand name with, 'Yes!' Nina disappears and Sophia whispers, 'She seems nice.'

'She is.'

'And I like her hair.' She punches my arm softly. 'That's for making her divorce you.'

When Nina comes out again, it's with a block of chocolate and her backpack. There's this awkward dance, where she says she really ought to go home and study, because she doesn't want to intrude. I don't want her to leave, but I also don't want Sophia to have to grieve with an audience. We go around in circles, but Nina cuts it short. Nina doesn't dance.

'I'll just hang in your room until you're ready?'

Sophia promises to be gone in ten, max.

'No, seriously, eat all the chocolate.'

'I will.' Sophia's wide-eyed and Nina believes her.

She brushes past my legs on her way out.

'This is the worst,' Sophia says. 'Thing is, I know if I call Ma, she'll try to reassure me, tell me Lara's doing fine. She'll say the vet's optimistic and whatever, but it won't give me hope. It hasn't happened yet, but it's like it has, and I just want to cry and cry and ... I have no idea how you do it.'

'I'm trying to ignore it.'

She thinks. 'I don't know if I can do that. If I only have a limited time with her, I want to be right there. I can't pretend it isn't coming. And it is, isn't it?' She looks to me for confirmation. I nod slightly. She keeps composed and stands. 'I have to go.'

We hug, and in an instant, she's out the door with a block of chocolate. I wait. Sophia's visit was a wrecking ball, and I need to rebuild myself. I recover, brick by brick, and start to retreat back to my bedroom. Nina's surprised Sophia's left so soon. I climb back on the bed beside her. She asks for details and I give them. We lie silently and I try to lose myself in her again. I can't though. I know my life is laid out in notes beneath us, and I can't pretend it isn't coming.

There is just us, now and then.

I push the bed against the wall and lay the notes bare. Mum must sense I urgently want to talk because she flutters around the house, busying herself with odd tasks, avoiding my bedroom like the plague just to mess with me. When she eventually passes my doorway, it's on her way to brush her teeth, dry her hair, and given how long it takes her, re-tile half the bathroom. I've sprouted an island-castaway beard by the time she comes in. She sees the yellow sticky notes.

'Oh, we've stopped trying to hide these, have we?' she asks.

I sigh. 'Why am I not surprised?'

'I vacuum your room. I've lost count of how many times I've sucked them up by accident, stopped the Hoover, fished them out without spilling dust everywhere and slapped them back down without you realising.'

I'm not even going to dignify that with a response.

Mum looks over the notes and then at me. 'How are things?'

'I did what you said —'

'You did *half* of what I said.'

'Mum!'

'Sorry. Got ahead of myself. Go on.'

I exhale. 'You told me to focus on the wind in my hair. I did. I knew something bad would happen to Sophia's cat, but it was completely off my radar, because I was so wrapped up in the now with Nina. I wasn't prepared. Sophia came over today, she wanted to know if everything was going to be okay and ...'

'You were useless.'

'I was useless.'

'What did I tell you?'

'Focus on the wind in my hair.'

'And?'

'And?'

'You can't see the future and be blissfully unaware.'

Damn. She did say that.

'People with two good eyes don't keep one closed for the hell of it. If they did, they'd see, but they'd lose depth perception. It's the same for us. We have three eyes; they're meant to be open, or else we wouldn't perceive the world as well as we can. You only knew you were useless because you knew Sophia would need you, and you didn't take advantage of that knowledge. Someone who wasn't like you, he wouldn't think he was useless. He would tell himself he was just doing the best he could. But *you* know you didn't do the best you could.'

'But if I don't ignore the future, then how do I build something with Nina without dreading how it ends?'

'The dread fades. Trust me, you'll come to appreciate the warning. If I went into marrying your father with rose-coloured glasses, I would have been shattered when he turned out to be a baboon. I saw what was coming and tapered my expectations.'

'That's bleak.'

Mum shrugs. 'As much as you might want to, you can't live like everybody else. Your life is your own. Let them be slaves to the moment. They can't see the forest for the trees. Sure, they don't have to contend with spoilers, but you ... you live with purpose. The shocks don't rattle you when they're spread thin. You anticipate them and have time to prepare for them, and the joys ... the joys last long enough for you to really savour them.'

'I haven't seen any joy with Nina.'

'See more, then,' she snaps. 'The first time your father and I have dinner, he walks me to my car. He doesn't kiss me, but he does hold my hand. Our fingers interlock and *whoosh*, I see the moment I kick him out. I can't get into the car fast enough. I'm adamant I won't see him again. I will avoid that future. Meanwhile, he's standing by the car, oblivious to all this. He thinks it's been a pretty good night. In his defence, it has been. He smiles at me. I catch it in the rear-view mirror and … Fuck, I really love that smile. All things considered, I shouldn't. I know he's going to disappoint me. But that's ten, fifteen years away. That's a long time for things to sour.

'I need proof it isn't all crap, but my control over my power is limited to knowing I see more when I skip a meal. My mother told me our minds stitch related memories together. All her memories with your grandfather, they were linked. When she wanted to know if his health would improve, she would conjure a recent memory. She would live it like we live our futures, sit on the edge of his hospital bed, feel the mattress sag beneath her, smell the disinfected air, and she would take control. She would ask him, point-blank, if he was dying. He would say, "No," and she would get a preview of their future. She kept asking whenever he took a turn, until one day, he said, "Yes," and there was no future.'

Mum pauses for a long, slow breath. 'I had tried that, remembering and then asking, never worked for me. She said that everyone's different. I had to discover my own way in my own time. Bugger that. I'm sitting in that car, and I want to discover it now. I grip the wheel, look at your father and see the patchwork of our recent past, the candlelight, the dinner, the wine. And I realise, if they're connected, I must just be able to go the other way. I stop travelling backwards and instead, go forwards, past the walk to the car, to ten, fifteen seconds ahead. I see him tapping on my window, asking if everything's all right. It's working. I push on — ten, fifteen days ahead. I see us sitting on the beach at night, he's in a suit, I'm in a dress, and we're laughing so hard our sides hurt. I try weeks, months. If I know it's not going to work, why do I still give us a go? Sitting at the wheel, I see you. And everything else suddenly doesn't matter. I sit back and smile. Your father taps on my window and asks if everything's all right. And it is. I have you to look forward to.'

I feel the story in waves. First, as a rare look into my parents' early, less messy life together. That wave recedes, and the second one hits with more ferocity: This is my solution. I have to spoil my life with Nina to keep me from spoiling my life with Nina.

I wait for Mum to leave for 'long brunch', and allow ten minutes for her to return having forgotten something. When she doesn't, I grab a fresh stack of sticky notes and every pen in the house in case a dozen inexplicably fail. I lie back on my doona.

I'm going to control my ability, no big deal. Mum did it in a car, under pressure. I'm on a bed, with no time constraints. Easy. And if I discover something I don't like, that's just a part of it. I've just got to spread that shock thin.

Besides, it's not as if I can find out Dad's leaving again.

I take a breath and shut my eyes. Right.

The thought of Nina sparks a patchwork of memories. I hug her goodbye on the porch. I lie beside her. She offers Sophia a block of chocolate. I … reverse the flow. I lie beside her. I hug her goodbye on the porch. I strain to remember forwards, past the present and into the future … Nothing. I open my eyes.

Yeah, the odds of what works for Mum working for me were slim, but I lived in hope. Maybe it skips a generation.

I shut my eyes.

The thought of Nina sparks my memory again. I hug her goodbye on the porch. I follow Gran's example and force myself to feel it like my futures. I step into my past self's skin. I can taste the strawberry on her lips. She's pressed into me. I can smell her, touch the streak in her hair. We pull apart, I take control.

'Will we have good times?' I ask her.

She smirks. Holy shit, it's happening. The memory's changing.

'I'm not telling you that,' Memory Nina says.

I open my eyes and curse a fuckload. I was close. I was *close*. I changed the memory. Related memories are linked, I just need to find a way to get from one to the next. And it's not as if I can walk …

Wait. Am I sure I can't? I mean, if related memories are linked, then all I need to do is find the edge of a memory and pop over into the next one. It could be walking around the block. It could be opening a door.

I lean back, eyes closed.

The thought of Nina sparks my memory again … again. I hug her goodbye on the porch. I can taste strawberry, it's sweet. I take control and pull away abruptly.

'What's wrong?' Memory Nina asks.

I make for the door. I open it and step through, into my future self, slow dancing with Nina under fairy lights. She tosses her head back and laughs. She looks so damn beautiful.

I snap back into my body and open my eyes. Holy shit.

Nina suggests the night markets. I'm game, and game enough to get there twenty minutes early. I wait by the Lebanese food truck on the outskirts. When she arrives, she's disappointed by the fairy lights. It's a bit too indie-movie pretty for her liking.

I tell her I don't mind them.

We wander through the stalls, collecting cardboard plates and splitting meals the other just *has* to try. We mix hot meats with ice-creams; Nina believes in concurrent dessert, and I'm a convert. We end up in the fenced-off seating area, nursing expanded waists. They're clearing the plastic tables and chairs around us.

'Should we move?' I ask.

'I don't think I can.'

The first thing I did after adding a *Dancing with Nina* sticky note, was YouTube how to do the foxtrot. Attempting the dance with an invisible Nina, I thought about what Mum said about needing to live with purpose. That has to be about more than simply preparing for it. The future might be inescapable, but I can control how I arrive there.

'So, I need to tell you something, and I'm aware of how bonkers it's going to sound,' I warn her.

Nina shifts in her seat. 'I'm always down for bonkers.'

I expect tests of the 'Guess which number I just keyed into my phone' variety, but, turns out, convincing her is as easy as convincing a pre-teen Sophia. Like, she just accepts it. It's kind of unnerving.

'Seriously?' I ask.

'Oh, it's totally bonkers,' she says. 'If it's true, I could be down with it. If not, I want to see your endgame.'

'This isn't a joke.'

'And that's exactly what someone who's playing an elaborate prank would say.'

She asks how it all works, and I try to explain. Her eyes glaze over, like she's bored, fascinated and a little terrified.

'My mum never told my dad,' I say, 'and I wanted to date differently.'

'You're not making this up, are you?'

I shake my head.

'Bonkers,' she repeats.

A guy leans into the front window of a nearby food truck and turns up the radio. I recognise the song from the future. Nina nods in time with the beat.

'Do you want to dance?' I ask.

She's firm. 'I don't dance.' And then something occurs to her. Her brow bunches. 'Do I really have a choice?'

I stand. 'Yeah, but I've already seen you make it.'

'You can't do that.'

'Do what?'

'That. I've seen you get up, so I assume Future Nina dances with you, so I don't really have a choice.'

'Were you not going to dance?'

'No, but … it's the principle.' She stands and takes my hands. 'You're lucky I like this song.'

I'm a little over-prepared. We don't so much dance as shift our weight from foot to foot. With each step, she gets closer until we're almost touching.

'So, the first time we kissed,' I start.

'Before you ran away.'

'Yeah, before that. I saw our future and it freaked me out.'

'What was it?'

I hesitate, as if not naming it might keep it from happening. But it won't. It is inescapable. It's amazing how far into the future you can get by leaping through doors and windows. 'We get divorced.'

'Wicked. Was I throwing a plate? I've always pictured myself as a throwing-plates kind of wife.'

'You threw the ring at me.'

'Choice.' She rests her head on my chest. 'How long do we last?'

'A while.'

Nina goes quiet. 'I'm gonna take you to the cleaners.'

'My lawyer is going to be a misogynistic arsehole.'

'I'm going to turn all the kids against you.'

'I'll make new ones.'

Nina tosses her head back and laughs. Fuck, I really love that laugh. It evolves into her humming along with the chorus.

'This song isn't bad. Who sings it?'

Nina answers, 'Brandy.'

In a Heartbeat

ALICE PUNG

The first thing I want you to know is that none of this is your fault. Ha, you can legitimately have the last word in every argument, you can use the excuse we've all been using with our parents since we were thirteen: 'I didn't ask to be born!' In your case, you don't know how true that is. It feels weird, writing to something that exists but doesn't yet, if you know what I mean. At the moment, I am just creeped out by the fact that I have two heartbeats. That's what the doctor told me when he put the stethoscope on my stomach. He said, 'Can you hear that, Kim, you have another heartbeat down there, listen, can you hear it?' his eyes shining dopily with awe over the miracle of life. Hell yeah I could hear it, it was going a million miles an hour, like my own heart when I found out the news. Shit, I thought, this baby's going to have sky-rocket-high levels of anxiety at the rate its heart is pumping, and then I wondered whether it was genetic, whether I had already passed on my own hang-ups and sink-downs, and I said to the doctor, 'It must be really stressed out,' and you know what he did? He laughed at me, the bastard, and patted me on the belly like *I* was the baby, and said to me, 'That's its normal heartrate. Their hearts beat faster because they are just so much smaller.'

Your grandma, sitting in the chair next to me, wasn't laughing, wasn't infused with the miracle of life, even though she was supposed to be. She just stared at the ultrasound screen with a face that was like, well, at least it's got arms and legs and a head in the right place; and then every time she looked at the doctor it was with a face that was like, *Doctor I had nothing to do with this*. And then driving home, she's at me.

'Why couldn't you have kept hanging around with those smart Asian girls at school? Nancy would never have got herself into this mess.'

Yeah, Nancy Lim. Your grandma always told me Nancy was fugly. Mum said God had spared Nancy with looks but had knocked himself out giving her brains, which was why her head was so massive. 'Such a strange big head on that small body,' Mum used to comment, and I would see-saw from malicious conspiring glee to being resentful of my mother for her pettiness. I looked at Mum from the corner of my eye. Her hands were tight on the steering wheel, like she was manoeuvring a tractor instead of our old Camry that Dad left behind, and I could feel the rays of her anger even before she began speaking.

'So stupid,' she spluttered, 'throwing away your future like that. Do you think you will now have happy ending with the boy?'

I almost laughed out loud. Your grandma's accent made her 'happy ending' sound more dodgy than it was. She kept yelling at me. I had learned long ago not to interrupt one of Mum's tirades; it was no use. It was like going underwater with waves above you. Sometimes you just had to let the waves pass before you could rear your head again, otherwise you'd just be hopelessly fighting a force beyond your control. 'You think he's going to stay around?

No, he's the sort who never want something like this to happen. He's the sort to marry a Nancy.'

I didn't say anything 'cause I knew your grandma was so obviously, blindly wrong. As if Luis would get with, let alone marry, Nancy! Aside from the fact that she looked like a walking cranium with her body only there to carry that cerebral matter from class to class, she was the first one I told about you 'cause I could trust her not to turn this into even more of a show than it already was. The others — Cassie, Nhi and Michelle — they were pathetic. I knew they'd be all squealy and *OMG, OMG, OMG* 'cause this would be the most exciting, terrible thing to have happened to them since Michelle's parents took her to Vietnam to get that secret cosmetic eyelid surgery 'cause she was underage for the operation here, and then she came back with one eyelid smaller than the other. Yeah, those girls were great at commiserating in misery, but this was not *their* terrible thing. It was mine, and I knew Nancy would not try to take ownership of my issue and be all drama queen about it.

So I gave her seventeen bucks and she walked into Chemist Warehouse and came out with the test, and we did it in the toilets at Footscray Library, and the test came out with strong traces of you you you in the two blue lines, and I said, 'Oh shit.' And Nancy didn't say, 'Don't worry it will all be all right,' or, 'Maybe it's wrong,' and she didn't pat me and she didn't make me feel better. I hated her a little bit then and wished I had told the others, because I knew that at least they would have surrounded me with the bullshit reassurances that a girl sometimes just needs to hear.

And you know what Nancy finally said when she decided to open her mouth? 'Abortion is legal in Victoria until up to twenty-four weeks.' WTF?! If I didn't believe she was seriously aspergic I would have whacked her one. But because since Year 7 I'd convinced myself Nancy had undiagnosed Asperger's (you know, Asian parents don't believe in that sort of stuff, so they never got her checked out), I knew she was just trying to be helpful. 'Nancy, we're Catholic,' I managed to say before the toilet door swung open and I shoved the pregnancy stick in the paper-towel bin.

We walked out of the library loos, and of course Nancy didn't understand me 'cause she was one of those 'fake' Catholics — her father only got her baptised so she could go to St Dominica's. The first day she rocked up to school, hanging around her neck outside her school-uniform jumper was a massive brown rosary with a swinging cross at the bottom. Her dad probably made her wear it. 'Hey yo, pimping for Christ!' I called out, and she turned as red as the sacred heart, bless.

Who knew that we'd end up hanging around after school at the library together — she was there to study, I was there mostly to kill time until Mum finished at Diamond Rose Fashions, where she worked selling nylon jumpers and viscose bridesmaid's dresses to Vietnamese women who all looked a little like variations of LaToya Jackson. Soon we formed a group with the other three girls from our school and my mum was real pleased that I was spending time in the library instead of loitering in Highpoint Shopping Centre with the boys from St Andrews.

Little did your grandma know, hell little did *I* know, that Nancy had a cousin, Luis, who was hot as. Looked like the lovechild of a Korean boy-band singer and Disney's Aladdin. First time he came up to Nancy and asked, 'Whatcha doing?' I felt a stab of envy — come on, he was approaching *Nancy*? Why would he hit on her when, come on, yours truly was there, helllooo.

Mum, still driving, interrupted my meanderings down memory lane. She was still going on about how Luis was going to abandon me for Nancy and her ilk, yadda yadda yadda.

'They're related, Mum,' I retorted. 'That's sick.'

'Those Chinese,' your grandma replied, 'it's nothing new, they all marry their cousins anyway, it's their way of keeping money in the family.' My mum, so racist.

It wasn't like Nancy was rich or anything, it was just that she wasn't so povvo like us. Your grandma made *interesting* choices: instead of spending $2000 on tutoring fees for me like the rest of the good Asian parents, she spent $2000 on my orthodontist. Don't get me wrong, it's not like I wasn't grateful for straight-as teeth, but priorities, you know. Mum was also always going on about me eating her out of house and home with my appetite, about me gaining weight and being 'unwanted', about me looking sloppy when I went out. Everyone wore hoodies, but she expected me to wear the sort of shit she sold at the shop, like, a lime-green blazer suit with a maroon sequinned top beneath, for crying out loud!

I swear, I'd been disappointing your grandma ever since I was a baby and didn't make it into the Bonds Baby contest. She was so sure I would win because she thought I would be the only 'mixed' Filipina-Australian baby. Poor Mum, little did she know about the Eurasian Invasion, all those other charming mixed-race babies who probably stood a better chance because their mums knew how to do tasteful and didn't enhance their onesies with hand-sewn sequins spelling out 'BEAUTYFACE'.

Well, turns out I didn't need the sequins, that I'd walk out in public and people would see the obvious. Not trying to be up myself or anything, but kindly old men in parks would say, 'Bless your eyes,' which I didn't find creepy, and men in business suits would stare at me on the train after school, which I did. Creepy as. And of course, the St Andrews boys, they loved me. You'd think a face like mine would be able to make it into the popular crowd at my school, but those girls were all stuck-up bitches. You know, the types to only shop in places where you'd come out with a cardboard bag with ribbon handles and lots of tissue paper on top, for one frickin' T-shirt. I couldn't imagine what they'd think of Diamond Rose Fashions. Ha! They were all wusses with colour, in every sort of way, even the token Vietnamese and the Sri Lankan girl in their group. They didn't dare dress in bright brights, and they didn't dare date in any shade darker than white.

Anyhow, once I established that Luis and Nancy were related, and I got talking to him, that was that. He was so smitten! He was so shy! Truth is, he'd probably been a dweeby kid, probably only come into his hotness in the last six months or so, and with no other girl to reflect his true image back to him except for cousin Nancy, he had absolutely no idea. At first we spent the afternoons in the library just talking crap, you know. 'Oh you're from St Andrews, do you know Edwin Patamisi?' I asked him.

'Yeah in Year 8 that arsehole squeezed a whole tube of wasabi in my Coke can when I went to the loo. Why?' He looked at me accusingly. 'Did you used to go out with him?'

I didn't know why I brought up Edwin Patamisi, except that perhaps maybe once or twice I might have kissed him. He was cute, in an Italian–Bieber kind of way, but he was dumb as. 'No!' I protested. 'I have better taste than that. Come on.'

'Anyhow,' he continued, 'I brought a water balloon filled with fish sauce to school the next day and put it on his seat before he sat down.'

I had to admit, that was pretty funny. I opened up my schoolbag because I usually got hungry at around this time after school. Brought out my illicit stash of Milky Ways, and handed one to Nancy. 'Do you want one?' I asked him. And suddenly, we were having this spontaneous little party at the back of the library, such sad losers. He unwrapped one after the other, eating five in less than five minutes, before he looked at a wrapper and commented: 'Hmm, "Fun Size". How can anything this small be considered fun?' And I had no idea where Nancy got this cool, hilarious cousin from, but suddenly after-school study sessions at the library didn't seem so boring anymore.

Although Luis was really, really smart, the thing that made me fall for him was that he could recognise that I was, too. He laughed at my jokes, and he listened to what I had to say about stuff. We pretended to study together for about three weeks, then gave up. Out of the goodness of our hearts we decided not to distract Nancy from her schoolwork anymore and nicked off to Footscray Park to — well, let's just say, engage in some self-selected extracurricular activities. Your grandma and his parents were the sort that were so strict that we spent the first month together behind the native flora section, just lying there on top of one another, in our school uniforms, like slugs, breathing, barely even moving, trying to meld ourselves into one person. So calming, so comforting. One whole month! See, your dad and I weren't making the beast with two backs, as Shakespeare calls it, right away. Give us credit. We had some class.

Then I figured out I was ready, or as ready as I'd ever be, and finally looked forward to going home to our flat after school, having the two whole hours before Mum got home to ourselves. Before Luis, I hated that place, it was the place where I felt Dad gone most deeply. When he pissed off, Mum just left all his stuff back at our old rental, and only took what we owned. Turns out, according to her, we owned stuff like the knives and spoons and forks in the drawers and even the half-opened packet of Toilet Duck flushables. Ha! To be honest, it didn't feel as good as it did in the park, which was all gentle and dreamy. I was worried my mum would unexpectedly come back. Anxiety kills libido, you know. We rushed it the first time, and afterwards we felt kind of spent. The sort of emotional low you'd get if you'd just scoffed down a litre of ice-cream 'cause someone was going to yank it away from you in twenty minutes.

But the more time Luis spent at my place, and the more I realised Mum wasn't suddenly just going to come home from the shop and pounce on us, the more relaxed we became. We became more experimental. Suddenly, a kiss would make me feel as if I were going down a roller-coaster with popcorn in my stomach. I mean this in a good way. I am saying it got better and better. Anyhow, we were pretty smart, we used protection and all that. *Most* of the time.

And that's how you came to be.

At this point in my story, you're probably thinking *ewww*. You may also be wondering why your dumb-arse mum didn't get the morning-after pill. Well, why question your miraculous existence arising from my deep-seated sense of embarrassment? Truth was, even though I googled the shit out of how to obtain it, there was no way I could show my face around all those Footscray pharmacists to *ask for it*. They all knew all the other traders, and news was bound to reach your grandma. I thought of catching a train to go to a pharmacy in a different suburb, or even the city. But you know what? I didn't end up doing it. I convinced myself that certain things would never happen to me.

And at first, nothing was actually happening. I wasn't getting any fatter, I didn't feel like having a vom every morning, I felt fine. The only difference was that I hadn't got my period in a month, then two. Turns out I was two and a half months along when Nancy bought me that test. Then I let a few more weeks slip by because still nothing *physical* seemed to be happening, and you know, the whole denial and fear thing, it's very powerful. It paralyses you. Also, some secret deadly curious part of me wanted to see what would happen next — you were a bunch of cells, and then an *idea* of life to me, and I wanted to see whether this idea was real — and some shit-scared part of me didn't want to do anything or make any decision, hoping it would all go away.

But no, now I have two heartbeats. Creepy as.

I was scared of telling your grandma most of all. When I did tell her, man, did the proverbial excrement hit the fan in such a massive dump that I'm still scraping it from my hair and fingernails (and when the metaphor wears off, you will have arrived, and then it will be literal! Fun!).

Mum went ballistic. She ranted and hollered and cried and took off her Homyped flat shoe, the shoe she had been standing in for eight hours that day at work, and threw it at me. I ducked. She took off the other one and chucked that at me, too. 'After all I have done for you!' she wailed. 'You do *this* to me! What a waste! What a waste!'

I had had enough. I calmly picked up my bag, my public transport card, and nicked off to Nancy's. Nancy's mum was sewing a whole stack of little light-blue shorts when Nancy let me in and we walked through the living room, which was filled with half-opened cardboard boxes and cardboard fashion labels. She gave me a shifty sideways glance, like I was evil incarnate come to corrupt her daughter. I looked down at the carpet and saw all the snipped-off threads, light blue against the dirty tan carpet. All those masses of swirls, loops and lines, rising to fill my eyes like artificial worms, like the floor was warm and alive with a million tiny veins. For some reason, they grossed me out. Really grossed me out. 'I'm going to vom,' I croaked to Nancy, and she dashed me to the bathroom, and for the first time in this pregnancy, I had a big, long vomit and cry. 'They won't let Luis anywhere near me!' I wailed to Nancy. 'They won't let him near me 'cause they didn't want us to keep it, those fuckers!'

Of course I knew those fuckers were his parents, the folks I had never met because they didn't want to meet me, not unless I followed their course of action. They took away his mobile, but he still found ways of getting in touch. The last time I had heard from Luis, he had texted me, *R U OK?*

Ya. R U?

Yes. I want to C U.

OK. Where & when?

Ftscry Lib. Wed 4 p.m.

I showed Nancy the texts and asked her to be my decoy, in case Mum wanted to interrogate me. When I left Nancy's and got home it was quite late. Mum had left dinner on a cold stove for me; she was already in bed. I was relieved. I didn't want to see her. I avoided her most of the week by staying behind at the library.

Wednesday arrived, and I rocked up at the library in my school uniform. I wasn't a mindless moron, but I had secretly been pinning my hopes on Luis. He was smart, I was smart, we could pull through. I could support him through school and vice versa. Also, Luis was nothing like my dad. He wasn't going to piss off on me.

So, your dad also rocked up in his school uniform. Saw me and his eyes widened a little. I think he was surprised that I still looked the same, that I wasn't already a massive heifer in a mumu. After the exchange of babe-I-miss-yous, he launched straight into it. No fingers gently touching, no crying together, no hands-on-the-tummy-prelude-to-intimacy shit that you read about in those pregnant-teen books with symbolic birds on the cover.

'Why didn't you let me know sooner?' he asked. His eyes seemed different. Harder. His parents had put him through some serious degree of hell.

'Why? So you could tell me to get rid of it?' I retorted. Oops. Who knew I was raging beneath? This wasn't going well, but I pushed on. 'I'm not getting rid of it.'

'I'm seventeen, Kim. This is my last year of school. I'm really stressed out. My parents are saying I'm never going to get into optometry now. What about the other options?'

We'd been through this already. All the bloody adults counselling me, asking me if this is what I really wanted, did I understand the responsibilities of having a child, yadda yadda yadda. Of course I did, which was why I was so depressed and miserable. There was no movie or book about this for me — it was either some newspaper tragedy about yellow girls who looked like me who were molested by their basket-eyed uncles, or *Juno*. As much as I wanted to be a wisecracking, smarmy sweetheart about this, I was not.

We had both sat together at the sexual health clinic, having this discussion after I told him the news, and when it was over and I refused to budge, his parents decided he couldn't see me again. They'd never even met me, didn't want to meet me, probably just imagined me as some cigarette-sucking skank loitering around Footscray Station in a Supre outfit, out to lure their glory boy.

This was the first time your dad and I had been alone since I found out about you, but we were fully clothed, no longer funny to each other, but suddenly too familiar in that terrible sick-to-death-of-you way.

'Why do you want this baby so much anyway?' he asked me, almost accusingly, as if I were the sole person responsible not only for having one in the oven, but for baking that cake, too. I looked into his stony eyes and immediately, with a vicious force that was almost visceral, wished it was anyone else's but his. At least that dumb arse Edwin Patamisi would have been more loyal.

It wasn't so much that I wanted a baby; it was the thought of getting rid of the baby that filled me with more fear and anxiety and guilt than anything else in my life. Maybe the childhood fear of the wrath of God. I used to roll my eyes at those precocious girls with braces who did serious school reports on issues such as being pro-life or pro-choice, those moralistic morons who never had to make such a decision 'cause they weren't getting any action until they were twenty-five.

But having two heartbeats, the thought of getting rid of one was horrible as.

It seemed now that having made a choice, everyone was treating me like some kind of naive imbecile. I knew I could not deliver you, like a pizza, to Jennifer Garner to take away to a cheesecake-coloured room. It was then that I realised — when bad shit happened, Luis lost all backbone. I could see the cogs behind his eyes, calculating, turning, working out the best way to minimise damage to his precious future. He was going to force me to do what his parents wanted. He was scared of them that bad. Whereas Mum, well, I wasn't scared of her, had never been scared of her.

Don't get me wrong, we were never the *Gilmore Girls*. But at least she stood by my decision. Once she stopped being pissed off at me and giving me the silent treatment for a week, she started yelling at me non-stop and telling me how stupid I was. She was kind of transparent, your grandma, doing Kübler-Ross's stages of grief to the book. That was two months ago.

And now she was in the car, still going through the stage of anger, driving me home from my ultrasound. 'Do you want to know if you are having a boy or a girl?' the doctor had asked, and just as Mum was about to open her mouth I quickly said, 'NO THANKS,' and the doctor asked, 'Are you sure?' I said, 'YES, and please don't tell my mum either.' My mother was incredibly mad, of course, said she had a right to know, and got all huffy and left the room, just as I thought she would. So predictable. Then I turned to the doctor and said, 'Yeah, I wanna know. Tell me now.' After I found out, I left the appointment and thought I'd find Mum outside in the waiting room, but she was actually in the car, sitting there, livid. I got into the passenger seat and could feel gales of anger radiating from her, hot enough to perm hair, which was probably the secret reason her hair always looked like Ronald McDonald's.

As Mum drove, she went on and on about that no-good Luis, all he cared about was his own self, asking me to get rid of it. 'Those Chinese, they're used to doing this sort of thing because of the one-child policy in China. Nothing to interrupt Luis's grades, oh no!'

Then she sighed. 'But life is life, no matter how hard it may be. You'd rather have it than not have it.'

Some days I looked at my mother like she was an illiterate third-worlder who couldn't adapt to a new country.

This was not one of those days.

Sometimes, my mum *got* things.

'You don't need Luis anyway,' she conceded.

This is your dad she was talking about. I thought about how after my dad left with the other woman, Mum decided she could not let us live in his house anymore, even if he had abandoned it to move interstate with the younger version of her, 'the fresh-off-the-boat version', as she bitterly put it. I remembered how she made us move, then she went out and found a job, even though after having me she'd never worked outside the home. I thought that after Dad left, her entire personality had changed from being the sweet, indulgent mother who was always there after school with maruya and ice-cream, to this nasty, bad-tempered grump without a good word for anyone. I had been so stuck on this idea of her that I barely noticed that every time I came home after school — even when I snuck Luis into the house — she'd always left a snack out on the kitchen counter for me: tamarind balls, leche puto, those American Hershey's lollies she always bought from the Filipino store that tasted a bit like brown crayons.

And then I thought about your dad — cowardly bastard — and realised that at least my dad stuck around until I was in my early teens. At least my dad had his priorities straight. Sure, he prioritised another woman over us, but at least that was a human being and not his frigging 'career'. I hoped to God that Luis would not get into optometry, but I knew he would.

I knew how your dad's career would pan out — he'd work long and hard and then in his mid-twenties his parents would suggest a docile, career-oriented dentist to him and they'd get married and make lots of money and take their kids on holidays in Europe. They'd do the shit we were meant to do together, the three of us. Every once in a while they'd write us a cheque — the two of us —

for child support, the *bare legal minimum*. Oh yes, his parents would make sure of that — he had told me his dad was an accountant.

'We'll raise this baby together. You can stay in school. It's only one more year to go.' We were almost home and my mum was now looking more exhausted than angry. I guess all her ranting wore her out. 'There's no way you gonna be a drop-out like me.'

I didn't think anyone would want me back at school, but Mum told me that she had spoken to the principal, Mrs Avery, and she was going to help me finish my high schooling no matter what. I had no idea that Mum thought or cared that I was smart. I'd always presumed she saw my looks as my currency through life.

I looked at Mum in her glittery rayon shirt and black slacks, her fake pearl earrings and diamante brooch. She wore everything carefully and treated her clothes better than those businesswomen on trains treated their designer coats and handbags. Her hair was still as black as her pupils, and it dawned on me that she was still only forty.

This was crazy as, but I began to imagine a future where I would be one of those single college mothers you always see in brochures, balancing a baby on one hip and a latte in the other, with a swag of books in a neat leather case across one shoulder. I would be the campus MILF, ha-ha.

'It's not that easy, you know,' Mum said, as if she could read my mind. 'But believe me, studying is so much better than working. You wanna study for as long as you can.'

'But what about your job?' I asked her.

'I can work part-time. If I look after your kid, I can claim carer's allowance. It's not as much as I am making at Diamond Rose, but I am getting crap pay there anyway.' I had no idea your grandma had been thinking so much about this, planning out practical things already. I wasn't so sure about Mum raising you part-time. I didn't want her to do shit like enter you in beauty pageants. But then again, she was gonna help me stay in school, so maybe those days of vicarious glory were over for her, too.

I knew one thing there and then — that neither me nor your grandma wanted the kind of future for you where you'd see us working crappy retail jobs and looking for people like your dad or my dad to save us. We'd show you that your dreams are boundless, whether you have straight teeth or not.

We arrived home, and I unbuckled my seatbelt. Stared straight ahead, and right after she turned off the engine, I said to Mum, 'It's a girl.'

I was going to tell her anyway. I just didn't want her to control *everything*.

Mum also stared straight ahead, not saying anything, but out of the corner of my eye, I thought I noticed a small twitch of a smile.

Someone had replied to my ad. Win.

The trouble with advertising was that a million other bozos were also advertising for people to share costs on the traditional post-graduation planet-hopping tour — schoolies time, right? — and they had more to offer than I did. I got sick of seeing words like 'luxury', 'carefree' and 'classy' in their ads. If my ad had been honest it would've had descriptions like 'almost trouble-free', 'comes with plenty of hard work' and 'probably safe'.

So, someone answering was a double-win, really.

I met her on the space dock, as far away from the *Port Vila* as I could manage. She was taller than me, and she had a really good, really white smile with none of that distracting tooth art. A tiny, tiny animated tattoo was on one ear lobe, but I couldn't make it out. She was wearing sensible space-going gear — shorts, T-shirt and bare feet — which was a good sign, and she had a canvas bag slung over one shoulder. It wasn't too big, either. If she'd rolled up with a couple of suitcases, some hat boxes and a bunch of garment bags, I would have known to back away.

'Is that you, Tekura?' I held out my hand.

She dropped her canvas bag on the deck and we shook. Her grip was firm enough without trying to make a point. 'And you're Damien Heong. When do we leave?'

'You don't want to see the ship first?'

'I've checked it out on the Stream.' She tilted her head. 'I've checked you out, too.'

'And?'

'You'll do.'

There's nothing like being tagged 'adequate' to get your day off to a good start. 'There's still work to be done before we can ship out. I warned you about that.'

She picked up her bag. 'I'm not staying on this station longer than I have to. Show me this deathtrap and we can get to work.'

She marched off. I stared after her, open-mouthed. Deathtrap? She was calling my spaceship a deathtrap? How dare she!

Uncle Jayden had lent me the *Port Vila*. It was a mini-freighter, one of dozens he had chugging their way around the solar system picking up and delivering whatever could make a profit. I'd spent some happy times with him and his crews, and that's where I learned to pilot, starting when I was fifteen, and soloing a year later. Not that there's a lot of real work to do these days, with the tame AI-running ships. Piloting between planets isn't hard, but I still remember the jeebies the first time Uncle Jayden let me dock at a space station. Everything you've learned about the way things move, change directions and stop has to be thrown out the window and a whole new set of skills learned. Mess it up and it's a few billion bucks and/or lives, including yours, at stake.

Pricey.

I caught up with Tekura in the airlock. Because it was the *Port Vila*, the airlock was cheapskate, supposedly licensed for two people, but it was really only comfy for about one and a half. It meant we stood face-to-face, far too close for strangers, trying not to do anything awkward with our hands.

Tekura sniffed. 'Smells.'

'All spaceships smell.'

'You should do something about it, you know.'

I whipped my doodad out of my pocket, expanded the display and poked away at it. 'There. It's added to the list.'

Tekura stared at me — or rather, at my doodad. When she saw me looking at her, she put a hand to her mouth. 'Sorry. I was being rude.'

I shrugged. 'I'm used to it.'

'It's just … You don't see many of those things, is all.'

'Yeah, we're a very select group, AyeAyes. Just me and a couple of hundred others, worldwide.'

'AyeAyes?'

'Implant Intolerance people. It's a special club. We won't have just anyone.'

Tekura squirmed a little. I could see that she was curious, but also that she knew how rude it was to probe people about conditions like Implant Intolerance. I held up a hand. 'Look, I know what you want to know so I'll answer before you ask. First of all, it's genetic and it can't be cured because I can't tolerate any of the gene manips that usually fix up genetic conditions. Second of all, no I can't access the Stream like everyone else. That's what the doodad is for.'

I didn't go into the third question that people ask, because I was sick and tired of it. How do I feel being cut off from the modern world and unable to join in like everyone else? How do you think I feel?

Tekura nodded. 'Kharaab kismat.'

Yep, bad luck in a bonus-sized package — but that was almost the last I heard of it. She rarely mentioned it again, and when she did it was in a way that made AyeAye sound completely ordinary and boring.

The *Port Vila* really was the bottom of Uncle Jayden's barrel, right underneath the clunkers, hacks and floating bombs that usually end up there. These mini-freighters were designed to run with a minimal crew, a dozen people maximum, and, as usual, the crew quarters were primitive. No private cabins, just a shared dormitory area with triple bunks and walls — bulkheads — a more-than-dull shade of metal grey. The ablutions area was three tiny, side-by-side shower cubicles. The kitchen — the galley — opened onto a tiny living/recreation area, with a table that folded away when it wasn't being used. Chairs likewise.

This was stripped down, pared back, a no-frills style taken to the extreme. If you ripped out every bit of flair, then sandblasted away every ghost of colour, then exterminated any idea of comfort, then you'd nearly have the *Port Vila*, the place Tekura and I would be spending the next three months.

Cosy.

So it turned out that Tekura was sensational with AI systems. When we got down to work, she thumped the *Port Vila* resident AI into shape in a couple of hours. She complained about it while she was working, going on about how cutting corners was the way to disaster and how some people wouldn't know how to set things up if their life depended on it. Mostly, I fetched and carried for her, while trying to wallop the life-support systems into working order, a job that got a lot easier after Tekura looked over my shoulder and pointed out exactly what needed doing.

She'd been on Banger Station for a month, which was about twenty-eight days too long, according to her. But it did mean that she'd made some contacts. She was able to lean on a drive specialist to come and recalibrate the *Port Vila*'s drive for mates' rates. I still nearly fainted at the cost, but the *Port Vila* wasn't going anywhere without a calibrated drive.

Things were actually going okay, until I got thrown in jail.

After some successful heavy-duty arc welding on some external sensor flanges, Tekura and I decided to take a morning off. It was the first downtime in two weeks since we'd started on making the old bucket space-worthy. We'd been working hard.

We left the space dock and since Tekura had had time to explore Banger Station with her mother before the massive argument and the storming off, she was able to lead the way to the tourist-trap sectors. Welcome to casinos, bars, music from holospeakers and buskers, restaurants, souvenir shops and other, seedier possibilities that you could only access through side alleys. Tekura pointed them all out, in a voice loud enough to get me blushing and to annoy the barkers, who stood at the heads of these alleys touting for business. It was noisy, colourful and about as classy as a two-buck yo-yo with extra glitter, and with Tekura there it was the most fun I'd had in ages.

Cheery.

Tekura was pointing out which of the burger joints used real meat and which used processed recycled algae, when a hunched-over figure shambled out from between two of the shops that lined the street. He had a flat hat that obscured most of his features, and a beard that finished the job, and overalls that only stayed on because of the amount of duct tape keeping them in one piece. And I had awful imaginings of duct-tape underwear. He glanced at us, then glanced around so furtively that I had to look to make sure we weren't being set upon by assassins. He was apparently reassured by what he didn't see, so he sidled up to us. 'Spare any change?' he growled out of the corner of his mouth.

We didn't get a chance to answer. Sirens sounded and lights flashed. Doors banged open. Three squads of different uniforms pounced on our beggar.

He didn't run. He put his hands to his face, threw back his head and howled like somebody who had lost all hope.

The yellow team reached him quickest, but not before half a dozen floating spy eyes homed in, hopeful of getting some juicy shots to make money out of on the Stream. The Yellows didn't slow down at all, bowling him over and grappling him to the ground. They wrapped him up in one of those elastic restraining webs, but it was the laughing and high fives that got to me. I stepped up. 'Hey, take it easy, he's not resisting.'

That was all it took. Bam. I was stunned, wrapped in another restraining web and locked up until I could pay the fine for interfering with lawful processes. And when I say, 'I could pay the fine', it actually meant Tekura paying the fine and getting me out because I had no money.

'Don't say anything,' she ordered when I was escorted out of the holding cell. 'Just come with me.'

I held it in until we were back on the *Port Vila*. I kicked the nearest bulkhead. 'Can't wait until we're out of here. Money-grubbing, soulless, heartless, brainless hellhole this station is.'

Tekura was looking off into the distance. She flicked left to right. 'There. I've hit your bank account with a request to reimburse me for the cost of the fine, and the accommodation. Pay it back when you get the money.'

'Accommodation? What accommodation?'

'You were in their cell for hours. User pays.'

I ground my teeth. 'I take it back. This place isn't heartless. It never had a heart in the first place. And what about the old guy? What happened to him?'

'There's nothing you can do, Damien. I made some enquiries. He was a stallholder, small time, couldn't afford to renew his licence, went broke and had no backers. His family left him, and finally he was reduced to asking tourists for money. A big no-no, that. The bounty hunters love scooping up those guys.'

'Bounty hunters?'

'It's a thriving business off Earth. No police, except in the really big places, so it's up to bounty hunters to snap up any law-breakers or loan defaulters. For the reward.'

'He won't be able to pay for his cell.'

'He won't go to prison. He'll become an indentured worker. That's supposed to mean he can work off his fine, but it really means he's a slave from now on and that's the way he'll die.'

I kicked a box of welding rods. It hurt. I did it again. 'That's not fair.'

'Out here, the market rules. User pays is God. Business is business.'

'Whatever happened to taking care of people?'

'Oh, that's okay. Lots of money in patient care, child care, geriatric care.'

'That's not what I mean.'

'I know.' She patted me on the arm. 'And it's sweet to find that some people are still naive.' She swung her arms wide. 'Travel the universe, remember? See other places and other ways. Learn about the differences that unite us.'

'Someone should do something about travel writers.' I thumped the bulkhead with a fist this time and scowled. 'They have a lot to answer for.'

In the end, what I thought was going to take a couple of months took a couple of weeks, thanks to Tekura. I felt awkward about it, as I hadn't put anything in the ad about getting the ship ready for the journey. She didn't complain, though. She complained about the stupid programmers, stupid engineers, the stupid systems analysts and the stupid cargo configurers, but she didn't complain about the work. She didn't complain about my cooking, either, but then again she would have had to be really picky to do that. I'm a great cook, even with the sort of basic ingredients that I was able to scrounge up on a limited budget.

That's when we talked most, I guess, over meals. At least, after about ten or fifteen minutes when we'd finished stuffing our faces. Hard work makes you hungry, right?

We raked over the usual stuff about where we went to school and what was on the horizon, ambition-wise, and about what we were looking forward to while poking around the solar system. I was glad she was looking for the same sort of out-of-the-way places that I was. She thought that visiting a mining colony on Calisto sounded exciting, and the prospect of a visit to Tycho Crater made her punch me on the shoulder, her eyes bright with excitement.

It was on one of these sessions that I finally made out that her ear-lobe tattoo was a little cat, one of those statue ones that wave their paw up and down. Once I worked it out, it was hypnotising. I couldn't stop looking at the way its paw bobbed, bobbed, bobbed.

Cute.

I got so comfortable I even told her about Uncle Jayden. I had to pick and choose carefully, though, because I didn't want her to think that I came from a family of total crazies.

Uncle Jayden is a strange mix of the old-fashioned and the new-fashioned. He owned a fleet of mini-freighters that ploughed all over the solar system, but he preferred old hardcopy books to text on display. He taught me how to cook by preparing and combining my own ingredients instead of printing out meals. And he wanted to be called 'captain', but he was happy with 'skipper' if no-one else was around.

He ran everything by the Law of the Sea, too. That's how he used to talk about it, with the capital letters. I think he really wanted to be back in the days of sail and oceans, to tell the truth. He had an antique brass barometer that he took with him onto every vessel he commanded, even though it was one hundred per cent pointless out in space. He loved buying old charts, unrolling them and poring over the details of sand bars and currents. His favourite books were by people like Melville, Forester and O'Brian, and he read passages out loud to me. Liked the sound of his own voice. And, like lots of people, he was into true-life history. His favourite stuff was maritime disasters. Shipwrecks, mutinies, castaways, especially those with a bit of cannibalism, lost-at-sea episodes that end up with people drinking their own urine, all that sort of goodness. He loved the idea of the war, too, in a way that was the opposite of my parents, most likely because it was so far away from the other side of the galaxy. He always had sensors on maximum gain just in case one of the spaceships from the Green–Blue war made it all this way and wanted to go hostile on us. Not that there was much we could do about it, since none of Uncle Jayden's freighters was armed. All we'd be able to do was turn tail and run.

So I gave Tekura an edited version of that and then remembered my manners. 'And you? Tell me about your family.'

Her face set like stone. 'My family is out of bounds.'

'What? Come on, family is juicy. Share all the embarrassing details.'

She shook her head. 'Promise me you won't go sneaking around my family, all right?'

'Now you're making it irresistible.'

'Don't be stupid. If you do, I'm jumping ship the first chance I get and you can whistle for your money.'

It wasn't the money I was worried about. Tekura was being serious. No fun stuff here, no playfulness, complete opposite of her normal self.

'Sorry. Didn't mean to hit a sore spot like that.'

She sighed. 'My family. Sore spot. That's about right.'

'And I've officially lost interest in them. I promise.' I yawned and stretched. 'What were we just talking about?'

Eventually, the *Port Vila* was ready. She squeaked through the space-worthiness test and I don't think the inspector was totally joking when she asked me for the name of my next of kin, just in case.

We were fully provisioned — at least as well as we could afford. I'd managed to scavenge some stuff that we might be able to trade, but I wasn't hopeful and it wasn't the main point of our journey. We were tourists, footloose and fancy-free, just having a good time following our noses across the solar system. I filed a departure request as soon as the inspector left and it was granted immediately. I took the pilot's chair. Tekura took the copilot's chair. We ran through our lists, double-checking each other.

'Looks like we're all set,' I said.

'There's one thing.' Tekura had tied back her hair and I could see more of her face and the waving cat. 'What's our first destination?'

'Mars looks lovely at this time of year.'

She grinned and strapped herself in. 'Mars it is, then.' She gazed off into space, then used a finger to flick in front of her eyes. 'No solar-flare warnings, but it looks as if the Greens have attacked several Blue-held systems in the fourteenth quadrant.'

'As if that's going to worry us.' The fourteenth quadrant might be one of the closest to our solar system, but it was still thousands of light years away. Before I was born, my parents — Rob and Daz — did a tour of duty as special advisers to the Blues. Now, they didn't want anything to do with that stupid war and the way it dominated politics back on Earth. Politics was banned in our house and that suited me because it was possibly the most boring thing in the whole universe, sports-star biographies included.

'Don't you care about the war?' Tekura asked.

I punched the engine-priming display. 'Nothing to do with me.'

Tekura gave me a look but didn't say anything.

Less than twenty-four hours out, I was still getting used to being in space again when I remembered what I'd forgotten. It's always like that. Whenever I go anywhere I'm always sure I've forgotten something. It burns away at the back of my mind until it hits me and then I swear a lot at how stupid I've been.

This time, it was a sensational forget: I hadn't organised entertainment. This might not sound like a big deal, but it was. It takes ages to get anywhere in a solar system. In fact, it takes less time to hop from star to star than it does to chug around planets. That's because once you get outside a star's gravitational field, the Asoka drive can be engaged. That's the one that folds up space and lets you travel light years in a couple of minutes. Without it, humanity wouldn't have spread halfway across the galaxy like it has. The downside is, though, that once you reach the planets circling whatever star you've arrived at, you have to use good old impeller drives. They're a whole lot better than the rockets they used back in the early days of space flight — those guys were basically strapping themselves on top of bombs, something I wouldn't do in a million years — but it still takes a long time to get from planet to planet.

On our trips together, Uncle Jayden could have happily spent the journey immersed in the Stream for entertainment, but he knew I couldn't. So when we visited Venus and the asteroid belt, he made sure to have the latest movies, plenty of books and lots of games aboard. He even interrupted his favourite between-planets pastime (making those stupid ships in bottles, naturally) to do stuff with me. Some of my happiest times as a kid were those long weeks between planets laughing away with Uncle Jayden at those old-time flat-projection classics like *Simple Jack*.

My wail brought Tekura running. 'I forgot the entertainment!'

At first, she didn't understand. Why should she? She had the Stream to keep her amused. 'Can't you read books on your doodad?'

She was right. I'd just associated good old-fashioned hardcopy books with long, boring space flight. 'Okay, okay, it's not as bad as I thought. Nice one. Thanks.'

'You don't sound very grateful.'

'No, really, it's fine. I like reading. I'll read a lot. See you when we reach Mars.'

The next day, Tekura dropped a large square of plastic shielding on our table. It was marked up in a square grid. 'I'm going to teach you Go.' She saw my startled expression. 'Calm down. This shielding is spare stuff. I didn't rip it off the walls.'

'Bulkheads,' I said automatically. 'On a ship — or spaceship — walls are bulkheads.'

She emptied her pockets of dozens of hexagonal nuts. Half of them were white. 'I found these right at the back of cargo bay two. I used nearly all my nail polish on them.'

'You don't wear nail polish.'

She rolled her eyes. 'You're not the only one who thought of trade goods. Someone on a lonely outpost would pay an arm and a leg for something like that.'

'And you used it to make white nuts?'

She looked at me very seriously and held one up. 'Stones. The pieces are called stones.'

And so began my initiation into the complex and meditative game of Go. Tekura was patient and knowledgeable, and put up with me asking the same question over and over again, like, 'What's a liberty?' She had an interesting approach, too, to welcoming a newcomer to the world of Go. She did it by thrashing me in every game. She could have been an expert, she could have just been a little bit better than me, I couldn't tell, but she definitely had no intention of letting me win a game or two to encourage me. At the end of each game she'd simply bow, grin and ask, 'Again?'

I'd almost always agree. This was an eye-opener, as I was never the world's most gracious loser. In games, I mean, not out there in real life. I could handle trying hard and losing out in a competition for a job, but there was something about the whole business of game playing that brings out the competitive streak in me. Uncle Jayden found that out early on and as a result we never played cards or anything like that. The only games we played were cooperative, where we were both working towards a goal, which would take days to complete.

Go with Tekura was different. I lost, but I never felt like jumping to my feet, flipping the board over and scattering the pieces — stones — all around the room. Maybe it was something about the nature of the game, or maybe it was who I was playing it with.

And didn't that open a whole can of worms that I wasn't quite ready to dive into.

Uncomfortable.

That was one of the things we hadn't talked about and continued not to talk about. We were both nominal grown-ups, healthy, who liked each other, and we were confined in a small space very close to each other in all sorts of ways. Shared dormitory, right? And yet neither of us suggested a really obvious way of passing the time. Reluctance? Awkwardness? Or was Tekura uneasy about my handicap?

Or was it just me?

I was working in the hydroponics section, the one that helped refresh the air and provide us with fresh veggies for our journey, and I nearly dropped my pH meter when the whoop-whoop-whoop of the alarm sounded.

I sprinted for the bridge, but Tekura was there ahead of me. 'A small ship of unknown origin has set off a repeating beacon. No other details,' she said. 'I've contacted the authorities. What do we do now?'

'We go to their aid.'

'We what?'

'It's the Law of the Sea. The nearest vessel to a vessel in distress is obligated to render assistance.'

'That's your Uncle Jayden, isn't it?'

'It's the right thing to do.'

I peered at the ship's display then jabbed at my doodad so hard I lost my grip on it, but I caught it after it bounced off the deck. 'Two, three hours, maybe less, we'll be there.' What sort of vessel would be all the way out here? It was millions of kilometres from the asteroid belt. No prospector in her right mind would be in this part of space. A smuggler? A schoolies trip gone badly wrong?

Mystery.

Nothing happens fast in interplanet travel, so we kicked back with the Go board. I practised my calmness while being slaughtered.

A few hours later Tekura lifted her head. 'Uh-oh. The distress call. It's loose on the Stream.'

'We're live? Spy eyes are all the way out here?'

'News sellers are looking for any news everywhere, all the time.'

It took me a minute or so, but my doodad showed me that a couple of spy eyes had picked up the distress call and had beaten us to the drifting vessel. Tekura interfaced my doodad with the ship's display so I could get a better view. It was a battered-looking spaceship of unfamiliar design but looked even older than the *Port Vila*. It was both rolling and yawing, and it wasn't a good sign. No captain would allow a ship to tumble like that if she had a choice.

My hands hurt and I realised that I was gripping the armrests of my chair really, really hard.

'It's Palmeenee.' Tekura was staring up and away to her right, making that twirly index-finger motion that I'd been told meant some serious data diving. 'War refugees.'

Wow.

Humanity has met very few alien species in our push into the universe. The Palmeenee were one of them and, as alien species go, they were about as alien as they come.

A Japanese exploring team found the Palmeenee world circling Kepler-186 and must have been overjoyed. Yorokobi was reasonably Earth-like, except for the lack of just about any dangerous animals or plants. It was such a paradise it took nearly a hundred years before the settlers realised that the planet was already home to an intelligent species. The Palmeenee hadn't been noticed earlier because there weren't many of them — and they kept to themselves, mostly in underground settlements. They were smart — incredibly so in areas like social dynamics — but they had no real curiosity and so never sought out the newcomers to their world. Even after first contact was made and a linguistic bridge set up, they weren't hungry for interaction. Trade, commerce, exchange of ideas didn't interest them. Dancing, swap meets and speed dating weren't even on the table. They weren't aggressive, and any dealings were almost painfully polite, but they left humanity to itself.

Strange.

The earliest contact did come up with one stunning fact, though — the Palmeenee had been a spacefaring species but had given it up 'a long time ago'. When the settlers had got over a bad case of the WTFs, they pressed the Palmeenee, who just mumbled vaguely about how they'd had enough space travel and couldn't see any point in going further.

Which made them the perfect collateral damage when the war spread to that quadrant. Neither the Blues nor the Greens avoided Palmeenee settlements when trying to smash each other. Casualties were high, but the Palmeenee never retaliated, which meant they continued to be overlooked and continued to take casualties.

Some of them, though, had had enough.

The Palmeenee ship shouldn't have made it this far. It looked as if it was made for short hops, and from the signs of damage on it, it had been caught in at least one skirmish. The *Port Vila's* AI managed to edge us alongside so Tekura and I could rig up a connection to bring the refugees into one of the cargo bays.

Describing alien species is tricky because they're alien. Which sounds stupid, but it's actually profound if you think about it. For a start, their biology works in different ways from ours. They've sprung from different origins, after all. And as for psychology and behaviour, that's spawned all sorts of research. Careers have been made out of trying to make sense of Palmeenee minds. Still, we make the mistake of assuming that aliens behave like we do. I guess we're trying to find some basis for connection in the grand human way.

But if I'm getting all philosophical, I say that there must be a few things that all life shares, and valuing self-preservation is one of them. If your home is being crushed by a disaster — and it doesn't matter if it's natural or something else — then you're going to want to get out of there, fastest. You'll want to look for somewhere else to live, somewhere that's safer. And — here's where I could be going out on a limb — most intelligent species seem to have some sort of regard for their offspring. They want to protect them, help them grow up and live a decent life. That has to give you even more motivation to get the heck out of a war-torn planet.

Sensible.

Physically, it's hard not to compare the Palmeenee to crustaceans of some kind. Insects, maybe? They have eight limbs and a hard exoskeleton at least. They spend a lot of their time with their spine arched back and the forelegs raised. These are their manipulators as they have sets of opposable claws. When upright like this, they can get to a couple of metres tall. I've heard them compared to praying mantises or scorpions, but now that I was seeing them up close I scrapped those comparisons. The Palmeenee were simply something else.

And they smelled like bread. Warm, fresh bread. Mmm.

Their contact with humans had taught them a few things. One of the taller Palmeenee pressed forward as a spokesperson. It — I wasn't going to even guess which of the four sexes the spokesperson was — tried a few languages in its whistling, clicking voice before settling on English. 'We have hurt. We have injured. We ask your help. Please. Please.'

A full-scale tourist spaceship would have a doctor on board, maybe two, and a nice shiny clinic. All the *Port Vila* could offer was a first-aid cabinet.

Tekura went into a near-constant Stream trance, diving for information on Palmeenee physiology and the best way to render first aid, working side-by-side with the Palmeenee spokesperson. I helped by finding blankets, bringing water, mopping up bright-red Palmeenee blood, sorting through our supplies to see what food would be acceptable, stopping Palmeenee trying to access the rest of the ship, and even holding Palmeenee down by their raspy shoulders while Tekura and the spokesperson went to work.

We had no anaesthetics that were effective on Palmeenee, so I found out what the Palmeenee sound of agony was, something I wish I could scrub from my memory.

Look, it was grim. I'm not going to pretend it wasn't, so if I've edited out some of the more awful parts, you'll understand. The stuff about the injured Palmeenee kids, particularly.

Tekura accessed the Stream in a way that made me jealous for about the billionth time in my life. She was even able to grab a few words of Palmeenee to help calm and reassure our guests. Me? I couldn't handle my doodad while I needed both hands to help carry a wounded Palmeenee, or shift pallets, or drag useful items from the Palmeenee ship to ours. I was dumb labour, mostly, but doing the best I could. How could I not?

All I could do was slap in a course for Mars, the nearest port. Get them there quickest and they'd have the best chance of surviving.

Time went blurry in the urgency. I don't know when Tekura dragged our Go board down from the bridge, but she found time after reading an article by one of the early settlers on Yorokobi.

I now know what excitement looks like among Palmeenee. When Tekura and I presented the board, there was a lot of straightening and tapping front claws together, almost like applause. Five of the little ones clattered over to us and the spokesperson had to herd them away to let us through. When we reached the spokesperson he/she/it/jher bowed. 'We are honoured. Will you take black?'

While just about all of the able-bodied Palmeenee clustered around, Tekura beat the spokesperson three games in a row. The spokesperson bowed. 'You play well.'

Tekura bowed in return. 'So do you.'

'We learned from the settlers on Yorokobi. Playing Go with them was good.' His/her/its/jher upper body rose and twisted from side to side. 'Do you know what happened to them?'

'The settlers?' Tekura bit her lip, riffling through the data in front of her. She went pale. 'None of them are left.'

Silence fell in the cargo bay, a stillness it hadn't had since the Palmeenee arrived. Eventually, the spokesperson tapped his/her/its/jher chest with a claw. 'Go is a worthwhile product of your civilisation. War is not.'

Soon, Go became the centre of Palmeenee activity in the cargo bay. As a distraction and a time filler, it was a winner. The Palmeenee organised tournaments and league tables in a way so complicated that my doodad gave up analysing it.

I found out something, too, that made me feel even warmer towards the Palmeenee. They had no access to the Stream. No implants, no doodads, no curiosity, remember? I had a whole bunch of Streamless buddies, and they were as alien as I sometimes felt.

Irony.

By this time, the *Port Vila* was well on its way to Mars and it was surrounded by a flock of spy eyes. All of the news dealers, looking to make a buck out of selling news to the universe, were desperate to know what was going on inside our vessel. Vultures? Scavengers? Bottom-feeding slime suckers? Honest workers? Who could tell?

One of the mid-size Palmeenee pushed a cup of water into my hands and herded me away from the chaos. He/she/it/jher took me to the corner of the cargo bay and waited until I slumped onto a stool before bustling off. I sipped and got my doodad to cast a display. The *Port Vila* was trending hotter than hot on the Stream, swamping just about everything else in the news sphere. Billions were talking about us, offering opinions, making promises and threats, wanting to proposition us, demanding to know our motives and how we felt about it all. I was even on a T-shirt.

We were the biggest thing in the solar system.

As tired as I was, I had to laugh. Without trying, we'd achieved something that half of humanity desperately wanted. We were scaling skywards, we were bobbing up at the top of news feeds, we were bumping celebrity weddings aside. Anyone who saw themselves as up to date with current affairs had to know about us. The history of the *Port Vila* was being searched as we worked. Even our backgrounds were being picked apart. I shied away from that. It took an effort, but I honoured the promise I'd made to Tekura not to probe about her family, even though there it was being kicked around the news sphere. I won't say I wasn't tempted, but then I saw that she had her arm around the tallest Palmeenee and she was helping him/her/it/jher to some bedding against one of the bulkheads. She was humming a song, gently, softly, as she eased the Palmeenee to the blankets.

I killed the screen of temptation, picked up a broom and started sweeping up old Palmeenee scales. Before too long I started humming, too. After that it was a short step to soft shoe shuffling a little, side to side, as I swept.

'You can do better than a broom for a partner,' Tekura said.

I jumped. I hadn't seen her draw near.

She held out a hand. I gave the broom to a junior-sized Palmeenee, who stared at it, and then Tekura and I were in each other's arms, dancing. We had no music, but it didn't matter much. For a few moments, our exhaustion disappeared and for a moment that was a bubble in time, instead of being caught up in a refugee emergency we were enjoying an end-of-year schoolies interplanetary trip.

'You can dance,' Tekura murmured.

My head was on her shoulder. She smelled good. 'You sound surprised.'

'Pleased, is all.'

'The Palmeenee are staring at us.'

'Let them stare.'

'They're good starers.'

'We're good dancers.'

Tekura and I shuttled between the bridge and the cargo bay that was now the Palmeenee sickbay and living quarters. We must have spent a little bit of time in the mess, feeding ourselves, I guess.

Our refugee rescue blew up a political storm. For years, the Earth government had backed away from taking sides in the whole Green–Blue war, but it was facing a general election in a couple of months' time so we became hot stuff. Real-time constant polling was showing that the government had been losing popularity for ages. It'd been in power for a decade and it looked as if people wanted a change, so the Palmeenee refugee situation was an opportunity for the government to show how strong it was. Commentators were frothing at the mouth and barking about keeping these aliens out, wanting to send them back to where they came from, and the government bigwigs were quick to respond.

Commentators? Who are they? As far as I can tell they're people who work totally from a 'no evidence at all' basis and simply say whatever comes into their head. Trouble is, people — and governments — listen.

Incredible.

Tekura was cynical. 'Okay, Mr Naive,' she said over a rare moment when we were drinking cups of coffee at the same time. I didn't want to start yawning as I thought I'd never stop. She had dark circles under her eyes from tiredness. 'Let me explain it to you. Xenophobia is fantastic for governments. They can use it.'

'Isn't it dangerous?' I was sitting down and I didn't think I'd ever be able to get up again. My head was made of iron and the table was a massive magnet pulling it down.

'Can be, but that doesn't stop them using it. It's the classic us-and-them ploy. They're going to come and grab our jobs from us. They have a different way of life from us. Our culture/heritage/breakfast cereal is going to be taken away from us by them.'

'That's stupid.'

'Yes. Yes it is. But it serves those who need to use it, like for elections. They manipulate the truth, keep it from people, and so xenophobia grows. The best way to overcome xenophobia is to share knowledge, to share the truth.'

'I thought we were going to be heroes, coming to the rescue like that.'

'Looks like we rescued the wrong ship for that.'

Mars wouldn't let us dock at Deimos Station.

I let the ship's AI put us into orbit while I scrambled to find Tekura. As usual, she was in the middle of a knot of little Palmeenee while trying to understand what one of the big ones was getting at and keeping an eye on the worst of the injured. Not far away, the Go tournament raged in silence.

You know, one of the more amazing things about the Palmeenee was how quiet they were. If this cargo bay was full of humans it'd be full of chaos. Noisy, too. The Palmeenee went about their suffering quietly. Maybe that was part of the problem. Too quiet for their own good? I'd hate it if that was how things worked.

Tekura's eyes went wide. 'They what?'

'The government back on Earth says that we can't bring the Palmeenee refugees into port. Deimos Station is closed to us.'

Tekura rubbed one of the little Palmeenee behind its ear plates. It jumped up and down and squirled. 'What are we going to do, Captain?'

I looked behind me, but then I realised that Tekura was being serious. I rubbed a hand over my face. How long had it been since I'd had a shower?

'Damien?'

Tekura was still waiting for an answer. 'We're going to follow the Law of the Sea,' I said. 'The Palmeenee refugees are owed assistance at the nearest port of call — and Deimos Station is the nearest port of call.'

✦

I tried arguing with the authorities. I cited international, interplanetary and interstellar law. I tried to lean on their humanity, but I couldn't find any. The government authorities controlled passage through Deimos Station, and they were standing firm.

I may have shouted a bit, too.

After kicking things and punching things and storming around for a while, I had an idea. Businesses down on Mars hated the way the Earth government controlled who could and couldn't land on Mars. In fact, most of the businesses on Mars hated the whole idea of government, but that's another matter. I had a sneaking suspicion that some of these mavericks might not mind breaking the government embargo — if there was a profit in it. And hosting a bunch of alien refugees and then selling media access to the highest bidder, could be a once-in-a-lifetime jackpot, enough to make company chairpeople dizzy.

So I had to wheel and deal with a whole bunch of people who were expert wheelers and dealers. After five minutes, my head hurt. After ten, I wanted to blow them all up. After thirty, I was in a dead zone and automatically playing one off against the other.

This was going to take some time.

The Palmeenee spokesperson asked for an update, wanting to know what was going on, but it wasn't through curiosity. It was through worry. While I could provide info, though, I couldn't supply explanations. Why were we still in orbit? What was taking so long? Why were the Palmeenee still suffering?

Politics. At least I had someone who was more expert than I was with that muck. I found Tekura tending to an old Palmeenee, helping to feed him/her/it/jher some of our last ice-cream. The Palmeenee loved ice-cream, especially vanilla.

'Tell me about politics.' I sat on a three-legged stool next to her.

She glanced at me with a 'what took you so long?' expression. 'Make yourself useful. Use a broom while you listen.'

'I can't stay long. I have a Martian logistics firm waiting for my response to their offer.'

'Sweep. Ask questions.'

I swept. 'So why is the government so keen to stop us from docking at Deimos Station? We've got injured beings here.'

'The government's making a point. Once refugees set foot on land — and a space station qualifies as land, apparently — they qualify for all sorts of legal status. They can appeal to courts, ask for representation, move from Mars to Earth, the sorts of things that would make it hard to get rid of them.'

'And the government wants to get rid of them?'

'The government wants to be seen as taking a tough stand on who comes to Earth.'

I had an answer for that. I'd been doing some research. 'But universal law states that refugees — of any kind — are entitled to seek safe haven.'

Tekura scooped up some ice-cream and ladled it into the Palmeenee's mouth. 'That's right. It comes from an agreement made way back in the early twentieth century.' She dropped the spoon in the bowl she was holding. 'Wars have been displacing people for ages and refugees have been refugees for ages. If we're going to be humane, and make any claim at being civilised, we have to help those in need. Who's more in need than refugees?'

I rocked back on my heels, then held the broom in front of me as a mock shield. 'Hey, I'm on your side, remember?'

Tekura frowned, then patted the Palmeenee on the shoulder and rose. She took my arm and steered me out of the cargo bay.

'Get ready, Damien,' Tekura said. 'The politicians are about to use every tool in their bag of dirty tricks.'

'That doesn't sound good.'

'It isn't. And we're caught up in it, like it or not. Be prepared to be trashed.'

'Me? What did I do?'

'Nothing, but that doesn't matter. Smearing someone is an ancient and effective tactic.' She sighed. 'Politicians are really, really clever, in some ways, at least. Find a hair, and they'll split it. They'll start to raise doubts. Are these Palmeenee really refugees? Are there Palmeenee aboard who could be criminals? Could these Palmeenee be carrying diseases that could spread? Could it be that some of these Palmeenee are just taking the opportunity to look for a nicer place to live, a place where they could make money? And what about the people piloting the ship they'd come on? Surely they're criminals of some sort or other. Accepting refugees would be condoning the activities of these lowlifes.'

'Wow.'

'Much wow.'

I leaned against the bulkhead near the entrance to the bridge. 'Can we do anything about it?'

'Sure we can.' Tekura's smile wasn't pleasant. 'The government's spinning stories, but two can play at that game. It's time we got the media on our side.'

So in between all her other duties, Tekura became our Media Liaison Officer. I even made her a badge out of an old Second Officer badge that Uncle Jayden had left lying around. She held it in her hands and studied it carefully. She turned it over and then back again. 'Thanks. But I think I need to tell you something.'

Uh-oh. 'Don't if you don't want to.'

'I don't want to, but I think you need to know that I'm sort of running away.'

'Aren't we all?'

'I mean it. My mum has no idea that I hooked up with you. She's been sending me angry messages, constantly, ordering me back home.'

'Ordering? Ouch.'

'She's like that. You get that way when you're important.'

Double uh-oh. 'How important?'

'She a minister in the government.'

'One of the big ones?'

'She's number three in the hierarchy.'

'Your mum is Minister for the Arts?'

'That's right. She was inspecting Banger Station to see about turning it into another artist studio cluster. She dragged me along to stop me jaunting off post-graduation.'

'And is this out there on the Stream yet? Minister's daughter saves refugees!'

'Not yet.'

'I bet your mum can't wait.'

'She doesn't know. Not yet.'

I rubbed my head. 'And you're telling me this now why?'

'It's going to come out sooner or later. Thought you might like to hear about it ahead of time.'

Tekura negotiated with some of the spy eye operators and allowed access to half a dozen. She managed things, of course, so that any video would show the Palmeenee as suffering calmly, as acting with dignity in their small family groups, of being no threat at all.

The best response came from showing the Palmeenee playing Go. That rated through the roof. More likes than a cat snuggling with a penguin while a duckling looked on.

I continued my sneaky discussions with Mars corporations, which impressed Tekura. 'Mr Naive becomes Mr Cunning? Nice.'

I wanted to see if any were prepared to send shuttles to dock with us directly and take the Palmeenee dirtside. Once they landed, Tekura assured me, everything would be different. The Palmeenee would have rights. 'But don't be surprised if the government goes to the next stage in the dirty tricks,' she warned.

'With the whole galaxy watching? What are they going to do? Blow us up?'

I didn't like the look Tekura gave me, but she was towed away by a gang of little Palmeenee. She was in the semi-finals of the Go tournament.

Not long after that, two things happened in quick succession. First, another Palmeenee ship drifted into our system. It was detected out near Neptune. It was in a worse state than the vessel we'd rescued, but it wasn't picked up by a merchant ship like us. It was picked up by the military, which started to tow it away, out of our system.

Everything went supernova.

You see, this crippled vessel started to come apart under the strain of towing and the situation turned chaotic. Soon, all over the Stream were government claims that the aliens on this vessel, the Palmeenee, had ejected their children, thrown them out into the vacuum of space in an effort to get the military spaceship to stop the towing and to take them in as refugees.

None of this actually happened, and that burned. Lies were told with perfectly straight faces. When spy eyes offered evidence that contradicted the government statements, they didn't apologise, didn't back down. The Prime Minister just got louder, denouncing such heinous actions and declaring that our borders were sacrosanct, that the decision about who comes to our worlds was ours.

Nice.

The Stream can't overload, but my doodad nearly had a nervous breakdown trying to cope with the flood of alerts I'd set up. Tekura managed better, but she said it was like trying to navigate through a swarm of bees. Bees that were on fire. With lasers.

Second, while the attention of the universe was on this other Palmeenee vessel and the little ones overboard, we were boarded by the military.

The hatch was blown off and the cargo bay started to decompress. This only lasted a second until a temporary airlock was snapped into place, but it was enough to throw everyone on the *Port Vila* into panic. Little ones climbed up as high as they could, squeaking and rattling. The mature Palmeenee stalked around, rattling claws. Loose items were sucked towards the hatch.

Tekura caught hold of one of the bulkhead struts and grabbed my arm as I stumbled and flailed.

The door to the temporary airlock opened and space marines in full battle gear marched in. They didn't point their weapons at us. Not quite. The leader surveyed the cargo bay and made one of those fist-pumping, pointing motions. They flipped their helmets back and I was relieved to see that they all looked embarrassed, uncomfortable and even apologetic. The leader could have been used in advertising — tall, with a good-looking skull, striking angular features. 'Who's in charge here?' she asked.

I looked at Tekura. She rolled her eyes and elbowed me. 'He is.'

I brushed myself down. 'Damien Heong. What's the meaning of this?'

'Just following orders, Captain,' the leader of the marines replied. She pointed to the Palmeenee. 'There,' she said over her shoulder. 'Secure the area.' She turned back to me. 'If you and your crew will leave the cargo bay, Captain, we can complete our business.'

I took a deep breath. 'And what is your business?'

'We're taking these illegal entrants to a safe place where they will receive the best care possible.'

'Mars? Earth?'

The marine shook her head. 'A safe place.'

I felt the heat rising in my face, but I didn't care. 'These are my passengers. I'm responsible for them. They don't just need the best care, they need immediate help. I'm taking them to Mars.'

'I'm afraid that won't be possible, Captain.'

'But the Law of the Sea says we must.'

'The Law of the Sea?' The marine frowned. 'What century are you living in, Captain?'

So maybe I shouldn't have sworn at a marine. And probably, certainly I shouldn't have pushed a marine in the chest. That's what caused me to be beaten up by a squad of marines, I guess. 'Restrained', I think they put it, but with a few well-placed punches and kicks just to let me know not to mess around with marines.

Groggily, from my position on the deck, cable ties around my hands and feet, I looked for Tekura. She was being cooperative, apparently, as she wasn't on the deck and cable tied. She caught my eye and gave me a grim thumbs-up sign. What for, I had no idea, so I fumed and struggled and swore and all I did was end up exhausted and bruised and ignored by the marines.

What they were doing was wrong. It was inhuman. All the good things like kindness and pity and sharing were thrown overboard just to help win an election by playing to the worst in us. The Palmeenee as bogeymen? Spare me. Evil outsiders, nasty others, we fear them … Well, the big guys didn't, not really, but they knew they could use the Palmeenee to scare enough voters into voting for them.

Smart.

I lurched from angry to feeling sick — gut-deep, punishing nausea. I lay there, helpless and ashamed, until the marines had gone and Tekura cut me loose.

The marines took the Palmeenee somewhere way out in the Oort Cloud, somewhere the government claims isn't part of the solar system, and so landing them there doesn't grant them any rights. No rights at all, no chance for anyone to learn about their hardships and suffering, no pity.

Tekura and I were left on a ship that was now allowed to dock at Deimos Station, but the cloud of spy eyes and actual news vessels gave me the shudders. Tekura and I put our heads together and set course for Saturn.

It's funny, but the *Port Vila* was back to how it was when we left Earth's orbit, but minus the Palmeenee it now felt so much emptier.

We talked a lot. Now, after everything, Tekura was able to share about her mum and about politics and what it had cost her. She laughed at the embarrassment all this had caused her mum. She said it was payback time. I told her about my parents, Rob and Daz, and how scarred they were from the war and how I'd like to stop that sort of thing from happening.

'We can change things, you know,' she said. I'd set up a wide horizontal display on the bridge to show us the way ahead. Saturn was a tiny bright dot, getting bigger.

'How?'

'Politics.'

'I thought you hated politics.'

'I've just seen too much of it much too close.' She shuddered, then grinned. 'But that's taught me a few things, like how not to do it.'

'Are you sure you're not just trying to surprise your mother?'

'Oh, it'll surprise her all right when we get a whole lot of people on our side and start a movement for change.'

'Lovely idea, but what's going to get people on our side?'

She pulled a spy eye out of her pocket. 'A nice close-up video of space marines beating up a heroic ship's captain who was only trying to do the right thing for dozens of despairing and injured refugees?'

'Heroic?' I liked the sound of that.

'It's the truth, and that's what we'll offer that old-style politics doesn't. We'll be open and truthful. No lies just to grab and hold onto power. We'll share what we know. We'll even answer questions when we're asked instead of talking around in circles.'

'You really have seen it up close.'

'You bet. Close enough to know that even if the truth is a sticky and uncertain concept, it's worth striving for.'

'What about the Palmeenee? The refugees? We have to do something for them.'

She was drumming her feet on the deck with excitement. Her cat tattoo waved at me. 'We have to help anyone who is so desperate they flee their home. How could we not?'

How could we not? That was something to live by. 'Let's do it,' I said.

'That means we won't be seeing Saturn.'

'Saturn can wait.'

Tekura's hand found mine. 'It's going to take us weeks to get back to Earth. What'll we do in the meantime?'

'I'm sure you'll think of something.'

She did. We used the time to plan how we were going to change the system.

With time left over for other stuff.

Sundays

MELISSA KEIL

9 p.m.

This is how it goes.

I am standing in a corner, 'cause I always seem to find myself standing in corners. Not in the centre of the sweaty, heaving dancers, and not in the back sunroom with the stoners and smokers. Definitely not too close to the front door — that would imply that I'm eager to escape, or eager to be seen. Party rules are vague and complex, but even I know that eagerness is never a good look.

I am holding a warm beer, handed to me ages ago by some guy in a baseball cap. He might've been one of Abdul's brothers, but it's hard to know for sure who lives here. I reckon there's, like, eighty bajillion people crammed into this tiny house, and, unlike our primary school socials, none of them are wearing nametags. Man — how many life situations could be clarified by nametags? Like, the guy hovering next to me with that smarmy look on his face? His nametag would read something like, 'Hi, I'm Ian! I'm gonna try to start a conversation by commenting on the juiciness of your lips, and will probably cop a feel of your arse as you try to flee.'

Yeah, and no doubt my tag would read, in pointy all caps: 'Gabrielle. Wicked crabby, despiser of parties, hater of mankind. Approach with caution.'

I take an accidental sip of beer. It tastes like what I imagine the Razaks' bathroom floor might taste like right about now: a soupy combo of dirt and cig butts. A hip-hop song is blasting, the walls and windows vibrating with bass, and the grind of dancers in the lounge are feverishly yelling the lyrics, as though there's some cosmic affinity between this ramshackle house on the edge of the Broadmeadows train line, and South Central LA.

I shouldn't be here. I should be hiding in the Razaks' granny flat with the other dorks who only score an invite to these things because their group, mysteriously, contains people who are considered cool. I should be exchanging snarky observations with Lara in front of Abdul's TV in said granny flat, or skulking with Tommy and his maths-nerd mates. I should be sharing silent, knowing glances with Louis, who went to round up our friends ages ago and has yet to return. Hell, if I were honest — I should be home, in bed, with a book and my daggy sixties music, which would reap me so much crap if these people knew it was the music I preferred.

I should be giving Ian my practised f-you face, 'cause even without looking I can feel him inching closer, the threat of mouth-breathing bearing down upon me.

Instead, my eyes are locked on the dancers. They're all silhouette and shadow, the dark broken only by the glow of a dozen mobile phones. In the middle of the space is Cameron, familiar floppy black hair a head and shoulders above almost everyone else in the throng.

There's nothing unusual about Cam being smack bang in the centre of the crowd. If there's a crowd of any kind — in

Year 12 Theatre Club, or the Chinese Youth Society soccer team his parents made him join — Cam will inevitably find himself in the centre, the rest of us mere mortals drawn to his smiling, too-pretty light. It's weird, 'cause in all the years that we have been friends, I've never found it intimidating — Cam is just my tall, affable, popular friend, who Mum likes to describe as 'our very own Gene Kelly'. I had to google that one, and no, I still don't get it. Though I suppose the shiny hair and perpetual shiny confidence do sort of fit.

Yeah, it's not unusual to see Cam grinding it up on the dance floor. Except, if this were any other party, Cam's side should be occupied by his beautiful girlfriend, 'cause Claire and Cam are never more than tongue length away from each other at these things. Claire and Cam are perfect, broad and tall and dark to tall and slim and light; kind and confident to warm and funny, and their babies would be adorable and flawless, like the mixed-race kids from a Bonds commercial. For four whole years, this is how it's been. Cameron and Claire are inevitable.

But now, as the music shakes the sticky floorboards, Cameron is kissing a tiny girl with bright-blue hair, and all I can think is this has to be some kind of elaborate Claire-and-Cam prank. My brain is doing strange things — well, stranger things than usual — but it seems to be telling me that one of my best friends is kissing some chick who is not one of my other best friends, and definitely not the person he is supposed to be kissing. My brain might be short-circuiting, but man, all I can think is that they do not look inevitable together. They are wrong, and incongruous, and would have some weird-arse-looking kids, with his cheekbones and her disproportionately long neck. Like photoshopping an otter's face onto a horse.

A hand grabs me lightly around the back of the head. I drop my gross half-beer with a squeal. Even through the pounding decibels, his low voice penetrates.

'Gabrielle? Are you hyperventilating? You look like you're hyperventilating.'

'Argh, Louis, let go!' I yelp. I straighten, fleetingly caught off guard by his calloused palm on my hair. Lou shoves his hands into his pockets. He's not much taller than I am, but is all shoulders and muscles and square, stubbly jaw, the boy my mum has always described, affectionately, as 'the thug one'. Though in Mum's estimation, Tommy is 'the nice one', and Lara is 'the chatty one', and Claire is 'the pretty boy's girlfriend', like my friends are characters in some lame-arse sitcom.

Lou's thick eyebrows furrow. He's wearing his uniform of faded jeans and a black T-shirt, a pack of smokes peeking out of his pocket. He smells faintly, familiarly, like tobacco and generic shampoo. I grab hold of his arm as my brain tries to hammer out some words.

'Gabe? Why's your face that colour?' Lou asks, dark eyes travelling back and forth between mine. 'You look like you've seen —'

But Lou is no longer looking at me. He's followed my gaze, and he's clearly caught sight of Cam, judging by his open-mouthed double take.

'Oh. Shit,' he says.

I grip his hand and use it to point through the crowds, somehow hoping that our combined power will cancel out whatever insanity is happening here. 'Lou — what is going on?' I yell. 'What's Cam doing? And who the hell is that girl?'

Lou has recently shaved his dark hair almost to the scalp, but a hand unthinkingly lifts to tug at the non-existent strands, his habitual nervous manoeuvre. 'Dunno. I mean, I guess him and Claire had a tiff or whatever, but —'

'What in the freaking hell is this?' A tinny voice squeals.

Lou and I spin around. Lara is standing next to us, hands on her hips, substantial chest heaving like she's sprinted here.

Lara rounds on us, an accusatory finger pointed. 'What is Cameron doing? Did you guys know about this?' she yells over the music.

'Lara, chill,' Lou rumbles. 'Look at Gabe. Do you think we know anything?'

Whatever is happening on my face makes Lara downshift from burly tempest mode. She has a smear of lipstick on one canine tooth, and it's normally my job to be on teeth patrol for Lara and her red lipstick, but none of that matters because the cosmic calamity continues as Claire materialises beside us.

I am frozen in shock, but Lara, always the more dramatic of the six of us, leaps in front of Claire. She grabs Claire and steers her around so that her back is to the dance floor. Lara shoots Lou and me a look of desperation; Lou takes a step back, disengaging as he is prone to do whenever any hint of emotional drama threatens.

'Listen, Claire-bear, let's go outside,' Lara says quickly. 'Tommy shouldn't be left alone with those guys from Lou's Greek school. Let's go find him before they dare him to chug a bottle of Sriracha again.'

Lou shoulders a little in front of me. 'Ah, yeah,' he says, his gravelly voice pained. 'Outside. Let's do that.'

Claire shakes off Lara's hand and turns around, pale ponytail swinging. It's like watching a car crash, a slow-motion building demolition; as disastrous as witnessing Tommy attempt to pull off a Panama hat for a month in Year 10.

Claire blinks at the dance floor. She smooths away an imaginary wrinkle in her dress. A pink-nailed hand reaches up to straighten the single heart on her necklace, a Valentine's present from Cam, which she has worn for as long as I can remember. And then she turns to face us again.

'Oh,' she says. 'So that's Isla. I kind of imagined she'd be taller.'

Lou superglues his shoulder to mine, tension humming through his skin. Lara's mouth opens and closes, but for once, Lara seems to have no words.

I round on Claire, my eyes bugging. 'Wait, what — you know about this?' I yell over the music.

Claire takes a nonchalant sip from her giant red cup. 'Well, yeah. I think Cam met her at the English exam last week.'

The three of us stare at Claire. She, quite painstakingly, avoids our eyes.

'But ... you guys ... you just had a fight!' I say. I hear the panic in my voice, and I know it's pathetic, but I can't seem to hold it back. 'You and Cam always fight, and you always make up. What ... Claire! You can't be okay with this!'

Lou looks kind of angry, or as angry as his deadpan face ever gets. 'Gabe's got a point,' he rumbles. 'It's not right. Even if you guys are on the outs, or whatever. He's being ... disrespectful.'

Lara nods vigorously, but Claire just gives Lou a swift, shrewd look that makes him scowl and avert his gaze.

Claire closes her eyes. 'Yeah, okay, look,' she says slowly, gesturing for us to huddle closer. 'We knew this was going to be tough for you guys, and I am a little pissed at him because we said we would talk to all of you together, but, the thing is ...' She crosses her arms defensively, and I feel a heavy, horrible weight settle in my guts. 'Cam and I have decided to break up,' Claire says flatly. 'It's been coming for ages. I'm sorry we didn't say anything sooner, but you guys ...' Her face scrunches, and even though my entire world is shifting on its axis, I'm also a bit flabbergasted, because I think Claire might be trying not to laugh. 'You guys are maybe just a wee bit invested,' she finishes with a grin.

My eyes ping-pong between Claire and Lara, Lou and Cam, but I think my brain stalled somewhere back at, 'So that's Isla.'

Claire sighs. 'Look, guys, this is gonna take some time for you all to process, but really, it's for the best.' She smiles brightly, like she hasn't just pitched a giant flaming turd bomb into the centre of our group. 'Come on, think about it. Uni starts soon, and honestly, I think we're both kind of relieved to be starting it ... free.'

No, no, no. This wasn't part of our plan. For four years it's been Claire and Cameron, ever since they hooked up at Tommy's fourteenth birthday party. Every movie night at Cam's house, bigger and nicer than any of the rest of ours, and every Saturday trip to the movies in the city; every lunch hour hanging on the edge of the soccer field watching Cam train; every after-school session at the greasy chicken-and-chips place at the train station. Every plan for next year, our first step into freedom, so close I can almost taste it — it's always been Claire and Cameron. Yeah, so maybe we are a wee bit invested. But, man, with the rest of our shitty, messy lives? Claire and Cam are the closest thing any of us have to a gravitational centre.

Claire gives us her best sympathy eyes. 'I know this is unexpected,' she says, her voice that patented, soothing Claire tone. 'But it's fine. Everything is going to be okay. It's all good.'

No. No, no. 'It's all good' is not acceptable for this situation. It's what you say when you fail a quiz that doesn't count towards final marks, or when Lou once again finds himself sleeping on Cameron's floor, 'cause Lou's mum is entertaining another Tinder date. It is not a satisfactory explanation for the only people in your life who are supposed to be rock-solid and unbreakable, one of whom is currently snogging a girl with indigo hair, who — oh my God — now has her hands right up the front of his shirt.

I close my eyes, trying to take myself to my happy place underwater with nothing but silence and my breath through my diving regulator. I haven't been to the ocean in months, what with exams, and my dad's wedding plans ballsing up my life. It's a little hard to visualise the peace of submersion with the brain-busting music, and Lou's too warm arm practically pasted to mine.

Claire shrugs. 'It doesn't have to change anything,' she says. The song switches to something even more thumpy and aggro, and someone on the dance floor hollers, dislodging the light fixture with an ill-timed arms thrust.

Claire casts one last look at the dancers and then disappears through the lounge-room door. Lara hurries after her.

The press of bodies has jammed Lou flush against me, enveloping me in his familiar smoke-and-shampoo scent. He looks uncomfortable, and totally thrown. Not a good sign, considering Lou dealt with the news of his own parents' divorce with nothing but a stoic shrug and a weekend *Fast and the Furious* marathon.

'Lou! This isn't right!' I yell, my voice getting lost. 'What are we gonna do?'

Lou cups a hand over the shell of his ear. He leans down, presumably to hear me better, the brush of stubble against my cheek briefly ticklish. I take a deep breath, trying to find the fortitude to repeat myself, just as someone jostles Lou, and my lips accidentally brush his ear lobe. Lou leaps back with a start.

Then a slurry, wet voice beside me burbles, 'Hey, has anyone ever told you you've got really sexy lips?' And Lou grabs my fist before I can launch it at gross Ian.

So this is what it's come to.

Stuck inside this crumbly house with a life that's suddenly crumbling, too. And for the first time, I can't be sure my friends will be there to salvage the pieces.

10 p.m.

Lou and I scramble into the kitchen behind Lara and Claire. It's like the last days of Casablanca in here, jammed with shouting people, every surface overflowing with cups and cans and the remnants of sausage rolls. Over by the fridge, Vanessa Nguyen is crying, noisy and damp, and her friends are scrambling around proffering paper wipes and fierce sympathy words. The usual party drama, fuelled by some crisis that'll no doubt be dissected to death over the next few hours. The magnetic letters on the fridge behind Vanessa's head have been rearranged to spell out the words: Hassan Fahed has a face like a cat arse. Commiserations, Hassan, whoever you are. You have my sympathy.

Lou scratches at his stubble, the raspy sound all too familiar when Lou is feeling beleaguered. 'Shit. Where'd they go?' he growls. 'And has anyone seen Tommy?'

The few people in the vicinity who know us shake their heads. The few people who don't offer some useless advice, and a few anatomical unlikely places where Tommy could be hiding.

Lou and I always find ourselves together at these things. Partly 'cause Lou is about as social as a hermit crab, or one of those octopuses who lug a coconut shell around, just so they have a handy place to retreat. I guess us social lepers and misanthropes must just gravitate towards one another; at least that's my explanation for why Lou and I, strangers then, ended up hiding together in the PE equipment room at our Year 7 formal, silently smacking a shuttlecock back and forth between us, tentatively bonding over the stupidity of the rest of the world.

The touch of cool glass against my neck snaps me back to the moment.

Lou holds out a bottle of Limonata, the top popped. It's my favourite, and not usually found in these parties of off-brand cola and cheap plonk.

'Where did this come from?'

Lou shrugs. 'Brought it from home, didn't I? Better than Abdul's stash. Didn't even know Romanian beer from Aldi was a thing.'

I take the bottle, weirdly unnerved by the gesture. 'Oh. Um, thanks, Lou.'

Lou shrugs. 'S'okay.' He clears his throat. 'We better find Tommy before he hears about this shit through the grapevine.'

There is a crash from the other side of the kitchen. A guy I vaguely recognise shoves his face against the pantry door, shading his hands against the slats. 'Oi, you guys!' he says to no-one in particular. 'Reckon someone's doing the business in here.'

Lou and I exchange a look. We hustle through the crowds, to find Lara and Claire trading whispered words inside the kitchen pantry in between bags of rice and cans of Spam.

Lara squints at us as light floods the cupboard. 'Get in here,

Gabrielle,' she hisses, hauling me and Lou inside and slamming the door behind us.

There's barely enough space for one normal-sized person in here, but with Lou's bulk and Lara's boobs, it's as crammed inside as a novelty clown car. I feel the pulse in my temple start to pound, in time with the shithouse club music.

'Suppose we couldn't have this conversation out on the street like normal people?' Lou grumbles. He lifts his arms above his head to make some space for me, and wiggles his backside into a shelf of tomato cans.

'Not my fault,' Lara snaps. 'Spend less time at the gym, G.I. Joe.'

I bristle. 'Hey, he's not the one with a skirt that could double as a circus tent,' I hiss, shoving the voluminous fabric of Lara's skirt out of the way.

Lara Saliba has lived three doors down from me since forever. She's my oldest friend, but weirdly, not my closest. It's like we're linked together only by proximity, and our stupid Mills & Boon names. Don't get me wrong, I love her to death, but her hectic energy and constant shoutiness are just a bit much to cope with, one on one.

'Yeah okay, sorry Lou,' she says, waving a dismissive hand. 'But, you know, forgive me for being a little bit tense. This is an emergency!'

'So what's the plan, then?' I whisper, 'cause urgent whispering seems to be called for in this situation. 'Lou, maybe you should go talk to Cameron?'

Lou grunts. 'And say what? You think I'm gonna be able to stop him pashing a rando? I can't even get him to stop putting McDonald's in his mouth —'

I elbow him in the ribs. 'How about, "Dude, since when has your thing been girls who look like cartoon characters?" Who even has blue hair —'

'Yeah, I reckon we could start by letting Is-la know she's peed on the wrong lamppost,' Lara says, crossing her arms. 'I haven't been in a fight since Year 7, but I still reckon I could take her —'

'Christ, you guys!' Claire yelps. It's dark in here, and I've been momentarily distracted by the gluggy sound of someone puking outside the door, accompanied by a few expletives, and a lot of cheering. I'd sort of forgotten Claire was even here. 'There's been no peeing on anything, Lara,' Claire hisses. 'Has it even occurred to you guys that this was my decision, too? Why are you all acting like I'm some sort of hopeless bystander?' Claire crosses her arms. 'I know you're upset, but that's actually really … freaking insulting. And, by the way, none of this is Isla's fault. That poor girl is not the issue here!'

The smell of vomit wafts into the pantry. I have a cast-iron stomach, but Claire's rant is making me queasy, and even in the dark I know Lou's face would be paling. I'm not sure that he's going to make it out of here without a sympathy hurl right into the Razaks' basket of cucumbers. Lou grabs my arm. He sways precariously sideways.

'Okay, we're done,' I say, yanking open the door. My friends may have crossed over into some alternate dimension of stupidity and obtuseness, but I refuse to spend another second of this hellish party trapped in a freaking kitchen cupboard.

I tug Lou's hand, and he follows blindly. I have no explanation for the giant ball of anger that coalesces as the kitchen light hits Claire's face, I only know that I need to get away from her before I say something I'm gonna end up regretting.

Outside, Brian Cheng from my chemistry class is face down on the floor, a puddle of bright vodka-and-orange sick near his head. His friends are pointing and laughing. One of them is in the process of tying his shoelaces together.

I step over his prone body, dragging Lou behind me, depositing the untouched Limonata on a bench as we pass.

'We're going to find Tommy,' I call over my shoulder.

Lou is holding his breath, his hand clasped firmly in mine. I've seen Lou gag after catching a glimpse of rubber novelty puke at Claire and Cam's last Halloween party, so I drag him quickly towards the laundry door, refusing to acknowledge Claire's anxious plea behind me. I know it's ridiculous, and yeah, probably a bit self-centred, this fury I can't seem to quash, that Claire's problems have upset my life. And, irrationally, all I really want right now is a hug from Cameron; Cam always has a ready hug for even the smallest of traumas, freely given and uncomplicated, one of the few people whose touchy-feelness doesn't make me squirmy.

God — I have been friends with Cam for way longer than I have known Claire. Does this mean that I'm supposed to be on his side? What am I supposed to do if these two people don't come as a pair now? I have this mental flash of my future, managing my friends like I manage my parents — conversations conveyed through me in terse Chinese whispers, and Cam hiding behind the agapanthus as he collects me for an awkward dinner that'll be filled with not-at-all-subtle digs at his ex — and I kind of want to join Brian Cheng in his epic kitchen-floor puke.

Instead, I hold tight to Lou's hand and cast a last look over my shoulder, leaving Lara gesturing frenetically at Claire, and Claire looking kind of resigned amid the Razaks' groceries. They can stay there for all I care.

11 p.m.

I lead Lou through the laundry, down the concrete steps and outside into the warm, smoke-filled air. It's a little less jammed here, the space beneath the carport hosting various pashing couples, and what looks like an impromptu game of tequila pong. At least, I think that's what's supposed to be happening; as far as I can see, the game seems to involve nothing but a bunch of giggling idiots sprawled across the table-tennis table, amid empty bottles of Jose Cuervo.

Lou lets go of my hand as soon as we hit the open garden, but he sticks close as we move through the crowd. It's like we're in some kind of shared daze, swapping occasional glances loaded with confusion. Lou's looking less greenish now, though the line of consternation between his eyebrows has yet to vanish.

'What should we do?' he asks as we head past Abdul's crowded granny flat.

I cast a glance around, but Tommy is nowhere in sight. Part of me hopes he has given up and gone home, but with everything that's been going on with his folks lately, I shudder to think what our normally cautious friend is up to right about now.

'Gabe …?'

'Louis, you reckon I have a plan?' I manage to reply. 'Dude, clearly you're getting desperate.'

Somehow, Lou and I end up wandering towards a group that has congregated behind Abdul's flat, a rectangle of grass that borders their neighbour's fence. The Hills Hoist stands near an overgrown lemon tree, school shirts and, like, a thousand pairs of boys' boxers flapping on the lines. If the Razaks' place is anything like mine, the clothes will hang there until someone runs out of socks or jocks — being rained on, and drying, and being rained on again, till they're stiff and crispy.

Abdul Razak waves us over. The guys are playing a game of Cards Against Humanity in the dim space, lit with phone torches and a few scarlet cigarette tips.

'Hey, guys!' Abdul says with a wave of his red cup.

'Hey, Abdul. Great party,' I say flatly, since spewing bile about what I actually think of this party would probably be impolite.

Lou plonks himself on the grass beside me, slapping hands with Abdul and a few other people from school. He glances suspiciously at the faces he doesn't know, his unconscious scowl and muscles enough to make a couple of guys drop their eyes.

'So I hear your boy Cameron gave his girl the flick,' Abdul says, sculling his drink. 'Man, thought those two would've been sending out wedding invites or some shit soon. What happened?'

Lou shrugs. 'Pretty sure it wasn't just Cam's call. But yeah.' He glances at me. 'Looks like it.'

Abdul whistles. 'Whoa. Who saw that coming?' He refills his cup from the nearby bottles of Bundy and Coke, managing to spill half of it on his jeans. 'So you reckon Claire's ready for some Abdul action?' he says with a lascivious grin.

Lou scowls again, taking in Abdul's over-processed hair, and jeans that don't look like they've seen a washing machine all year. 'Somehow I don't think you're her type,' he says dryly.

Abdul doesn't seem fazed. He waves his cup at me. 'So how're you doing, Gabrielle? Suppose this means we're not gonna be seeing you around soccer training anymore, yeah?' He peers at me curiously through hazy booze eyes. 'What … are you into again?'

It strikes me that I have no idea how to answer that question. Not even my mum has a nickname for me. I am not the pretty one, or the funny one, or the smart one — I am too awkward to be the future superstar, too scrawny to be the thug. Suffice it to say, I am definitely not the nice one. I am the one who circles behind the others, who keeps myself locked tight in case anyone sees that I'm part of this group for no reason other than fluke circumstance.

God. I'm not just going to lose some of my friends, however this plays out. I'm going to lose the only parts of my personality that anyone cares about.

Beside me, Lou shuffles a little closer. 'Gabe's into plenty of stuff,' he says, with a look at Abdul that makes him return hastily to his card game.

Lou tucks his feet awkwardly beneath him. His brow is furrowed again, and he looks like he wants to say something to me, but then Rema Jabbar appears, stepping accidentally into the pile of cards and sending them flying. There is a chorus of swearing and curses, but Rema brushes them off with a shrug. She drops down beside us.

'Hey, you guys — ah, you might wanna go check on your friend Sowinski? He's not looking too great.'

Lou sits up straighter. 'What?'

'Yeah, the guy with the ranga hair, right? He's one of yours? Think he's passed out in the hallway. Last I saw someone was drawing a Sharpie face on his arse. And what's the deal with his dad?'

Lou and I exchange an alarmed look as we leap to our feet. 'Tommy told you about that?' I ask.

Rema grabs a drink from Abdul. 'He's telling anyone who'll listen, but he's not making much sense. Something about his dad running off to Queensland with a chick from accounts? Sounds harsh.'

But Lou and I are already hurrying back through the garden, ignoring the calls behind us and the now half-naked tequila-pong players.

We find Tommy Sowinski in the hallway near Abdul's parents' bedroom, carrot hair sticking up like some mad scientist, wire-rimmed glasses askew, pants attempting to free themselves from his arse. His typically placid face is shiny and animated, his normally shy grin very slightly deranged. Beside him is Cameron, sans blue-haired Isla. Lara is hovering on his other side.

Awesome.

Lou makes a growly sound. He pushes a few people aside and clears a path for us. And then he slaps Tommy on the back of the head. 'Sowinski — what are you on?'

Tommy just giggles. 'Lou! Nothing, man. Just had a couple of beers with your friends. And wine. And, oh, I think someone had Campari? Man, that stuff tastes like mouse wizz. But your mates are cool, dude.'

Lou turns his back on Cameron, pointedly ignoring him. 'They're not my mates, Tommy. And since when do you get shit-faced?'

Tommy giggles again, but there's a hint of pain in his eyes, too. 'Yeah, well, what else am I gonna do? Go home to the crying and yelling? Hang here with these guys?' He waves a hand in Cam's direction, and hiccups. 'Can I just say how excited I am for more crying and yelling? So great!' he yells, his jeans wiggling even further down his legs.

Lara attempts to secure Tommy's pants. Cameron gives us a cheeky smile, but there's something defiant in it as well. He slings an arm around Tommy's shoulders. 'Dude, there's not going to be any crying or yelling. Claire-bear and me are fine.' He gives

Tommy a squeeze. 'Come on, man,' he says with a laugh. 'It's not the end of the world.'

I've always had a soft spot for confident Cameron, but right at this moment, all I want to do is kick him repeatedly in the ball sack.

I close my eyes, desperately trying to dredge up whatever vestige of underwater peace I can find. But this corridor is stifling and stinks like beer and sweat, and nothing of ocean calm is forthcoming.

God, could I be any lamer? Still dreaming of becoming a marine biologist, which is so incredibly childish and pathetic, not to mention impossible with my spectacularly average final score. It's juvenile, like wishing for a castle and a pet unicorn. Like wishing for me and my friends to all end up living together in a pretty house with a picket fence and a pair of labradors.

Tommy slides down the wall. Lou and Lara grab him under the armpits and haul him upright. Cam stands back, observing their efforts with his smile that's always seemed kind and genial, but now just seems crap-eating and smack-worthy.

I consider, briefly, just walking out of here. But then Tommy looks up at me through his coke-bottle glasses, his woozy eyes all lost and sorrowful, and my feet find themselves not moving anywhere.

Midnight

I don't want to be here.

If my world is going to fall apart, I don't want it to be in this place of booze and grime, forced laughter and preening selfies, while two guys in their undies dance on the hallway sideboard.

Did I mention I really don't want to be here?

I could go home. My place is less than four blocks away. I could easily take myself and my shallow, feckless heart home to bed. But then what? It's Saturday, without even the distraction of school on the horizon. No, scrap that — the clock has ticked over, placing me smack bang in the midst of Sunday morning.

Sundays are the worst. Sundays are supposed to be family days, filled with lazy breakfasts and morning TV and slumming in pyjamas till late afternoon. I remember Sundays being market days, and when I was little, zoo days and park days and movie days, back when Mum and Dad were still Mum and Dad, and not the warring pair of strangers that they've morphed into.

Sundays are, like, the most pointless days of the week now. There's nothing more depressing than waking up and knowing that nothing at all is going to happen today, that getting out of bed is optional, 'cause it doesn't make a scrap of difference to the world whether I'm in it or not. The only reason Sundays are ever bearable are the bored mid-afternoon drop-bys from Tommy or Cam, the impromptu homework sessions with Lara and Claire, or the last-minute invites to breakfast at Lou's house with his mum and grandma. Maybe I never fully appreciated just how much I relied on the steady presence of my friends. I should have guessed even that would be fleeting.

Lou wraps an uncertain hand around my wrist.

'Hey,' he says quietly. 'I reckon Tommy's gonna need the loo in the next thirty seconds 'cause I'm pretty sure whatever he's drunk is on its way back up. Um ...' He clears his throat. 'You doing okay?'

I glance down at his hand. His thick, stub-ended fingers curl almost fully around my skinny wrist, and even though he's not holding on tight, I feel the heat from his skin like a brand. It feels, in this moment, that the only thing stopping me from running out onto the street with a hysterical banshee scream is the warmth of Lou.

As though my hand is operating independently of my brain, I lay my palm over his. It's like, just for this moment, I can't bear to lose the contact. Gooseflesh on Lou's skin pebbles beneath my fingers.

Tommy chooses this moment to unceremoniously remove his pants again. He moves surprisingly fast for someone who still can't seem to figure out how gravity works, brushing aside a laughing Cam as he whips off his jeans and throws them at the guys still dancing on the sideboard. The pantsless dudes whoop and yell back incomprehensibly, that special vocab only recognised by the chronically drunk and stupid.

Lou lets go of me and grabs hold of Tommy. I collect his jeans from the place they have landed on the Razaks' umbrella stand, trying not to notice that Tommy is now wearing nothing but faded Simpson boxers with a hole in the left arse cheek.

Lou shoves a shoulder under Tommy's arm, and Cam does the same on Tommy's other side. Lara hustles some people out of their way, clearly now in charge of this expedition.

Lou shoots a harried look at me. 'Just a warning, Gabe — he pukes on me, and you're gonna be helping clean sick off two of your mates,' he says with a wry grin.

I fling Tommy's jeans over my shoulder. The little patch of pale arse skin that's visible through his boxers seems to wink at me.

'Yeah. That seems about right,' I mutter, before following them into the bathroom.

1 a.m.

Lou and Cam hoist Tommy into the bathtub, thank all the gods, now with his pants on again. Someone bangs on the bathroom door, yelling something unintelligible. Lou bangs back wordlessly, but his meaty fist is threatening enough to make the frantic thumping pause for a moment.

'Shit, Tommy, you need to start hitting the gym,' Cam says with a laugh. He clears away some cans and bottles and shoves Tommy's legs over the stained rim of the tub. He scans the disgusting swamp floor, and fishes Tommy's glasses from beneath a pile of soggy loo paper.

Lou grabs the glasses from Cam, not too gently, and lays them between the half-empties on the vanity. 'Lay off him, dude. At least some of this is your fault.'

Tommy giggles, then groans. 'Oh, dude, you should see your face,' he says, waving a hand at Cam. 'I dunno why there's three of you, but all your faces look like they've swallowed poo.' Cam peers incredulously down at Tommy. Tommy squints up at him. ''Cept, why is the left one of you so furry-looking?'

Lou shoves past Cameron, but then hovers beside the tub like he's not sure what to do next. 'Great,' Lou mutters as Tommy giggles at nothing in particular. 'So much for lookin' out for him. Right, Cameron?'

Cam rounds on Lou, his smile disappearing. He may be the sportiest guy among us, but Cam has never been an aggressive dude. Now he puffs out his chest, his shoulders thrown back. 'You got something to say to me, man?'

Lou straightens to his full height, too. He tucks his hands into his back pockets, the muscles in his arms popping. 'Nah. Not much I can say to my mate who's acting like a giant dick bag.'

Cam takes a belligerent step towards him. He's way taller than Lou, but thinner, and the menacing effect he's going for is kinda diminished by the flapping piece of toilet paper stuck to his shoe. Lou holds his ground, the muscles across his back tensing. There's barely enough room in here for the five of us, much less Cam and Lou's puffed-up posturing, and I want to do something, say something that'll wind back this madness, but I have no experience with my guy friends behaving — well, like guys. It's Lara who steps between them.

'Seriously?' she growls. 'It already stinks like a mortician's compost in here. We don't need the added stench of festy testosterone, thanks very much.'

I manage to unfreeze long enough to insert myself bodily between Cam and Lou as well. I place one hand on Lou's chest, ignoring Cam's glare. 'Come on, Lou. This isn't helping,' I say weakly. 'Tommy needs us right now.'

'Tommy needs a reality check,' Cam says, eyeballing Lou over the top of my head.

Tommy waves a hand, scattering the row of novelty soaps on the edge of the tub. He struggles to sit up, unfocused eyes suddenly cheerless.

'Okay, how's this for reality?' Tommy bleats. 'Everything ends. Life is meaningless and relationships are pointless. No-one sticks around and nothing lasts. We're all going to die alone anyway.'

Cam grins at him. 'Much better,' he says brightly.

Tommy hiccups. He leans over the side of the tub, dry heaving, before collapsing onto his back. Lara sits on the edge of the tub and rubs tentatively at his shoulders.

Lou gets right up in Cameron's face. 'See this? This is your fault. You couldn't just wait to sort out your business till Tommy was more solid? You know the last couple of months have been shithouse for him, and you still couldn't care less, could you?'

Cameron throws up his hands. 'Lou, are you seriously saying you wanted Claire and me to pretend to be crazy in love, just to make Tommy feel better about life? What is this, some shitty screwball comedy? Is one of us wearing a fake moustache in this scenario?'

Lou moves in front of me and shoves Cam in the chest with a thick index finger. 'A moustache might improve your face, arsehole.'

Yeah, Lou has never been quick with the insults. Cam bursts out laughing. Even Lara, busy mopping at Tommy's forehead with a wet chunk of toilet paper, chuckles. Lou looks filthy, like he's not sure whether to storm out of the bathroom, or punch Cam in the head.

I, on the other hand, am beyond over this party. I grab hold of the edge of the vanity, the anger and uncertainty that have been building all night boiling over. I'm fully sober, but the world beneath me is spinning and spinning —

'Argh, for fuck's sake, stop it!' I yell.

Cam and Lou recoil. Lara's eyes widen. Tommy stops his dim-witted giggling. Even the relentless pounding on the bathroom door ceases.

'Enough,' I whisper, instantly deflating. 'That's enough. There's no point … it's done, and over, and blaming Cameron isn't going to fix anything.' My eyes are locked on Lou's worried brown ones. 'It's no-one's fault. It just … is.'

And I realise, as I'm saying it, that the words are true. No-one is to blame here. Not Cameron and not Claire, and, God forbid, not Isla. It's not Cam's and Claire's fault that the rest of us have clung to them like desperate barnacles, too scared of the boundlessness of our futures, too afraid of being cast adrift. But Tommy is right. Everything ends.

I take a deep breath, willing myself to be a grown-up and sensible, but no amount of mental pep talks can seem to stop my eyes filling with tears.

Lara jumps up, but it's Lou who is suddenly at my side. He drapes a hesitant arm around me, all smoky traces and solid muscle. I wrap my arms around his middle, trying to convince myself that I'm holding on tight for his sake as well as mine, since Lou's face becomes a delightful shade of puce as Tommy retches in the bathtub.

What is going to happen now to the six of us? How can we still function with a giant fracture down our middle? I know I should be more concerned with my own total lack of a plan or purpose. But all I know is that these five people are my anchors, and one by one, it feels like they're cutting me free.

2 a.m.

Tommy is asleep in the tub now, snoring, his face tucked into a cushion that Lara found in a bedroom. She brushes his hair back with an affectionate huff.

Cameron, wisely, decided to vacate the bathroom. Who knows where Claire has gone? I can't even bring myself to care anymore.

I'm perched on the closed toilet seat, peeling the label off one of the Razaks' shampoos. Lou is leaning against the door, tapping his packet of cigarettes distractedly on his forearm. I can all but see his fingers itching to light up.

I don't know how long we've been sitting here, mostly silent, lost in our own worlds. Outside, the party continues, the beat still shaking the house, and despite the fact that the cops have now visited twice, it's still so loud that I know it'll be ringing in my ears well into the day.

Lara stretches out her legs from her place near the tub. 'Christ, you guys,' she says with a groan. 'How long do we let him sleep it off? This tub isn't exactly ergonomic.'

I wiggle my butt on the uncomfortable toilet lid, and I remember a conversation that the six of us had one night at Cam's house a few months back. Claire and Cam were planning to look for a house near the city, one of those sweet terraces that we pass on the tram when we occasionally head out east. They'd been talking about it since Year 11, but time was ticking, and their vague plans had suddenly started becoming real. Tommy was going to rent a room with them, already saving money from his shifts at KFC, and claiming his mum's old couches before she sold them on eBay. Lou wanted to stay close to home, not knowing if he could afford anything else on a mechanic's apprentice salary, and Lara's parents were still freaking at the prospect of her travelling into the city for uni, let alone moving out of home. I had made no plans, but I wasn't worried; content with the fizzy exhilaration of hearing my friends sketching out our future.

For some reason, it's the thought of Tommy's couches that finally snaps whatever composure I was holding onto. Two blue, sunken, Fantastic Furniture rejects, safe under plastic wrap in his parents' shed, waiting for their new home, that I see turning to dust before my eyes. Maybe his mum will just put them out on the street with the rest of his absent dad's junk. And the couches that should have been the centre of movie nights and pizza nights and random sleepovers will be relegated to the unknown of someone else's life.

I stand and back up till my backside hits the bathroom wall. And then I shove Lou aside and pull open the door, pushing past a girl doing a pee dance in the corridor, and I bolt for the nearest exit.

3 a.m.

I stumble into the front yard, stepping over a guy snoring beneath a rose bush, and around a couple whose tongues are so far down each other's throats that I don't know whether to avert my eyes or offer them a round of applause.

I bolt to the edge of the garden, gulping in the warm air. From here, I can see the whole expanse of the narrow road — the house across the street with its pin-neat garden, and the one next door with the overgrown grass and collection of beat-up cars. A little way down there's a house almost identical to this one, with peeling cladding and a concrete porch. At this moment it's filled with couches and a group of big guys, all beers and booming laughter. Everything is too close together here, everything looking one step away from the decayed neighbourhood in some soon-to-be apocalyptic wasteland.

I slump against the wire-mesh fencing and sink to the ground. The Razaks' house seems to throb, the walls pulsing with music and the dying remnants of a party that'll no doubt be repeated in some other house next weekend.

I close my eyes, with a lump in my throat that I can't seem to swallow. Our neighbourhood is never properly quiet; even now, the early morning is overlaid with the voices of the guys across the street and the sound of distant car horns. I hate this place. But I can't help loving it, too. And in my whole entire life, I've never been able to decide which emotion is going to win out.

My eyes are still squeezed shut when a warm body drops beside me. The faint hint of smoke follows in his wake.

'What do you want, Lou?' I mumble.

I open my eyes and glance sideways at him. His too-large frame is squished between me and the rhododendron bush near the letterbox, pink flowers haloing his shaved head. Despite everything, a rusty laugh escapes me.

Lou wiggles himself into place. 'You okay, Gabe?'

I sigh. 'I dunno, Lou. Probably not. I'm sorry about the dramatics though,' I say, waving a hand in the direction of the house. 'Everything just really ... sucks. You know?'

Lou's head turns at the choking sound on the other side of the lawn, as the pashing couple disengage with way too much saliva than is probably hygienic. He snorts.

'Yeah.' He shrugs. 'But whaddya gonna do? People are gonna do what they want, right, not what we expect them to do. I reckon you've just gotta roll with it. You can't control everything. Or everyone.'

I rub my hands over my eyes. 'Yeah, I know that. I know I'm being stupid —'

He nudges my shoulder. 'Hey, I never said that.'

'You didn't have to,' I say, sitting up straighter. 'I realise I'm being ridiculous. But it's not just Cam and Claire though. It's everything.' I tug at a handful of dry grass, rubbing the russet stalks through my fingers. 'I just really hate this feeling that nothing at all is ... permanent. You know?'

I rest my head against his arm with a sigh. Lou tenses slightly beneath me. 'It's over, isn't it,' I whisper. 'Cameron and Claire ... and the rest of us, too. Nothing is going to be the same, now. Is it?'

A faint chuckle rumbles through Lou's chest. When I look up at him, I don't think it's me he's laughing at. He looks kind of sad, and resigned. He looks like the same old Lou, pragmatic to the core, rolling with whatever crap life throws his way.

'Gabrielle,' he says quietly. 'It's kinda scary having the … the rug pulled out from under you, or whatever. I get it, you know I do. Not everyone stays, right? But, you know, not everyone leaves either.'

I blink at him. Lou looks away, hastily fishing out his cigarettes and patting down his pockets for a lighter. I take the pack from his hands before he can light up. 'Ugh, and speaking of permanent — when are you gonna quit, Louis? Don't know if you've heard this, but these things aren't exactly extending your lifespan.'

'Huh. So does that mean you want me to stick around?'

I turn to look at Lou properly, only to find that he is staring down at me, his face close, eyes kind of weirdly dilated.

I swallow. In the dark, Lou isn't easy to read. His eyebrows are drawn, tight and tense, and if I didn't know him so well, I'd almost peg that look as dangerous. But I do know Lou, and to me he looks nothing but bewildered. His mouth looks strangely soft, lips slightly parted, even though he barely seems to be breathing.

For the briefest instant I think he's going to run, or I am. But somehow, insanely, I move forward, not backward, my brain figuring out what is happening just a few moments behind my body.

Kissing Lou is weird, so weird, like adjusting to breathing under the ocean; not instinctive, not at first, but not totally unnatural either. There's no choir of angels singing, no exploding fireworks; I can feel every touch of his lips and every move of his tongue, 'cause I'm totally here and present in this moment. I open an eye to the sight of one familiar thick eyebrow, and the feel of raspy stubble against my cheek, which is all kinds of odd, and, strangely, kind of nice, too.

Lou pulls away from me. His breathing is heavy, the dusky skin of his cheeks stained pink. He looks away quickly, but then he seems to steel himself. He draws his shoulders back and looks me square in the eye.

'I've wanted to do that for ages, Gabrielle,' he says. His voice is even huskier than normal.

'Oh,' I say quietly. I feel my face crack into a strange, shy smile. 'For how long?'

Lou's eyes widen. He grins at me. 'Since, like, Year 8?'

I straighten my back against the wire-mesh fencing, schooling my face into neutral, even though inside I'm feeling all crazy and buzzy. 'Oh really? Even with the braces and glam-rock hair?'

Lou chuckles. 'Yeah. Think it might have been the hair that did it for me. 'Sides, I can't talk. Remember my blond phase?' He shudders. 'Ma said I looked like a Greek Dolly Parton. Can't believe you stayed friends with me after that, Gabe.'

I nudge him back, leaving my hand resting alongside his. 'What can I say, Lou? My tastes have always been questionable.'

Lou touches the edge of my fingers, warily, his smile disappearing. He scratches at his stubble with his other hand. 'Gabe?' he begins uncertainly. 'Um, so … what should we do now?'

I glance at the Razaks' house. I think about my friends scattered somewhere inside; Cameron and Lara and Tommy and Claire, all doing their own thing, wherever they might be. Lou's question feels like it's loaded with more than I know how to answer.

I leap to my feet. And then I reach down and I offer him my hand. He stares at it for a moment before grabbing hold and letting me pull him up. This is probably my cue to let go, but I hold on to Lou, winding my fingers through his. Screw letting go. Maybe I'm just a wee bit nervous — okay, make that a wee bit gigantically terrified — but I refuse to let go until he does.

'Louis? I have no idea what we should do now. But I think — no, I know — that I could really use a cheeseburger.'

Lou smiles at me and squeezes my hand. He leans down and pecks me on the lips, just briefly.

'You want to go?' he asks.

'Yeah. I suppose we should go back for a bit and see who we need to drag with us. But either way — I think I'm ready to leave now.'

4 a.m.

This is how it goes.

We're walking down the street as the first hint of a watery orange sunrise stains the edge of the sky. Lara is propping up Tommy as they stumble in front of us, her heels in her hands, his glasses lost somewhere in the disaster that is the Razaks' house. Tommy is using Lara's entire body as a man-crutch, since he still seems to be incapable of coordinating his legs. Around us, stragglers from the party drag their feet towards the train station, laughter and groans and a few honking cars hustling alongside. We left Cam and Isla catching a ride with one of his friends from the soccer team, Cam's arm defiantly around Isla's shoulders. Claire left a while ago; apparently she took off with those girls from the debating team for 7-Eleven slushies and doughnuts hours ago. She's texted me though; I guess I'll text her back at a more civilised hour. Lara is still grumbly, although whether it's caused by the Cam-and-Claire drama, or the fact that her heels are now covered in Tommy's spew, is anyone's guess. And Lou is holding my hand. Or I'm holding his. I can't remember who was responsible for the hand-binding situation, who grabbed on to whom first. I'm not sure if it's all that relevant.

Every now and then we will catch each other's eye, a surreptitious sideways glance that makes Lou blush and my stomach tumble. Every now and then, Tommy will turn around and squint at the two of us, like he needs to keep checking on the continuation of our existence, and Lara will cast a glance over her shoulder, this dumb, gleeful smirk on her face.

Lou squeezes my hand. 'So how long do you reckon we're going to cop shit for this?'

I shake my head, with a bubble of laughter that I can't contain. 'Um, I reckon summer holidays are going to suck? I wouldn't plan on them letting this go anytime before uni graduation. Maybe keep, oh I dunno — say the next decade free?' And then I realise what I have said, and my entire face fills with heat.

But Lou just grins and squeezes my hand again. 'Yeah. Sounds okay to me.'

Then Tommy trips over and face-plants into a bush. Lara stands over him with a sigh.

'Thomas, I swear to God, you're like a bloody cautionary ad for underage drinking.' She grabs the back of his T-shirt and tugs him upright.

I turn my face to the sky. Graffiti covers the fences here; in this crumbly early light it almost looks organic, like it's grown from the red brick and concrete itself.

I don't think I'll ever not feel sad about Cameron and Claire. I'm guessing these last few years of our lives are always going to make me feel wistful; this moment tonight one of the many little pieces of sadness that amass over time like scar tissue.

But I look down at Lou's rough hand in mine, and I think that, maybe, it's not just the sad stuff that accumulates. New stuff builds, too. I suppose not all of the unforeseen things that shake your foundations are going to suck.

Lou lets go of me and hurries to rescue Tommy, who is now, for some reason, sitting on the footpath and singing a rousing version of the national anthem. Lara rocks back on her feet with an incredulous laugh. Lou all but throws Tommy over his shoulder, and he looks at me with a weary, happy smile.

Will it last? Who knows? Maybe forever is a ridiculous concept, like wishing for mermaid fins or a life in a magical city under the ocean.

'So,' Lou says with a huff as he falls into step beside me, Tommy bobbing happily over his shoulder. 'Breakfast?'

Oh right. It's Sunday morning. Still a lazy day, a nothing day.

But I take Lou's hand again, content for the moment with breakfast and possibilities.

Missing Persons

ELLIE MARNEY

When you stand out in the front yard of your family's dilapidated white stucco house and look forward, and all you can see is a street view of more dilapidated houses, with a panorama of traffic, and warehouses, and power lines above and beyond that … it's safe to assume that your home is not what it was anymore.

'Going for the don't-give-a-shit look on your first day, eh?' Mike's eating a jam sandwich out of one hand, he has a clipboard full of delivery invoices tucked into his armpit and his driver's shirt is unbuttoned. With his hair sticking up like that, he looks as if he just fell out of bed.

I give my brother the stink-eye. 'What do you care what I wear to school?'

He scratches his head, which only exacerbates the hair problem. 'Just sayin'.'

'I could go in my underwear. Or a wetsuit. Or a toga. It won't change the fact that I'm *going to school*.'

'Jeez, Rachel. Wear whatever you want.' Mike gives me a meaningful glance. 'Wear a delivery driver's outfit.'

'Oh ha-ha.'

Mum walks over in the old jeans she uses for house-cleaning. Her eyes are on the weedy front-yard lawn as she twists a scrunchie around the hair at the nape of her neck.

'… and I told your father I'd be getting a ride in to work after we dropped you at school, so I hope he's remembered to —' She sees me, and her hands drop. 'Oh, Rachel. Please tell me you're not wearing a flannie shirt and cut-offs on your first day. And the knotted hair … You've got such *lovely* hair, sweetheart, why don't you wear it loose?'

'Yeah, Rachel,' Mike says, grinning. 'Show us yer lovely hair!'

I mouth, '*Rack. Off.*' at my brother. I'm about to turn and say a highly modified version of that to my mother when there's a distraction: Dad pulls up in the taxi.

'All passengers!' Dad does a very lame-arse impersonation of a train driver out of the rolled-down passenger window. 'Come on, girls. We don't want Rachel to be late for class.'

'You're turning this whole first-day-of-high-school business into a thing.' I bundle into the car, with Mum beside me. 'You'll give me a complex.'

'I'm sure your first day will be wonderful,' Mum says. 'It'll be a breath of fresh air after Year 11 distance ed.'

'Right,' I say, because there's such a thing as fresh air in the middle of *Melbourne*, not to mention in a classroom full of sweaty teenagers.

It's not like I haven't seen North Coburg Secondary; I did the tour there with Mum and Dad a week ago. The impressions I got consisted of: halls with lino floors, run-down buildings, concrete lunch benches, and hundreds of people my age, like I'd walked into some sort of Teenager Convention. I've never actually been around large groups of people that much — except at the Ouyen

Races or the Farm Expos — and it turns out they make me nervous.

Now I'm regretting I ever shared that information with my brother.

'Don't stress, sis.' Mike winks at me as he shuts the car door. 'You'll be fine.' Which is Mike-speak for *They'll rip your head off,* I think.

Mike heads for his delivery van, Dad rolls up the windows and turns on the radio, Mum fiddles with her scrunchie and casts glances my way as we drive along Summoner Street towards Sydney Road. And I sit with my satchel on my lap and pretend that I'm anywhere but here, in this huge city, where my world has become infinitely smaller.

'Hot guys,' Mai Ng says.

I look back at her. 'Pardon?'

'I was just getting your attention. I have to explain the rooms for your classes now, so I figured I'd wait until you were listening.' She smiles, not unkindly. 'Although I totally get the desire to zone out when people talk about this stuff. I almost fell asleep during induction when I arrived here.'

My cheeks warm. 'I'm sorry. I'm listening. I need to know where I'm supposed to be going.'

'Relax,' Mai says. 'You *won't* know where you're going for a while. Everybody gets lost at first.'

We're walking through one of the lino-floored corridors. Out the window, three junior boys play handball against a brick wall, kids eat their snacks underneath a bunch of straggly trees, and more students chase each other towards someplace I think might be the canteen. People bloody *everywhere*.

'I'm just not used to … all this.' I wave at the view. 'School, I mean.'

'You're from the country, yeah?' Mai leans forward. 'What's that like?'

'Different,' I blurt. Then I think about it. 'I mean, the distances are big, and it's nowhere near as populated. But we probably do pretty much the same things as city kids.'

'You hang out, watch a movie, listen to music?'

'Sure. Or you play games, or text each other if you've got reception. Or you can drive around in someone's car. Go swimming in the dam. Get together and make a bonfire — a twig, we call it.'

Mai raises her eyebrows. 'We don't do much of that in the city.'

'Guess not.' I look at her sideways. 'We have hot guys in the country, too. They pop up on occasion.'

She laughs, until she's distracted by the view outside. 'Speaking of …'

I follow her line of sight. 'The blond one? Or the one with the soccer ball?'

'Soccer ball,' she replies dreamily. 'Gus Deng. Incredible shoulders. Smart. Nice — like, really sweet.'

'Seems perfect.' I grin.

'We're on friendly terms, but yeah. He's not Vietnamese. My mother would have apoplexy.' Mai sighs, returns to my paperwork and adjusts her black-framed glasses. 'Okay, lemme show you where you need to be for your next two classes. And we have English together, so that's a win.' She gives me a smile. 'I think we're gonna get on well.'

'Me, too.' Mai's smile is open-hearted; mine is more just relieved.

'Don't commit too soon,' Mai warns. 'You haven't met my friends, you might hate them.'

'I'm pretty easygoing.'

She snorts. 'You haven't been introduced to Mycroft yet.'

⁂

Not everything about school is awful, but still. At least two of my teachers seem to be incapable of modulating their voices above a drone. The bells that ding at unexpected intervals make me jump. And in my biology class, some crazy guy up the back sets fire to his class notes within five minutes of arriving and is immediately bundled out to the principal's office by the teacher, Miss Paulsen. I catch a glimpse of the guy's dark hair and hear his fruity accent before his departure, and table him as someone to avoid.

At lunch, Mai ushers me towards a bench seat near the library. She waves to about forty different people along the way. In my entire life in Five Mile, I don't think I even *met* forty teenagers.

'So when'd you move?' Mai asks, unboxing her food.

'Two weeks ago.' I find an apple in my satchel. 'After the farm went bust, my dad and my older brother came down to organise a rental place and find work, and then we all just … pulled up stumps.'

'That blows.'

'Yeah. Can't say I'm in love with the city experience so far.' The bench seat we're on is underneath a big scribbly gum. Leaf litter is scattered around us and the tree's roots have buckled the concrete, as if trying to escape. Even the trees want out.

'Melbourne can be fun,' Mai says. 'The little cobbled alleyways, the secret cafes … You'll get the hang of it.' She scans the area and the roofline beyond, unfazed. This is all normal for her. 'You just need to find your tribe. The people around you can make a big difference.'

'You have a tribe?'

'A sort-of tribe. A small one. A tribelet.' Sunlight glints off her purple bangles. 'I get on okay with a lot of people, but my friend Dani moved to Sydney last year, so now I'm mainly tight with Mycroft. He's the investigative scientist, I'm the punk geek girl — we both speak fluent snark.'

Her black T-shirt has line drawings of a variety of objects — a toaster, a phone, a banana, a llama — with the slogan *Not the droids you're looking for.* I grin, pull the knot out of my hair to tidy it. 'You keep the geek-girl shtick. I'll be the country bumpkin.'

'You're on.' Her smile transforms into a gasp. 'Shit, your hair is *long*. Ever thought about some streaks? There's this great burnt-orange colour that'd be perfect with your shade of deep blonde —' Her gaze strays behind me. 'All right, finally. My tribe approaches.'

I turn my head in time to see a … whoa. Okay, so he's tall. Lanky, with dark curly hair. No backpack in evidence. Tight, slightly stained black jeans with a white T-shirt and a red trackie jacket, unzipped in front. This guy doesn't look like the scientist type — more like the dictionary illustration of Urban Boho Chill. *This* is Mai's tribe?

I haven't retied my hair yet, and I probably have apple bits between my teeth. I may not be ready to cope with this guy on my first day. I try to imagine him walking down the street in

Five Mile, hands shoved in his jeans pockets, and … nope. Not possible. I take a breath as he swaggers in our direction, and —

There's a yelp, and a spectacular windmill of flailing limbs, as Mr Urban Boho trips on the stairs and face-plants on the concrete.

'Oh, *crap*,' Mai says.

'Oh, crap. It's okay,' I say, as we both rush over. 'I have some first-aid training.'

'Awesome,' Mai says, 'because blood makes me sick. Mycroft? Are you still alive?'

A groan — he's still alive. I kneel on the hard ground at the guy's shoulder, turn him over. In spite of the gushing red cut on his forehead, his eyes are open. They're as blue as a Mallee sky.

Mai gags a little at the blood. 'God, Mycroft, are you okay?'

'It's all right. I was saved from an undignified brain injury by my face.' He's talking to Mai but looking straight at me. 'Wow. Hello.'

'Hi.' I check the rest of him, but the cut seems to be the biggest issue. 'You might be concussed, you should stay still.'

'I'm staying still,' he points out. 'I'm lying flat on my back, that's about as still as it's possible to be.'

Shit — the fruity accent. This is the bozo from my biology class, the one who set his notes on fire.

My hair falls heavily in front of my eyes and I shove it back. 'How do you feel?'

'Perfectly fine. Brilliant.' He grins through the mask of blood on his face. 'Mai, would you do the honours?'

'Oh, God,' Mai says, tilting her chin up. 'Mycroft, this is Rachel Watts. Rachel, Mycroft, and Jesus, I think I'm gonna spew.'

'*Don't spew*,' Mycroft and I say together.

We look at each other for a moment before I yank off my flannie. 'Better put pressure on that head wound.'

'My head wound is fine,' Mycroft says, extending a hand. 'Let me up.'

'I don't think you should —'

'I'm all good. Let me up.'

I blink at him. 'Okay.' This should be entertaining.

I take his hand — large, over-warm — and ease him into a sitting position. He's heavy, and his face goes predictably white within two seconds of being upright.

'Ah, no,' he says. 'Let me down. Let me down again —'

'She did warn you,' Mai says.

'Shouldn't we get a teacher?' I settle her friend back on the concrete, shove at my hair again. 'Or maybe an ambulance? He's bleeding a lot.'

Mai rolls her eyes. 'He always bleeds a lot. Stay here, I'll go find Mrs Ramen.'

'Oh no, Mai, come on,' Mycroft starts. 'Ramen's *hopeless* —'

'Are you guys okay? Mycroft, what have you done now?' Gus, of the incredible shoulders, has walked over. His backpack is slung on one strap, and he's still carrying the soccer ball.

'I didn't do anything,' Mycroft says. 'I was walking along, minding my own business, and the ground jumped up and assaulted me. I'm offended that you think I did this to myself.'

I see Mai straighten her tartan flip skirt as she stands. 'Oh, hey. Just a bit of an accident.'

'Accident?' Mycroft whines from ground level. 'I'm bleeding to death.'

'You're not bleeding to death.' I look up at Gus. 'Hi, I'm Rachel.'

'Hi,' Gus says. He turns to Mai. 'Yeah, maybe you should get Mrs Ramen. I can walk up with you, if you like?' The way he says it, just a little too casually, makes me think she might be in with a shot.

'Um, lemme check with Rachel.' I nod, and Mai's expression glows. She turns back to Gus. 'That would be great, thank you.' She glances at Mycroft over her shoulder. 'We'll be back in a sec. Hold tight, okay?'

'*Mai* —' he starts again.

Ignoring him, Mai strides away. Gus is sticking to her like glue.

Mycroft groans. 'Ramen won't help! She never helps! She has haemophobia!' But they're already too elsewhere to hear.

I shift on my knees. 'What is that, fear of blood?' I'm surprised this guy's still accessing higher brain functions, let alone spouting words like 'haemophobia'.

He sighs. 'Yes. Although Mrs Ramen's fear is more to do with getting blood on her clothes, which is different and slightly more misanthropic.'

'Well, I don't really give a rat's about my clothes, and I don't have haemophobia.'

'Clearly.' His eyes, that surreal shade of blue, gaze up at me, and I suddenly feel weird kneeling here — Mycroft must be getting a great view of the underside of my chin.

'Okay.' I huff out a laugh. 'This is kind of an unusual way to meet someone on my first day of high school.'

'Isn't it?' Those eyes again. 'You've already told me you're not a misanthropist before we've even gotten to know each other.'

Mycroft's breath is soft on my inner arm as I hold my shirt in place. I wet my lips and glance away.

'Wait, did you say this is your first day of high school?' When I look back, Mycroft is still pale, but his expression is animated enough. 'Mai said something about it, but I didn't think she meant your first actual day of high school *ever* —'

'Yes,' I say. 'It's my first actual day of high school ever. I moved from the country. I was home-schooled via distance ed before now.'

'Incredible.' He shakes my free hand, while lying in that peculiar position. 'You've managed to evade formal education for a significant period of your life. Congratulations and well done.'

'Are you taking the piss?'

'Good God, no.'

A breeze stirs the leaves of the bench-seat tree, and a couple of other students wander by. I can't imagine what on earth we look like, with Mycroft lying on the concrete and me sitting next to him, pressing my shirt to his forehead.

'Are you sure your head's okay?'

He gazes off somewhere above my shoulder, considering. 'Well, obviously it hurts.'

'You *could* have concussion.' I frown at him. 'Recite the alphabet or something so I know you're still functioning.'

'Hydrogen. Helium. Carbon ...'

'You're reciting the periodic table?'

'It soothes me.'

'Are you nauseous?'

'No.' He tilts his chin a little. 'Are you always this capable?'

Are you always this odd? I want to ask. But unlike Mycroft, I have a brake pedal attached to my mouth. I'm going to give him the benefit of the doubt, too, 'cause he's just fallen down and clonked himself, and it's possible he needs stitches.

'Was your previous place of residence a total backwater?' he asks suddenly. 'Is that why you shifted to Melbourne?'

Screw 'benefit of the doubt'. I glare at him, and wait for Mai to get back.

The upsides of going home are that first, I get to go home. Second, I get to ride the tram. The city looks different out the tram window; more contained, almost manageable. Third, it's Mai's tram, too, so we ride together, although she goes a number of stops further on than me.

The downside, I discover, is that Mycroft lives along the same route. He has three butterfly closures over the now blackened gash on his forehead, but he bounded onto the tram along with every other student travelling north along Sydney Road.

'Okay, what offensive thing did he say to you?' Mai asks, from the seat opposite mine. 'Actually, wait, don't tell me, it doesn't matter. Mycroft manages to offend everybody at least a few times a day. He's unbelievably bright, but he has no "off" switch whatsoever. Don't take it personally.' She looks sideways just as the tram slows and Mycroft galumphs down the aisle towards the doors. 'Um, isn't this your stop?'

Jesus. This just gets better and better.

Mai snags me as I rise. 'You should come over. Not today, but, y'know, once you're settled in.'

'I'd like that,' I say, smiling back. 'Oops, gotta go.'

I tumble out of the tram doors and cross the busy road to Summoner Street. Mai said it makes a difference, the people you have around you in the city. I think I'd like to be in Mai's orbit.

I have Carly and the others from distance ed on email, but I'm in the Big Smoke now.

That thought flattens me out a bit.

I sigh when I realise who else is now in my orbit. Mycroft lopes just a little ahead, arms swinging like he hasn't suffered a recent head trauma. My steps slow; maybe he doesn't know I'm following. With a bit of luck, we won't have to converse at all. I said I was easygoing, but the backwater comment still stings.

We pass the electricity pole near the corner, then the scraggy yards in front of various houses. A few metres further on, Mycroft pulls a squashed pack of cigarettes out of his jeans pocket, pauses to light one. His pause is just long enough for me to catch up. When he spins around, I realise he knew I was following all along.

'Hello again. Are you stalking me?'

'What? No.'

'Really? I was hoping you were stalking me. I've never had a stalker before.'

What *is* it with this guy? 'I live here.'

'In this house?'

'On this street.'

'I don't believe you.' Mycroft's eyes narrow. 'What number are you?'

My back stiffens. 'I don't think I want to tell you.'

He grins. 'It's fine, y'know. I'm harmless. Mostly harmless. I mean, I talk a lot. Are you the blue house?'

'The white one,' I admit.

'Excellent! So we're street-mates.'

I gape for two whole seconds. 'I think the word you're looking for is "neighbours".'

'Yes, neighbours. Wonderful.' He sighs happily, waves his cigarette around at the street. The houses are cheap, mostly rentals, and there's a skip spewing garbage down on the corner. 'So, you're poor, then.'

I bite my lip, but there's no disguising it: this street is a dump. 'Looks like it.'

'Excellent,' Mycroft repeats. 'We're neighbours in penury. Here, let me give you the tour.' He points out houses with his cigarette. 'Mr and Mrs Ahmuddin — they're always working, kids in child care down the block. Mrs Gantinas — retiree, grows lovely tomatoes. Those people I don't know. Mr Sutton — unemployed, sits on the front step a lot in summer, you've gotta watch out for his dog. The rest are mostly a revolving door of short-term leases I can never keep up with, including the lovely couple in number twenty-six, who seem to do nothing but argue at high volume ...'

He stops at the expression on my face.

'Oh, hey now.' He steps closer. 'C'mon, Watts, it's not that awful.'

What's awful is that I'm standing here, close to tears, in front of a guy I've just met who doesn't seem to understand that this is not a *game*. This is my life now. I've exchanged pink dirt and leaf litter and swollen blue skies for *this*.

'Thanks for the tour,' I get out, bolting for my house.

'Sorry about yesterday,' Mycroft says, on the tram to school the next day. 'Didn't mean to put you off. I was about to invite you to come over and watch YouTube videos with me, but you ran away ...'

'Yeah, sorry, I was a bit tired from school.' I look at the world outside the tram. Is there a word that's the opposite of agoraphobic? Like, if you can have a fear of wide-open spaces and huge skies, what's the name for the fear of busy streets and encroaching buildings? What's the fear of cities?

'I have something better, anyway,' Mycroft says, grinning. 'I've made some sodium acetate, and you should *definitely* come over and see that. Magic.'

The air here feels canned. I suppose it has something to do with the level of pollution. It's like you're breathing in something that's been recycled a thousand times over, even outside, even when you're — 'What?'

'This afternoon,' he says conspiratorially. 'It's one of my favourite experiments, 'cause the results are so reliably spectacular. You mix it up and pour it out onto a solid surface at room temperature —'

'This is a science experiment.' I wriggle up in my seat. 'You're talking about a science experiment.'

'Yes. So the saturated liquid —'

'You do science experiments in your room?'

'Regularly. But on this very special occasion, to cheer you up.' Mycroft gazes out the window. 'And me. Most days need a bit of cheering up, I reckon. Sodium acetate is highly cheering, because —'

'Where did you get the British accent?' I ask suddenly.

'From the British People factory,' he shoots back.

I squint at him. 'You're a very peculiar person.'

'And you're a mystery.' Mycroft's eyes aren't chasing the scenery anymore. They're bathing me in blue. 'I quite like mysteries.'

I have to turn my head away. 'I'm still getting used to being here. In Melbourne, I mean.'

'Mycroft, did you do the English homework?' Mai asks, disentangling from her headphones.

'Yes.' He twists in the seat to face her. 'And I'll look over your maths questions if you'll correct my spelling.'

Mai pulls a notebook out of her backpack. 'His spelling is *atrocious*.'

'I'd argue that point, but I can't spell "atrocious",' Mycroft says. 'You'll get used to it. Melbourne, I mean.'

I realise he's looking at me again. 'Everyone keeps saying that.'

'Everyone is right. I only arrived seven years ago, and look at me now — *thriving!*'

He throws out his arms in a parody of a city-wide embrace.

We get into the habit of doing homework right after school, while it's still fresh. If I was doing this as usual, with distance ed, I'd have it staggered at different times of the day, to suit around home stuff, like lambing days, and sheep inoculations, and checking the perimeters in the morning. But I'm not, so I'd better not think about it.

Mycroft hums while we work, and finishes faster than me. He gets up and pokes around in the fridge, like it's his own house.

'What's for tea, then?'

'Sausages and chips.' My head is still down, my right hand scrawling. 'Salad, too.'

'You've got to get some greens in there somewhere, don't you.' He sighs.

I sit up and stretch my back, then hear the banging of Mum coming through from the front. She makes straight for the kitchen after she dumps her cleaning gear in the living room. It's funny how we all head straight for the kitchen, still, even though it's not as central as it used to be in our old house.

'Thank God I'm home,' she says, sounding like she really means it. 'I thought that last place would never end — three toilets. Hello, Mycroft. What are you doing in our fridge?'

'Oh, the usual,' he says.

'Hello, sweet pea.' Mum kisses the top of my head, which makes me feel like I'm about five years old.

I turn in my seat so I can side-hug her. 'I was just about to start the dinner.'

'Make your old mother a cup of tea first?'

I give Mum my chair, fill the kettle and light the gas on the stove. Mycroft has closed the fridge and, in a burst of helpfulness, popped a teabag into a mug.

He sits back down at the table and starts packing up his books. 'All right day, then, Mrs Watts?'

'Oh, you know, dear. So-so.' Mum looks tired, and smells strongly of Pine O Cleen, where before she used to smell of lanolin and baking bread.

'D'you want chips and salad, Mum?' I start defrosting the sausages in a sinkful of water. I try to lift my tone: I sound almost as tired as she does, and I've only been at school.

'Yes, love, that'd be great.' She stands slowly, like someone who's spent all day kneeling and bending over. 'Okay, I'm going for the shower. By the time I get out I might feel human again. Where's your father?'

'Outside. He's digging around the Hills Hoist again.'

Mum makes no comment, just exhales a big breath through her nose as she walks in the direction of the bathroom off the hall.

Mycroft comes over to the kitchen benchtop and leans against it. He doesn't say anything about Mum, or Dad, or any of it, for which I am profoundly grateful. He takes the iceberg lettuce off the bench and starts stripping leaves into the salad bowl, until I stop him.

'I'm doing it. It's fine.'

'I don't mind —'

'*No.*' I take the lettuce out of his large hands.

He steps back from the benchtop. 'Okay.'

For a moment, I'm too miserable to think properly. Then I remember something to say. 'Tell me about the next article.'

Mycroft rocks on his feet. 'Well ... I'm tossing up between posting the one on bio-LED trees in place of streetlights, like they're doing in Taiwan, and another one on recovering fingerprints from cold-case evidence by vacuum metal deposition. I could post either of them at *Chemistry World*.'

'I like the idea of sparkly tree streetlights.'

'I like the fingerprints.' He looks strangely fierce when he says it.

'Why forensics?' I ask. 'I mean, what is it about forensics that you find so ...'

'It's interesting.' He looks out the kitchen window, tucks his hands in his jacket pockets. 'It doesn't matter anyway, 'cause they'll both be pseudonymously posted.'

'But you'll know who wrote them.' My shoulders relax as I look at him. 'And me.'

'That's two people.' Smiling in a subdued way, he grabs his backpack. 'Gotta go.'

'Loads of sausages tonight. I might drop by yours with a plate.' We both know there's no 'might' about it. It's been three weeks since I got to know him, and Mycroft's level of self-neglect still bothers me.

He pauses. 'Would you like to come to the zoo with me tonight? I mean, y'know, later.'

'I don't know if I'd be allowed ...' The lettuce is still in my hands. 'Won't the zoo be closed?'

'Yes. We don't go inside. Sorry, that sounds weird.'

'A bit.'

He grins. 'Come on, Watts. I'm offering the finest park-bench experience available in Melbourne. You'll meet the cream of the dero elite. We can cadge a ride on the tram.'

'Now you're tempting me.'

His smile blooms in full as he hoicks a cigarette out of the pocket of his trackie jacket. A bellow sounds from the living room. My brother, just home from work, barrels into the kitchen and grabs Mycroft in a headlock.

'Put it away!'

'I will —'

'Put it away!'

'I am! Honestly, look —'

'No cigs inside. I get enough of that shit at work.' Mike noogies Mycroft with his free hand. 'This bloke giving you trouble again?'

I grin as I slice the tomatoes. 'Nothing I can't handle.'

Mycroft shakes free and straightens his clothes. 'Right. I'm leaving now.'

'See you later.'

'Cool.' He bites his lip over a smile; he knows I'm coming to the zoo.

'Funny guy,' Mike says, after Mycroft closes the front door. 'Why doesn't he just stay for dinner?'

'Don't know.' I shrug. It's not my business to share.

'Is Mycroft really his first name?'

His first name is James. I found out when I saw a whole-school photo in the admin corridor. 'Mm,' I say.

'How're you going, anyway? With school and stuff?' Mike picks up an apple and chomps into it.

'Oh, I'm thriving.' I wipe my hands on a tea towel. 'Go get Dad out of the garden. Tell him I've started cooking and he's only got an hour and a half before work.'

Four weeks in.

When it gets too much, I go over to Mai's place, or walk with her and Gus to the park, or visit Mycroft, who makes sodium acetate fairy-tower sculptures on request.

Sometimes I catch the tram up to Fawkner cemetery — it's quiet there, and there's trees, and space to breathe.

'I've figured it out,' Mycroft says, during recess. 'Watts, you're a Martian. I googled "west of Ouyen" and found these pictures — it's all desert and salt lakes and endless flat paddocks. Seriously, it's a lot like Mars, especially if you use the right filter —'

'Show me,' Mai says, grabbing the phone he's waggling, and I see the photos. Homesickness cuts through me with a stiff, serrated blade.

'No wonder you're struggling so much with urban life,' Mycroft goes on. 'You're a stranger in a strange land. If *I'd* come from … Watts? Watts, where are you off to?'

I don't really know where I'm going. I just need to go.

'*Watts!*'

I hear Mai say, 'Now look what you've done,' but I'm already halfway towards the school gate. Energy zips around my body. My bones feel like they're vibrating.

I need to walk. I want to follow my legs to the back paddock, boots crunching past the mallee scrub and the windmill, moving onward. Walking, walking, until I'm walked out. No voices nearby, no noise pollution from traffic, no people, no smells of exhaust. Just the sound of my boots clomping all the way to the dam.

I'll shed my boots there, and my socks and flannie and tank and cut-offs. I'll step into the mud on the bank, plunge straight into the cool brown water. This feeling will ease away, float off into the dam like so much oily scum, and my mind will spring back into shape. Everything will be manageable. Everything will be okay.

The rhythm of moving, stretching my legs, actually makes me feel better. The only problem is, no matter how far or how fast I walk, I can't reach the back paddock or the dam. And I'm on Sydney Road, so voices and noise pollution and traffic exhaust are a given.

I want to get out of here. But no amount of walking is going to get me back home.

I end up in the only place I know will be quiet. By the time I arrive I'm thirsty, and plastered with sweat. I have a drink from a tap, then wander around the rolling green grounds before picking out a plinth to lie down on. Just the fact that I can see trees and sky makes something ease in my chest.

I lie in the sun, try not to think, read a book. After a while, there's the sound of shoes scuffing gravel, back behind me.

'When you die, do you want to be buried or cremated?'

I sigh, but I've had enough time and space to calm down by now.

'Cremated.' I speak up to the clouds. 'I want my ashes to be scattered on the little hill in the west paddock.'

'I thought you'd say something like that.' Mycroft walks over to the side, so I can see him even while I'm lying down. 'Me, I've always thought maybe a sea burial. Everyone standing on the ship, looking out over the waves while they say all the words, then they push your coffin off the side and — plop, you're gone.'

'A sea burial?'

'Yes.' He leans on a headstone, pulls a cigarette out of the pack stashed in his T-shirt sleeve. 'D'you think the coffin just sinks straight to the bottom, or would it float around for a while?'

'You'd know the physics better than me.'

'I think it's to do with air pressure.' He taps the cigarette on the pack, leans to light up, blows smoke as he slips the pack away. 'Maybe they leave holes for the water to get in, or add weights to the bottom. I guess they must sink reasonably quickly. Otherwise you'd have all these coffins floating around the ocean, like plastic bags ...'

'I think they sink, Mycroft.'

'I'm sorry,' he says.

'It's okay.' I roll on the granite plinth, until I'm sitting up with my legs crossed. 'But I don't know why I'm your friend, sometimes.'

'Is it because I'm your neighbour and you can't get away from me?'

'You're too insightful. You open your mouth and all these razors come tumbling out.'

'I'm not that insightful, Watts. If I was, I'd have the insight to censor my own bullshit.' He sits on the plinth beside me. 'It's disturbing that you came to a cemetery.'

'I just needed some time on my own.'

'Surrounded by all the dead people, yes.'

'I just needed ...' I pause, but then all the words tumble out. 'I'm *stuck* here, y'know? I'm trapped. With thousands of people all living in the one place. And yes, there's action, and twinkling lights, and things happening, but I feel like I'm watching this endless cycle of people getting up, and eating, and going to work, and watching the same TV shows, and saying the same things, with this backdrop of bitumen, and cement, and all this stuff on repeat, with me standing outside watching it, fighting against it, *all the time*. Like, where am I? Where the hell am I? And there's no space to move, and I can't see the sky, and everything gets this pickled-in-aspic feeling, like you could slice into it and each slice would be the same cross-section, this thick grey jelly ...'

I slump on the plinth, exhausted from explaining it all.

'Christ.' Mycroft leans his shoulder against mine. 'It's fucking depressing, when you put it that way.'

'You were right.' I scrub my hands against my cheeks. 'I feel like an alien here. Or a, a missing person. D'you know what I mean?'

'I know,' he says solemnly, and I realise that he does know. I'm the way he was seven years ago.

'I'm *lost* in this city,' I say miserably.

'It's okay, Watts. I found you.' Mycroft puts his arm around me, curls me in. 'I found you.'

Oona Underground

LILI WILKINSON

Oona stands at the mouth of darkness, her hair full of sunset, her mouth full of smiles. She belongs to the day, to fresh air and warm breezes.

'Come *on*, Meg,' she says.

She's wearing sensible denim overalls, a white shirt and bright-red gumboots. Her hair is twisted up in a crown of golden braids, and strings of yellow beads hang from her neck.

'I just don't get why you want to go in there.'

'I told you. I want the witch to tell me my destiny.'

Her smile is teasing, but there's something else in her eyes. A longing for answers to a question I don't know.

We've all heard the stories about the Witch Queen. She dances in the drains, and if you bring her a treasure, she'll tell you your destiny. There's a guy at our school who knows another guy who will sell you a map of the drains so you can find her. Sometimes the Year 12s head there before their exams, hoping for a miracle. When they come out again, they don't talk about it. They act all mysterious, but I don't reckon they ever go down there at all. The mystery is just there to cover up the fact that they chickened out.

I don't believe in witches.

Oona charges forward. I hesitate. I'm afraid of what we might find in there. Cold fingers brush my ankles.

'Why now?' I ask. 'It'll be dark soon.'

'Because she can't be found during the day. You know how these things are.'

More nonsense.

'Please.' Oona turns back to me. 'I can't go in without you.' She reaches out her hand. I reach back and our fingers entwine.

I would follow her anywhere.

I've always followed Oona, ever since we were kids running squealing in our knickers under the sprinklers. For a while in primary school I tried to *be* her — I wore my hair the same way and got my mum to buy me the same dresses and shoes and accessories. But it never worked. I always looked like a cheap knockoff, paling in comparison to the real thing. By high school I had grown into the role I was born to play — the sarcastic best friend. I stood by Oona's side, and made sure I never took up any of her spotlight. If that meant shivering in her shadow sometimes, while she shared the light with someone else, then so be it. It was a small price to pay.

Oona texted me on the first of January, asking me to meet her in a cafe. It was important, she said. She'd had an epiphany. We ordered iced coffees and sat by the window, watching people clean up the debris of their new year celebrations.

Do you believe in destiny? she asked.

I don't believe in fate any more than I believe in witches. But it's hard to say no to Oona.

I don't know, I said instead. *I think we make our own destiny.*

Oona nodded. I stirred my iced coffee and waited.

I want to fall in love, she said, and my own heart thrummed with hope. But she shook her head and frowned. *It isn't working. I'm looking in all the wrong places.*

Look *here,* I wanted to tell her. Look at me. But I didn't. I never do.

But last night I realised I'm doing it all wrong. I've been trying to barge into love. To break it open and force my way in. But what if love doesn't work that way?

My hope shrivelled into resentment. *You're overthinking it,* I told her.

Oona ignored me. *What if love is something wild?* she said. *What if you have to surrender to it? Surrender to your destiny?*

I rolled my eyes.

I'm handing it over to fate, she told me. She dug in her bag, pulling out a Sharpie and her wallet. She selected a ten-dollar note and wrote I LOVE YOU in tiny, neat letters — across the bottom of the note.

Whoever gives this note back to me will be my true love, she declared.

Then she flashed me an impish smile and headed over to the counter, passing the note to a waiter and telling him to keep the change.

We walked home together as the sun grew high and hot, parting at the corner as usual. She gave me a hug and I breathed in her sun-warmed hair.

As we step into the tunnel, a gush of stale, muddy air eddies around us, drawn up from deep below. It smells like old dirt and things best left undisturbed. I don't need to ask Oona why she's here. It's been nearly a year since she surrendered to her destiny, and she's getting impatient. She's been on a few dates with boys in our class, hoping for the reappearance of the note. But of course there's been nothing, because there's no such thing as destiny.

Oona carries a blue backpack of supplies — a torch, extra batteries, a family-sized block of top-deck chocolate, a litre of water and the map she bought from a guy behind a 7-Eleven last Thursday. I offer to carry the bag because I'm a sucker, but Oona gives me a cheerful grin and says we'll take turns.

The tunnel slopes gently downwards, round and large, easily tall enough for us to walk upright. A trickle of water runs through it, only an inch or so deep. The grey concrete is barely visible under layer upon layer of graffiti, tags and messages and animals and girls with big eyes holding umbrellas. The graffiti snakes down the drain before us, squiggly lines converging into blackness. I turn back and look at the mouth of the tunnel, lit blazing gold and orange. Ripples of sunset dance towards our feet, swirling into the colours from the graffiti, reflected on brown water.

We walk. Oona hums to herself. The light grows dim, and I switch on the torch. It's like moving back in time, as the graffiti becomes faded and the bands it refers to grow more and more dated. NOFX. Linkin Park. Mötley Crüe. There are other things on the walls, too — snatches of poetry, spells, wishes. I see a few references to something called the Witch's Ball. Dark mould blossoms across the pale concrete ceiling like my grandma's Florence Broadhurst wallpaper. We pass under a black grate, and pause to soak up the last rays of sunset. I can hear the clamour of roosting birds and the rumble of cars. The light turns Oona's braids into a glowing crown. Rusted metal rungs lead up the slimy concrete walls to the grate, and I long to climb them and escape the damp darkness.

'What are you going to ask her for?' Oona asks, her voice bouncing off the concrete walls.

'Who?'

'The Witch Queen.'

I shrug into the darkness. 'I don't know,' I say. 'I haven't really thought about it.'

'How can you not have thought about it?' Oona sighs with exasperation. 'What are you even doing here?'

I don't respond, as in my opinion, it should be entirely obvious.

'Remember Harvey Webb? I heard he came down here and asked the Witch Queen to make him swim faster. And now he's going to the Olympics.'

I do remember Harvey. In Year 7 he'd lent Oona a pencil for a maths test and I'd seen my own longing mirrored on his face. Everyone loves Oona. Had he really come down here? Had he walked through the same brown sludge?

We pass a tributary that can't be too long, because twilight spills down it into the main tunnel. I can tell it's getting late; as Oona stands silhouetted at the mouth of the tributary, she doesn't seem golden and glowing anymore. The light is fading and turning grey and ominous. Oona's figure is empty black, and I fight the urge to rush to her and press her flesh, just to make sure she's still real and warm. She consults her map, and we head down further into darkness.

The light from the torch passes over opening after opening, each one slightly different. Some are curved and smooth, like tubular waterslides. Others are jagged with white calcification and mud. Graffiti teeth and lips encircle one, making it a gaping mouth swallowing up the darkness. Floating in the muddy stream at our feet are several sky-blue feathers and a scrap of black lace. I can smell roses. Painted signs indicate landmarks that Oona checks off on her map. Godzilla Point. Cactus Island. Tram Room. Under each of these signs is a large white square painted with a grid — a guestbook where urban explorers leave their names. *Combo. Sharkyshark Proserpina. Woody, Dougo* and *Sloth.*

'I wonder what she eats,' Oona muses.

'The Witch Queen?' I ask. 'Probably nothing because she doesn't exist.'

Oona's chuckle echoes off the walls. 'Maybe she eats the unbelievers,' she suggests.

'Maybe.'

There's a pause. 'I wouldn't let her.'

I know she wouldn't. Oona has always looked after me. Countless times some popular group has tried to lure her away, but she never lets me go. She is fierce and loyal and true, and the fact that this isn't enough fills me with self-loathing.

I hear a rhythmic sound, like a steady drip, but sharper, dryer. It gets louder as we continue downstream. Irrationally, I wonder if someone has planted a bomb down here, under the streets. My throat closes over as I imagine being buried here, crushed by dust and rubble and earth. The drain curves sharply, and I see the source of the ticking. It's a clock, hanging from a bent and rusted nail up on the wall. It reads 7.44. I pull my phone out of my pocket. There's no signal down here, but the clock still works. It confirms it really is 7.44. I wonder if my parents will be worried.

Above the clock, a beautifully calligraphic sign reads PARK LANE. Oona consults her map, and we continue, up a slimy flight of stone steps and into a large square tunnel. For the first time since entering the drains, the ground underfoot is dry.

'I guess this must be a disused section of the system,' says Oona. 'Overflow or something.'

There are signs of humans here. A shopping trolley laden with bags and bundles. A filthy mattress. A rusted kid's bicycle.

'Wait.' Oona grabs my sleeve and points.

A narrow tunnel leads off to our left.

'What?' I ask.

In response, Oona switches off the torch. And I see there's light coming from the tunnel. Not daylight, it's too late for that. This light is weak and warm and close.

'Come on,' Oona whispers, and switches her torch back on.

'Are you crazy?' I hiss. 'There could be someone in there.'

'I know. That's why I want to see.'

She trots off down the tunnel, and I drag myself after her.

The narrow passage widens at its end into a kind of room. Old pallets have been fashioned into shelves that hold pots and pans, spices, and sealed canisters of rice and pasta. I stare. We appear to have stepped into someone's home.

A camping stove sits on another pallet, and beside it, a narrow bed, neatly made with a faded Care Bears doona cover. There's a man lying on the bed, reading a book in the glow of one of those clip-on book lights. He squints as the torch sweeps over him, and sits up.

He's small and bald, wearing a business suit that was probably once very expensive but is now ragged and worn through at the knees and elbows. His fingernails are long and dirty.

'Visitors!' he says, looking pleased.

'Um, hi,' says Oona. 'We're sorry we disturbed you.'

'Not at all!' says the man. 'Have a seat.' He indicates two milk crates. Gingerly, we sit. The man perches on the corner of his bed and beams at us. His eyes seem too large for his face.

'Looking for the Witch Queen?' he asks. 'Or are you just going down for the ball?'

'What ball?' I reply.

'The Witch's Ball. Didn't you get an invitation?'

I shake my head.

'We're just here to see the Witch Queen,' Oona explains.

The man nods. 'It's hard to find her without an invitation to the ball,' he says. 'But I can tell you which way to go. Once you go on from here, it's very hard to come back. You have to be sure.'

'We're sure,' says Oona firmly.

The man springs to his feet again, and I notice he has a tremor in his right hand. 'Want a Milo?'

I open my mouth to decline, but Oona says *yes please* before I get the chance. Of course she does. The man goes over to his makeshift kitchen and produces three chipped mugs and a tin of Milo. He lights the camping stove.

'Have to be careful with the gas,' he says, looking nervously at the ceiling. 'Can't leave it on too long or it eats up all the oxygen. But a few minutes to make Milo is okay.'

He places a small saucepan of water on the stove, and grabs a few of those individual cups of long-life milk that you find in crappy buffets. He dumps two into each mug, along with a few spoonfuls of Milo.

'What do you do all day?' asks Oona.

'Sometimes I go up to the park, or the library,' the man says. 'Or if I can't be bothered I just stay down here and read.'

He waves his hand towards another milk crate, which serves as a bedside table. It's piled high with battered paperbacks.

I spy Stephen King's *On Writing* in the pile.

'Have you read *Cujo*?' I ask. 'It's my favourite.'

The man shakes his head. 'I don't like horror,' he says. 'Gives me the creeps.'

He turns off the stove and pours hot water from the saucepan into each of the mugs. He stirs the Milo with a plastic spoon before handing a mug to each of us. I notice he has no arm hair – no hair anywhere, as far as I can tell. I take a sip of the Milo, and even though a part of me is worried about poison or drugs, I immediately feel better. Warmth spreads right through me, into my cold fingers and numb toes.

'So you two,' says the man. 'You're friends, or ...'

'Friends,' I say, and the bitterness of the word overwhelms the sweetness of the Milo.

'*Best* friends,' says Oona, and I immediately feel guilty for wanting more.

The man looks wistful. 'It's good to have a best friend.'

'We've always been friends,' Oona explains. 'Meg is the kindest and best person I know. She's patched up my heart more times than I can count.'

She looks at me sideways and there is an intensity in her eyes that is unfamiliar. I remember when we were little and her parents split up, how small and broken she was. How tightly she'd clung to me as she'd sobbed. How I knew I would do anything if it would make her smile again.

'How long have you lived down here?' Oona asks the man.

'Oh, nearly forever,' says the man. 'At least a hundred years. I came down here looking for something I'd lost. Something precious. I'm still looking.'

'Why don't you go see the Witch Queen?' Oona asks. 'Maybe she can help you find what you're looking for?'

The man looks at her, and I see something in his eyes. A warning. 'The Witch Queen doesn't work that way.'

'What do you mean?' I ask. 'Have you met her? Is she real?'

The man chuckles. 'Depends on what you mean by real.'

I tip the mug up to get the last sweet dregs of Milo.

'Are there others?' Oona asks. 'Living in the drains?'

'Sure. Old Snake lives just around the corner. He's been here for longer than me. Longer than there've been drains. He lived here when it was just caves and underground rivers. There are others. Not everyone is social. There are more people now because it's summer. It's nice down here. Cool. But it can get real ugly in winter.'

'Does it flood?'

'Not often. This part of the system is overflow — only floods if there's a real bad storm. It's happened two or three times since I've been here.'

'What happens to all your stuff?'

The man shrugs. 'Washes away. It's only junk, it doesn't matter.'

I'm still thinking over what he said about the Witch Queen. I still don't believe in her, but I have a feeling there's something the man isn't telling us.

'Is it far?' I ask. 'To the Witch Queen?'

'Yes.' His tone is frank. 'Very far. You have to really want to find her.'

'I do.' Oona's voice throbs with conviction, and I look at her sharply. She is staring at the man, and he is staring back at her, and I feel like they are sharing some unspoken communication that I'm not a part of. Jealousy stabs at me.

'Well, then,' says the man. 'If it's like that, you'll find her. But be careful. Look out for spiders. The eels should stay away from you, as long as you don't step on one. And don't worry about the green glow. I used to think it was radiation, nuclear waste or such like. But it's just plankton. *Noctiluca scintillans*, they're called. I looked it up in the library. "*Noctiluca scintillans* exhibits bioluminescence when disturbed". That means they glow when you mess around in their water.'

'Thanks,' says Oona. 'Is there anything else we should know?'

The man doesn't answer, just stares down into his Milo, as if he's hypnotised by it. After a few minutes, Oona and I glance at each other, wondering if we should just leave. I put down my mug and start to rise from my milk crate. The man flinches, looking at us blankly with his giant eyes, like he had forgotten we were ever there. His expression is lost, confused.

'Do you ever wonder if you're already dead?' he asks. 'And you just haven't realised?'

Oona reaches out and pats him gently on the shoulder. 'Thank you for the Milo,' she says.

The next tunnel is tall and thin and hexagonal, shaped exactly like a coffin. Oona tells me it's called Mummy's Walk on her map. I shudder as I feel something brush my ankle, and think about eels and spiders and ghosts. Narrow pipes emerge from the wall and ceiling like the roots of great metal trees. Some of them trickle with icy water that runs down the back of my neck and under my collar. We trudge on for what feels like hours, around snaking bends and sharp corners. Oona stops regularly to consult the map — this section of the drains, she says, is called The Maze. We eat all our chocolate and drink all our water. The air grows cold and stale, and I wonder how far below the ground we are. It's hard to believe the outside still exists at all.

Every now and then I think I hear something. Snatches of music or bursts of laughter. I'm not sure if it's real, or if my mind is playing tricks on me. There are strange smells, too. Wafts of warm incense, or candlewax, or roses, suddenly overpowering but gone in an instant.

Without warning, the torch winks out. Oona, who is carrying it, lets out a little scream. I've never experienced such darkness. My eyes start playing tricks on me — things reach from the walls, grasping Oona's hair in front of me. Shadows dart across my vision, running around the tunnel and up the wall.

'The bag,' says Oona, and her voice is close and distant and strange in the darkness. 'There are batteries in the front pocket.'

I swing it from my shoulder and grope for the zipper. Oona has sensibly stored the batteries in a ziplock bag to protect them from getting wet. I pull out two, and reach for her in the darkness. I find her fingers, cold and clammy, and hear her fumbling with the torch as she clicks open the battery compartment and removes the spent batteries.

It seems to take forever. I can hear Oona's breathing grow shallow and fast, and I know she's starting to panic. I don't know how we'll ever find our way out of here if we don't have a light.

I reach out to steady myself on the stone wall, and adjust my stance. The water moves around my ankles, and just like the ragged man said, a green glow ripples out around my feet. The water shines with a thousand tiny lights, each one a tiny body, a tiny life. I hear Oona move her own legs, and see her dark outline against the glowing green water. I feel like a giant planet, floating in the glittering endlessness of space.

'It's so beautiful,' Oona says softly.

I hear a click and the torch comes on. The lights in the water fade, and I see Oona's face. She's closer to me than I'd thought. Close enough that I can feel her skin humming next to mine, and hear the rise and fall of her breath. We stare at each other and it feels like she's waiting for something. But then Oona turns away and pulls out the map again. Pinpricks of white light glint above us. For a moment I think we are outside and that I can see the stars. But it's just little balls of white polystyrene stuck to the ceiling. Oona looks up at it, too.

'How did they get up there?' she wonders out loud, and I feel a shiver of unease.

The tunnel curves around, and we climb down a series of terraced steps that form a kind of shallow waterfall. It's quite tranquil, the tinkling of water as it spills over the steps in a gentle slope.

But the tranquillity evaporates when the tunnel ends abruptly, a slimy rail preventing us from going any further. On the other side of the rail, a deep, dark shaft plunges down into nothingness. I shine the torch up to the sign above the shaft.

THE PIT OF DEATH. A long metal ladder is attached to the railing with a chain. It looks strong and cold. I glance at Oona, who is very pale.

'Is there another way?' I ask.

She shakes her head. Then she takes a deep breath, tucks the torch into the pocket of her overalls, and swings a leg over the railing.

This is seriously dumb. We could die down here. And for what? A stupid ten-dollar note? Oona steps onto the ladder. The slack-hanging chain pulls taut, swinging the ladder backwards with a jerk. Oona screams, clinging to the rungs. But the ladder holds. Oona's eyes turn to me and I see panic and relief and desperation. And I realise it can't just be about the note. There has to be another reason why she's here. There's something else she needs to know. Slowly, carefully, she climbs down the ladder, and I watch her get swallowed up in blackness.

Eventually, I hear her call up to me, and I want to run away *so badly*. I want to climb back up to the real world, where everything is bright and alive and full of air.

'Can you hear me?'

It's the tremble in her voice that is my undoing. The wavering uncertainty. There's a part of her that really thinks I might leave her down there, abandon her to The Pit of Death. And I can't bear that she doubts me. So I climb down after her, following her deeper into the underworld.

When I reach the bottom, Oona wraps her arms around my neck and pulls me close. I can feel her trembling. 'For a moment I thought you weren't coming,' she whispers.

'Don't be ridiculous,' I say, trying to sound confident and indifferent. 'Come on, it can't be too much further.'

We hear the Witch's Ball long before we see it. Strains of music bounce off the curved tunnel walls, creating ripples of echoes. It's impossible to tell which direction it comes from. But it gets louder as we trudge through the silt, until eventually we stumble out into an enormous chamber, our mouths hanging open and our eyes wide.

This part of the drains feels old, older than should be possible in this city. Red brick walls curve gently up into darkness, so high it's hard to make out the ceiling. Stone pillars support the ceiling. There are maybe a hundred people down here, ankle-deep in muddy brown water. They look like fairytale characters, elaborately dressed and decorated in feathers, sequins, lace and leather. Women wear jewel-encrusted bodices and hooped skirts. A man in a skin-tight knitted jumpsuit in bold-coloured stripes is dancing in front of me. His hair is spiked into a neon-green mohawk, but as he whirls past I see that the mohawk is woollen, too. He's dancing with a woman with a tall woven hairpiece that seems to be made from brightly coloured drinking straws.

The walls are crowded with hundreds of tiny candles — they'd be unsafe anywhere else in the drains, but here the ceilings are high and a row of ancient rusted grates lets in fresh air. Yet more candles swing in glass lanterns hung overhead, casting roaming shadows on the brick walls.

A band is playing up on a ledge — a violinist wearing a gown of gauzy greys and blacks that make her look as if she is wreathed in smoke. Another woman in a black leather corset with a diamond-studded eyepatch is wrapped around the curves of a double bass, and a man covered in black feathers with a beaked, pointy nose clutches a trumpet in black fingernails shaped like claws.

Oona's hand creeps into mine, and I feel a little more complete.

'How did they get down here?' I ask.

She shakes her head.

Another woman twirls past, wearing a dress of origami, paper angles and points crisp and white at her shoulders, but slowly disintegrating around the knees, as the muddy water wicks up from the ground. She spots us and holds out her hand. Her face is painted chalk-white, her eyes and lips rimmed with gold. Oona takes a half-step forward, but the paper woman whisks away, drawn back into the press of bodies.

Oona looks at me, her eyes shining. 'Come on.'

She draws me into the crowd, and we are caught up in the music. I see a face spattered with metallic paint, like gold freckles. Long eyelashes with articulated bends, like spider legs. A man wearing a moulded breastplate, shining iridescent black-green, like beetle wings.

Despite our exhaustion, it is impossible not to dance to the wild, skittering rhythms. We give ourselves in to it, and almost instantly it swallows us whole. My feet splash in the dark water, and my protective shell breaks open. Oona's cheeks are flushed and I feel bold and reckless. I pull her to me and she laughs, delighted, her hands curving up my back and shoulders. We dance breathless, chest-to-chest, our hearts beating together.

We dance our way to the opposite edge of the crowd. There are maybe twenty tunnels leading off this chamber, with no signs to indicate which is which. Oona touches a man on the arm. His skin is so dark he almost melts into the dark of the tunnel behind him. He is painted with glinting stars and colourful whorls of galaxy. Oona leans up on tiptoe to shout a question into his ear, and he nods and points to one tunnel, the smallest one, little more than a narrow opening in the wall.

Oona pushes through the crowd, heading in the direction the galaxy man indicated. She doesn't look back to see if I'm following, but I do anyway.

The tunnel is red brick, too, and oval in shape, like a skinny egg. It isn't large enough for an adult to stand up in, and my shoulders brush the sides as I follow her. I hear her breathing tighten — this is the smallest space we've been in. Water trickles at our feet, and the walls seem to pulse with the sound of the music from the ballroom. Spiders scuttle overhead, and I turn my torch onto the wall, letting out a strangled sound when I see the bright-red splashes on their backs. There must be thousands of them, popping in and out of the cracks between the bricks. Easily enough to kill us both.

'Maybe we should go back,' I say.

She pauses and for a moment I think she's going to say yes. The surface tugs at us, promising fresh air and safety. We don't belong down here.

'No,' she says at last, her voice unsteady. 'Keep going.'

The tunnel shrinks. We hunch over until we are bent double, then drop to our hands and knees. It squeezes us, like wet cloth being wrung dry.

'Oona,' I say, my voice high and strained. 'I can't breathe.'

Ahead of me Oona stops crawling. The tunnel is too narrow for her to turn around, but she reaches back between her legs and grabs my hand.

'It's okay,' she says. 'You're okay.'

I'm not okay, but it's too late to go back. We can't go back. This realisation makes my chest constrict again, panic flooding my lungs. I squeeze Oona's hand, and feel her strength flow into me.

I follow her. I have no choice. But even if I did, I'd still follow her.

The tunnel opens out into a small chamber, the oldest part of the drain system. It is made from dusty bluestone blocks, a round column of a room that rises and rises above us out of sight. Candles gutter in the gaps and bumps in the wall. Wax drips long stalactites, translucent fingers and tentacles reaching down to us.

There is a kind of altar in the centre of the chamber, a stone slab mounted with a huge bull's skull, curving horns reaching up to the stone ceiling. A clay dish of burning herbs releases tendrils of pungent smoke. Rose petals are scattered over everything, floating red in the water.

Behind the altar dances a solitary woman. She is large-breasted, her face painted with white lines and swirls. Green spectacles glint over her eyes. She wears a top hat and a dress made from hundreds of strips of coloured lace that float around her, like hair underwater. A necklace of tiny skulls hangs low from her neck. She holds out her arms to us, and I see they are ringed with tattoos that seem to writhe and shift in the candlelight.

The Witch Queen turns her head to greet us, her spectacles flashing.

Oona steps forward bravely. 'Witch Queen,' she says. 'My name is Oona and I've sought you from ... from afar.' She digs in the backpack and I realise I never asked her what treasure she brought to offer. I guess I never thought we'd get this far.

Oona's hand opens, and I catch my breath. It's the purple origami unicorn I made for her in grade five, when her parents were breaking up and she was so sad all the time. I spent a whole weekend watching YouTube tutorials trying to get the folds just right.

I can't believe she has kept it, all this time.

I can't believe she's giving it away.

The Witch Queen takes the purple unicorn and tosses it on her altar without looking at it. It's gone within seconds, a brief flare of yellow flame, and then just ash.

Oona glances at me and licks her lips. 'I want to know my destiny.'

The Witch Queen raises her eyebrows. 'I don't deal in destinies,' she says. 'All I can tell you is the reason you came down here.'

'Okay.'

The Witch Queen takes Oona's hands and they sink into a kind of dance, a sweeping back-and-forth waltz around the altar. Oona's eyelids grow heavy, and it's like she's hypnotised. As their dance speeds up, Oona's face changes, becoming unfamiliar to me. The Witch Queen bends down and whispers something to her, then spins Oona out from her embrace, letting her go so she twirls off through the water and the rose petals, and slumps against the stone wall.

I move to help her, but the Witch Queen stops me with her arm.

'Leave her,' she hisses. 'The truth sends you wild, but only for a time.'

'Will she be okay?'

The Witch Queen doesn't answer, she just holds out her hand. 'Now you,' she says.

I take a half-step back, shaking my head. 'Oh no,' I say. 'I'm not here to — I'm just here for moral support.'

'Don't you want to know your destiny?' she asks.

'I thought you didn't deal in destinies.'

The Witch Queen's mouth quirks in the faintest hint of a smile. 'You are bold,' she says. 'But you still want to know.'

Her hand is still outstretched, waiting.

'I didn't bring anything,' I say. 'I didn't bring a treasure.'

But that isn't true and she knows it. A mouse tattoo runs around her wrist, circling it three times before coming to rest right on her pulse.

I can't give it to her. It's my only chance. A fool's hope, I know. But if I hand it over, then I'll be giving up.

In the corner, I hear a low growl coming from Oona. I glance over and see her, hunched and twisted, her back heaving with animal breath. I need to get her out of here. My hand moves to my pocket. I'll give it up for her. To save her.

The plastic of the ten-dollar note is smooth under my fingers.

I unfold it carefully, and read the words one last time. Then I give it to the Witch Queen. She flashes her teeth at me, and holds the note to her face, inhaling its scent. Then she casts it onto her altar, where the burning herbs melt and curl it into black smoke and twisted remains. I feel my heart curl and melt and shrink along with it.

The Witch Queen grabs me around the waist and pulls me up against her full, hot breasts. She leans closer, and I can see dark eyes behind the green glasses. The scent of sweat and smoke and roses is overpowering. She cocks her head to the side, and then runs a long, warm tongue up my face, from my chin to my temple. I feel dizzy.

'You came here for her,' she says. 'You would follow her anywhere. She is your first love and your last.' Her voice is as thick and slow as molasses.

And even though I already knew that, now I really *know*.

And I realise what I've done.

I stole Oona's destiny. When I turned back from our corner and returned to the cafe. When I swallowed my embarrassment and asked the waiter if I could swap her note for one of my own. I took Oona's destiny and locked it away in a prison of false hope. She is down here because of me. I am not the wisecracking sidekick in this story. I am the ogre, the dragon, the wicked stepmother.

I look over at the altar and see the melted plastic that was Oona's fate. I have destroyed it. It is as black and shrivelled as my own heart. I reach over to it, and it disintegrates at my touch, the pieces crumbling away and scattering in the muddy water at my feet, mingling with the floating rose petals.

I scatter, too. Bits of me come spilling out into the night. I feel my eyes grow large, hair sprouting along my spine. I turn my head up and howl into the darkness. It's too much. The roses and water and everythingness of it all.

The Witch Queen grabs my chin and forces my head up to meet her gaze, jerking me back into the little stone room.

'A storm is coming. Find shelter above the stars,' she says, and whirls away with a surge of fluttering scraps of lace.

And suddenly it's just me and Oona in the room.

'Oona?' I call.

She looks up at me, and I feel a cold chill of fear. Her hair has fallen loose from its braided crown, and her teeth are bared. A growl rumbles low in her throat. Her eyes are inky-black. A gust of warm wind lifts my hair from my shoulders and I shiver.

We never should have come here.

I grit my teeth and grab Oona's hand, scared she will scratch or bite me. But she doesn't, and allows me to lead her back through the narrow tunnel. As it widens enough for us to stand, I stumble and reach out to steady myself on the wall. I freeze, terrified the spiders will swarm all over me. Except the wall is bare and smooth. The spiders have gone.

We find our way back to the ballroom, but it is empty. No dancers. No music. The candles still flicker on the walls, illuminating feathers and sequins floating on water that glints with a rainbow film of oil.

Oona turns her face towards me, and I'm relieved to see that she looks normal again. Her eyes are wide and her face is pale. She shivers as the dark tide laps at her thighs.

'Meg,' she croaks.

And that's when I realise that the water has risen higher.

'We have to go,' I tell her.

There are eight tunnels that lead into the ballroom, and they all look the same. I don't know which one we entered by. The water is flowing stronger now, no longer a trickle but a stream with a steady current.

'Downstream,' I mutter. 'If we follow it downstream we'll find our way out.'

The water has climbed even higher, and it's bringing other things down from the surface, too. Autumn leaves, sticks, empty chip packets and beer cans. The refuse tugs and scratches as the pressure of the tide pulls us further and further down the tunnel. It's up to our waists now. I can hear thunder rumbling, getting louder and louder.

We have to get out.

'There.' Oona points at iron rungs in the wall. We scramble up, past a crust of tiny polystyrene balls. There's a manhole up there, and Oona darts to the top of the ladder and pushes, but it is heavy steel and concrete and she can't budge it. I squeeze up next to her, and we both set our shoulders beneath the manhole and strain. It's no use.

Find shelter above the stars.

There is a ledge just above the line of white polystyrene balls. It's only a foot or so of recessed concrete. Oona and I drop down onto it. I shine my torch down into the foaming water. The thundering sound is almost deafening now, and the water turns white and churning. It fills the tunnel, and I can see enormous shapes sucked along with it — a battered rubbish bin, an old TV, a shopping trolley. I hope the man with the Milo is okay.

Oona and I cling to each other with numb fingers, and I can feel her heart hammering the same desperate rhythm as my own.

'I'm sorry,' I yell over the thundering water.

'No, *I'm* sorry!' she yells back. 'I never should have made you follow me down here.'

'But it was all for nothing.' I can't yell anymore, but I need to say it anyway. 'You didn't get what you came for, and it's my fault.'

Oona's expression softens and she looks puzzled. She says something, only I can't make it out over the roaring below.

And then somehow we are kissing. She curls her body into mine and we just *fit*, hands and lips and skin and sodden clothes.

Oona tastes like sunshine and I forget about the flood and our imminent death because despite all odds, this cold, wet, dangerous prison is exactly where I always wanted to be.

When the water eventually subsides, we help each other down from the ledge. Astonishingly the torch still works, but the map is useless now, soaked into mush, and anyway, we have no idea where we are. We follow the flow of water at our feet, in the hope that it will eventually lead us outside. I desperately want to know what Oona is thinking, how she feels about what happened. But she is silent, her shoulders small in front of me as she picks her way through the debris. With every step, the taste of her fades, and I grow cold and shivery.

Eventually there is a dim, grey light ahead. We follow it, and it grows brighter and brighter. The water grows deeper, and I realise that this tunnel opens out onto a large brown river. It's early morning, and I can hear birds and the rumble of cars.

I wonder if the world has changed much, since we've been gone. I can't imagine anything will ever be the same.

Oona steps out of the drain into the river, waist deep in muddy water. She scrambles up the bank, grabbing onto weeds to haul herself up the slope.

And I hesitate again, because going back out into the light means going back to the real world. The world where she and I are best friends and she holds my hand and I long for something I can't have. I want to stay in the darkness, just for a few minutes more. I reach into my pocket before I remember that I gave Oona's note to the Witch Queen. But my fingers touch folded thin plastic, and I pull out the note. It is grimy with silt, but the letters are still there.

I LOVE YOU.

I saw the note burn. It melted into a black lump. I saw that happen.

'What did she tell you?' I call out.

Oona turns around, squinting to find me in the shadows. Her overalls are brown and grey, wet and clinging to her stomach and thighs. Her hair is drying into fuzzy ringlets, lit up pink and gold by the rosy fingers of dawn. She hesitates.

Red gumboots slide down the bank and she plunges back into the water again, making her way over to me. When she is close, I hold out the note and see her eyes widen as she takes it.

'Why did you go down there?' I ask.

Oona drops the note, and it floats away on the muddy brown tide. When she speaks, her voice is low, barely more than a whisper. 'I wanted to know if you'd follow me anywhere.'

She presses her body up against mine, her face tilting to my face, her mouth to my mouth. She feels warm and alive as she takes my hand, our fingers sliding together. Then she leads me out of the drain, up the embankment and into the sunshine.

The Feeling From Over Here

GABRIELLE TOZER

LUCY
5.53 p.m.

Blisters burn the backs of Lucy's ankles. She thuds along the footpath parallel to Northbourne Avenue, a veil of sweat decorating her forehead, but she doesn't bother to wipe it away. Turns out shoes fresh from the box and a school uniform aren't the best choices for sprinting through the streets of Canberra.

The bus is shuddering by the time she charges into the Jolimont Centre, suitcase rattling on the tiles and vice-captain badge swinging from her uniform collar. She watches, still puffing, as the last of the passengers pile onto the swollen bus. Heart pounding, Lucy squats down on the concrete to unzip the suitcase. Her hoodie and tracksuit pants are folded on top, in half, then in half again; her attempt to be organised before the trip.

Before this afternoon.

Before the spare hours between class ending and arriving at the bus stop had dissolved, thanks to helping her coach pack up the swimming gear after last period and fielding calls about the Year 12 formal every five minutes from the school captain.

Swearing to herself, Lucy tosses the hoodie and tracksuit pants over her left arm and wheels her bag to the back of the bus line.

The driver saunters over. 'Wagga or Albury?' he asks, grabbing her suitcase.

'Melbourne.'

'In it for the full eight hours, huh?'

'Yeah. Brave, right?'

'Brave's one word for riding the overnighter.' He chuckles, warming up a little. 'Alrighty, Eight, onya get, find a seat. Better get this milk-carton-on-wheels movin' before the roos take over the highway.'

Lucy nods. 'Is there time for me to run inside to change into my ...' She gestures to her tracksuit, voice trailing off as she spots the driver's raised eyebrow. 'Never mind.'

She tugs at her uniform, cringing at the saucer-sized stains radiating from her armpits.

5.56 p.m.

The bus is packed. Lucy squeezes down the aisle, sucking in a breath as she dodges dangling feet and a juicebox-throwing toddler. She strains towards her seat at the back, her imagination whirring as she panics about which brand of awful she'll be wedged in with. A man obsessed with watching dirty YouTube clips on his iPad without headphones? Or maybe a child who loves nothing more than screeching in people's ears?

Row after row, Lucy passes the passengers — no signs of anyone clipping their nails onto the floor yet, like her best friend Nate had warned her — although anything seems possible after eight hours trapped together in the dark. Lucy grins when she reaches her seat: there's not a whisper of another human in the spot next to hers.

6.01 p.m.

The bus rumbles as Lucy dumps out the contents of her bag onto the empty seats.

Buzzzz.

Her phone.

Again.

The twins. Simone, the eldest of Lucy's family by seventeen minutes, tells her not to worry about packing shampoo 'cause Ana is addicted to collecting the free little bottles from hotels during her work trips. Too late.

It buzzes again.

Nate moaning, '*The Olivia Bensons miss youuuu, Lucy Maree Faris*' in their group's chat.

And again.

More from Nate, this time sending selfies with Tamiko from the back seat of his parents' car on the way to Maya's farm for Shabbat dinner and a sleepover.

Lucy runs her fingers through her thick ponytail as she fights the twinge in her chest.

It's band practice for The Olivia Bensons tomorrow, so they'll be working their way through the Stones, AC/DC and KISS's back catalogues. Although Lucy wonders whether it'll even happen without her nagging everyone into position, drumsticks in hand, smashing at the kit until they stop sliding around in their socks in Nate's garage. Probably not.

If they're the bricks, then she's the cement.

6.04 p.m.

The bus driver walks up and down the aisle counting passengers. Yawning, Lucy curls up against the window, using her bunched-up tracksuit as a makeshift pillow, clamps her eyes shut and jams in her earphones to block out the thick, throaty laughter from a woman a few seats ahead. Lucy buries her face further into the material, nose crinkling at the faint waft of chlorine.

A tap on her shoulder.

Her eyelids strain open.

Through twisted lashes, Lucy sees the bus driver beaming, his scrawny arm leaning on the headrest in front of her. 'Evening, Eight. We've got ourselves an incoming.'

Lucy's gaze follows the driver's fingers as he points towards the front of the bus. In the aisle, right next to the driver's seat, stands a tall guy in skinny jeans with a backpack hanging off his shoulder. His hoodie is pulled down low over his forehead and he's absorbed by his phone so Lucy can't see his face, only a hint of his profile.

'Better late than never, I s'pose,' the driver continues, 'although a second later and he'd've missed the party.' The unflattering lights sparking a bright-white glow through the bus aren't helping Lucy get a better look. Pretty cute, Lucy notes, although she thinks all guys look pretty cute in a hoodie and skinny jeans. A bad habit, really.

'Scoot over, then,' adds the driver.

'What?' Lucy rubs at her eye.

'I can't strap the big fella to the top of the bus, can I?'

He squeezes his way back down the aisle, announcing to the passengers with a gruff laugh that it's almost time for take-off.

Lucy rechecks her ticket.

Aisle seat.

Damn.

As Lucy sweeps her stuff back into her bag, grimacing at her sticky school uniform, she doesn't know whether to be irritated she has to share her precious spare seat with someone, or panicked that *someone* is a guy in a hoodie and skinny jeans.

A maybe pretty cute guy.

The pressure.

A passenger with a toenail clipper would be welcomed right now.

She looks up to see the *maybe pretty cute* guy standing in the aisle next to her. The hoodie's slipped off and he's not *maybe pretty cute* at all. He's *definitely actually cute*, but that's not the problem.

It's Cameron Webber.

His shoulder-length hair is cropped off, but it's him.

Cam.

Webby.

The World Wide Web.

BBQ.

BBQ Sauce.

Smoky BBQ Sauce.

Smoky.

The guys in his group had too many nicknames to keep up with. Smoky was always Lucy's favourite — it matched his eyes — until it felt wrong and she could only think of him as Cameron Webber again.

Lucy's jaw tightens.

'Hey,' Cameron says, breaking into a smile as he readjusts his backpack.

'Hi.'

'How's it going?'

'Fine, thanks.'

She holds her breath as Cameron squeezes past her to the window seat.

He's said hello, he's asked how it's going, but Lucy can't tell if he's making small talk with that girl he used to know or if he's just being friendly to the grubby stranger on the bus. Maybe he doesn't even remember her. When Cameron is settled into place, earphones in, thumbs drumming against his jeans, Lucy reaches for her phone. Not that it'll be any use: Maya's farm has Australia's worst mobile reception.

But still Lucy's fingers dance on the keyboard.

SOS, Olivia Bensons, she types, biting her lip. *Trapped on a bus with Cameron Webber. Benson #2 down. I repeat: Benson #2 down.*

6.19 p.m.

He keeps sniffing.

Long, crackly sniffs that sound like he's trying to snort something up his nose. Lucy wriggles her earphones in a little further, wondering how deep they can go without busting her eardrums. She sniffs as payback, drawing in a long, loud breath, but it only makes her torso hard from nose to gut and she explodes into a coughing attack, burying her mouth into her soft fist.

Cameron raises an eyebrow — an *everything all right?* eyebrow — but Lucy forces a small smile, still spluttering into her fingers.

He settles back in his seat. Another sniff. Then more drumming of his thumbs to the beat pounding in his head. Fast, hard drums, the type of song Lucy knows she'd rip up on stage if she and The Olivia Bensons ever got the chance.

She curls her body away from Cameron's, wiping her hand on her uniform when he's not looking, then fluffs the tracksuit beneath her head. It slips down from the headrest. Sighing, she flops the other way to try to get comfortable, until she realises she's now arched in towards him.

He spots her before she has time to shift.

'You okay?' he asks, taking out an ear bud. 'You seem kinda —'

'What?' She sits up a little straighter, lips pursed.

His bottom lip twitches. 'Nothing. So you're okay?'

'I'm okay.'

'Then okay.'

He turns up his music but he still hasn't said her name. Lucy Faris. It's not that hard. Four syllables. He has to remember it. You don't just forget the name of someone you used to know. Although, to be fair, she hasn't said his either.

Lucy wonders if the sound of his would catch in her throat if she tried to say it out loud.

Oh, how she'd fantasised about spitting it in his face.

Or just spitting in his face.

Now she's here, centimetres from Cameron's skin, close enough to smell the peppermint on his breath, and she can't look past the invisible bubble around him; her skin prickles every time he tries to hold her gaze for more than a second. Frustrated with herself, Lucy's eyes lower to snoop at the scribbling on his hand. A blue chequerboard on the ruddy flesh below his knuckles. Two red stars on his little finger. And the word 'tiny' scrawled up his left thumb in mottled black ink, running into the quick of his chewed nails.

Clearing her throat, Lucy makes a big deal out of retrieving her phone from her bag, hating herself for not handling this better. But Cameron's said less than twenty words to her and none of them are 'I'm sorry'.

'Sure you're okay?'

'Yep. Still okay.'

'Then okay.'

Twenty words.

Still no sorry.

6.54 p.m.

I'm dying, she types to the group. *Dying ... dying ... please send help before I'm dead. Benson #2, over and out.*

She frowns at her phone, willing someone to do the impossible and reply.

But no-one answers her SOS.

7.01 p.m.

Still nothing.

It's just her, Cameron Webber and six hundred kilometres of highway, she thinks, grasp tightening around her phone.

7.03 p.m.

Lucy's thoughts are so loud she worries the whole bus can hear them. Arms folded across her chest, she glares out the window across the aisle; Cameron's shut their blind. Not that she would've dared peek out past him anyway.

It's been three years since Cameron showed up at her school in the middle of Term 1 and promptly disappeared a few months later. Plenty of the guys in Year 9 had cold porridge for brains, but he seemed like a different breed with a soft tone that made it sound like he was trying to swallow his words before anyone heard them. Cameron played a ton of sport — the number-one currency in their corner of Canberra — so after a few days of bouncing between groups, word spread about his sprinting and kicking game in PE and it landed him in with the popular guys. The footyheads. The jerks, according to Lucy. *According to just about everyone who was brave enough to admit it.* Cameron wouldn't say much when the loudmouths — the Mitches and the Daveys and the Matts — talked rubbish; he'd just nod and tuck his shoulder-length hair behind his ears, cracking jokes that everyone pretended to get.

Lucy would see him at the local pool on mornings before class. Green swimming cap on, he'd power through the water, his enormous feet kicking up and down, propelling him through the fast lane. He would see her, too. One day he complimented her backstroke style, the next day she mentioned his fast tumble turns, and they soon fell into a habit of propping each other up whenever they saw each other.

A smile. A wave. A flattering comment.

Lucy didn't understand how a nice guy like Cameron could hang with such a group of jerks; Mitch was a walking, talking detention slip with more than one suspension on his record.

Then came Soo-Yin's fifteenth birthday party. The jerks, the in-betweeners, the drama kids — everyone who wanted in, was in. Cameron had found Lucy by the bonfire with The Olivia Bensons and he'd wedged himself into the conversation, not that Lucy had minded. She'd locked eyes with Nate across the group, hoping this was the night he'd learn to read her mind.

Be my wingman.

It must've worked, because one by one, Nate, Maya and Tamiko snaked back inside to fill up their glasses. Lucy and

Cameron laughed about sports and movies and Mr Haber's new toupee until Cameron's eyes watered. He filled in the edges of a mounting silence by stammering that she had 'long eyelashes', which Lucy liked. Before she could reply, he rushed to say that she looked really pretty with her hair pulled back into a long plait, too. It was a fishtail braid, but Lucy wasn't about to correct him. Instead, she stepped in closer until their warm breath was intertwined and she kissed him, not bothering to say any more words. Not about his lips tasting like peppermint, not that she liked the way *his* hair fell to his shoulders and he should wear it out more often. Judging by the feel of his lips and tongue softly moving with hers and his hands fumbling on the small of her back, tracing their way to her hips, he didn't mind one bit.

But day by day, week by week, Cameron stopped showing up to the pool as often. It didn't take long before Lucy stopped watching the entrance to see if his big, broad figure would come loping in, towel draped around his shoulders.

He was no longer one of hers, he was one of theirs.

Yet when Lucy and Cameron passed in the halls, he'd squeeze out a smile like they'd shared the sweetest secret in the world, but he'd never hold eye contact long enough for them to take anything further. Lucy wore her hair in a fishtail braid after the kiss, but when Cameron started to vanish out of her orbit, she swapped it to a messy knot plopped on top of her head.

7.17 p.m.

Lucy bumps her head on the bus toilet's ceiling as she attempts to untangle herself out of her school uniform. Arms caught in the pocket holes, she wriggles and hops around until it slips off onto the bathroom tiles. She snatches it up. The edges are wet.

Don't think about it.

Don't imagine what might be on the scungy toilet floor.

Lucy drags on her dress — a low-cut number that was packed for tomorrow's dinner with Ana and Simone but was now hugging her skin since Cameron Webber found his way onto the bus. She catches her reflection in the tiny, cracked mirror and fake-pouts her lips, wishing Nate was crammed into the cubicle to tell her she's ridiculous for squeezing into the dress. She swears again, realising she's been fussing with her hair for so long that Cameron probably thinks she has some sort of life-threatening intestinal disorder.

Not that she cares what he thinks.

7.21 p.m.

My life is in the toilet, literally, she texts, cringing at the wet paper towels clogging the drain of the bus bathroom's sink. *It's Friday night and I'm in a smelly toilet with nothing but a door and a few lousy metres distancing me from that jerk-off. This is not okay, you guys!*

She pauses then spritzes perfume onto her wrist and neck.

7.23 p.m.

Lucy drags on her hoodie over her dress, pulling it down to try to hide evidence there was any attempt to look nice for Cameron Webber. She wipes at her wrist with a damp paper towel.

7.27 p.m.

Still avoiding eye contact with Cameron, Lucy slides onto her seat. Her thoughts are drenched in sarcasm as she imagines Mitch and the bros whispering about her, just loud enough so she can catch the echoes of their words. *Faris is a six out of ten today,* she pictures them saying in muffled tones in the back of Year 9 English. *No really, she's an all right sort, the kind you'd be happy enough to hook up with, even if the lights are on, but you wouldn't brag about it.*

Her skin prickles.

This bus is the time machine from hell, she thinks, glaring at her knuckles as she berates herself for thinking about Mitch's cruel rating system for the first time in ages.

The categories were brutal.

Hottest Girl.

Best Legs.

Most Improved.

Prawn ('Smokin' hot body, throw away the head,' Mitch'd say, his upper lip quivering into a smirk that made Lucy's stomach whip with anger on behalf of his latest victim).

Eleven out of Ten.

Negative One Hundred.

And they're only the ones she can remember.

The system was created by Mitch, who took pleasure in pitting all the Year 9 girls against each other by ranking them based on their looks and personalities, and giving out awards for the 'winners' at a party at his place.

It was a process that was months in the making.

It was a process that should've been illegal because it felt like a crime was going down every time word spread through the school about the latest batch of unwilling nominees. The Olivia Bensons sat close enough to the jerks that they'd occasionally hear a familiar name thrown out from Mitch or Davey. But it was the screeches of laughter and thigh-slapping that made everyone pray to the high school gods that their name wasn't mentioned.

One day during English, Lucy heard Mitch mutter Maya's

name to Davey. She told herself it was nothing. That she'd imagined it. But then she heard it again.

Once Mr Burgess turned his back on the class to scribble on the whiteboard, Lucy sucked in a breath and walked to the desks where Mitch and Davey were shaking over their pages, failing to hold back their sniggering.

Mitch's mouth folded into a thin, crooked sneer when he noticed her standing there. He leaned back in his chair, running a hand over his greasy coffee-coloured quiff. 'Whaddya want, Faris?'

Lucy's jaw clenched. 'Just wanted to borrow something ...'

'Too povvo to have your own stuff?' Davey said, crossing his thick freckled arms across his chest. 'Although I guess your dad's not getting much coin making tabouli, huh?'

Mitch snorted.

Lucy nodded, pretending to turn the idea over in her mind, then snatched the page from Davey's desk. She tore back towards her spot, eyes dancing over their messy handwriting. Her thigh smacked into the corner of a desk, but she didn't care until later when she realised a bruise had painted her olive skin purple.

Maya, 8/10 (hot legs, kinda stupid).

Tamiko, 9/10 (bangin', ice queen but).

Faris, 7/10 (boobs on legs, bit of a bushpig).

Then, next to it, an addition to Lucy's: *+1/2 (loves a lacy bra).*

She felt her cheeks roasting, then stormed back to their desks, no longer caring if Mr Burgess noticed.

'*Bushpig?*' Her voice was low. A hiss.

Mitch didn't blink. 'It's creative writing.' His pink mouth locked into a firm line. 'This is English class, remember? You speak English, don't you, Faris?'

'What did you say to me?'

His lip flickered. 'Oh, you don't understand?' He was fighting laughter. 'I know your dad was born in Beirut so I'll talk … slower … next … time.'

'Grow the hell up, Mitch,' Lucy said, scrunching up the page and pegging it at the nearest bin. 'Yeah, I'm half-Lebanese … and you're a full-freaking-arsehole.'

The kids at the desks nearby laughed under their breath, and a few caught her eye, impressed that someone had finally stood up to him, but Lucy's heart raced so hard she felt like she was about to explode all over Mr Burgess's classroom. When the bell rang, she powered towards the door, focusing on nothing except getting to her next class. But she hadn't even made it to the quadrangle before Mitch called out behind her.

'Oi, Faris, wait up, got something for ya.'

Rules didn't seem to apply during these in-between-class moments and there weren't any teachers monitoring the hallway, so Lucy didn't slow down.

'Faris, come on!' he tried again. 'I wanna say sorry.'

Lucy paused and turned around, only then realising Mitch had collected a group of mates, who'd slipped out of neighbouring English classrooms. Matt, Davey, Lee and Cameron all dawdled behind him.

A pack.

A mob.

Sheep.

'What do you want, Mitch?'

'Sorry about the list, hey. That class gets my imagination running wild, ya know how it is.'

Lucy rolled her eyes. 'Whatever.'

'Here.' He passed her a comb. 'For you.'

Lucy took the comb, confused. 'This? Why?'

Mitch and Matt cracked up laughing, while Davey snapped a photo of her with it. Cameron and Lee looked at their scuffed school shoes, looked at the canteen sign, looked anywhere that didn't involve looking at Lucy.

'It's for your mo.'

Lucy's eyes narrowed. 'Excuse me?'

'It should work on those caterpillars, too,' Mitch said, pointing at Lucy's eyebrows. 'So, like, did your mum do it with a bushpig or was it your dad who —'

Lucy swore as she pegged the comb at him, but he just sniggered, until he realised Lee and Cameron weren't joining in.

'Right, boys?' he said. Still nothing. 'Whaddya think, Webby? Reckon you'd hook up with a bushpig?'

Cameron cleared his throat. 'What?'

'You heard me, bro. Up for an oinker?'

Cam paused, unable to look at Lucy. 'Ah ...' His cheeks were smeared with a rich burgundy. 'I dunno.'

'We're all friends here,' Mitch said, stepping in closer. The top of his head barely reached Cameron's forehead, but he didn't break eye contact with him. 'Would ya go there or what?'

Cameron swallowed. 'Nah ... nah,' he said, voice catching on the middle of his sentence.

Lucy sucked in a breath.

Liar.

Mitch laughed. 'No way, huh? Come on, bro, don't be shy. We've all got different tastes.'

'Nah,' he repeated, as Lucy's skin crawled at the memory of Cameron's hands and lips on her. 'Wouldn't want to ... choke on a hairball.'

Lucy's chest felt so tight it was like someone had run laces through her ribcage and yanked on them, pulling her in on herself.

'Friggin' lethal, Webby!' Mitch hooted. 'Check out the quiet assassin, hey, boys. You're not wrong, though, I wouldn't either.'

While the boys snorted, Cameron's eyes found Lucy's for a second. She could feel her cheeks flush red, and she held her breath to try to stop tears escaping down her cheeks. *Undo it, Cam*, her mind pleaded, but he just stood there. Silent. While her eyes watered, he stared at the crack that carved through the concrete in between his Vans. His lips flickered a little, like he was building up to say something, but he said nothing.

Coward.

Lucy watched as Cameron kicked at the ground then walked off, stepping in time ahead of Mitch and the rest of the pack as they lumbered out of sight around a corner. Seconds later Davey moonwalked back into view to holler at two Year 10 girls leaning against the drama-room door, which ignited a fresh round of whooping from Mitch and Matt. Jaw tightening, Lucy retrieved the comb and snapped it in half. *Animals.*

Later that afternoon, in the back aisles of the library, Nate wiped away her tears. 'Babe, we're only stuck with them for a few more years —'

'Jesus, don't remind me.'

'But, Luce, then you and your spectacular brows never have to see them again. And they're stuck with themselves and their teeny-tiny brains forever. Talk about a life sentence.'

Lucy liked that part.

Things didn't get easier straightaway though.

It's a cruel fact of life that things often get worse before they get better.

The photo of her with the comb, with the newly added captions of 'Lucy Hairis' and 'Hairball alert' were shared around the school and online under an anonymous account the next morning. The boys stayed quiet as teachers tore down the posters, but everyone else figured who was behind it. The next day, gossip got back to Lucy that Mitch was spotted storming out of the principal's office, red-faced, hunched over, spitting on the concrete as his dad thundered alongside him. He didn't show up for class the next day or the day after that. By the end of the week, word had spread that Mitch's rap sheet of suspensions over the past three years had added up, and the king of the jerks had been brought down. Mitch was expelled. His reign was over.

In the coming weeks, Lucy lost count of the classmates who bailed her up in the hallways, whispering, 'Thank you' as though Mitch's expulsion was all part of a grand master plan that she'd personally orchestrated.

She only wished she could take credit, because with Mitch gone, the mood around school was lighter. Slower. There wasn't a need to be on high alert. But then Cameron would lumber past her on his way to the gym and she'd hurry to look in the opposite direction, counting the seconds until he was off in the distance and she could walk the halls without her stomach lurching. Because she couldn't forget what he'd said. And when Cameron was presented with a state sports award at assembly a few weeks later, she scowled at her lap while everyone else whooped like he was some kind of hero. Like popularity was contagious.

Cameron and his family left Canberra not long after so Lucy didn't have to speak to him again.

Until today.

7.39 p.m.
Lucy exhales.

Bushpig.

The comb.

Hairball.

She'd almost forgotten.

7.42 p.m.
Anyone out there?

7.55 p.m.
'Wakey-wakey!' the driver calls out over the loudspeaker. 'We're pulling into Gundagai, folks. I'm making good time so run don't walk to your suitcases.'

He waddles off the bus and a handful of yawning passengers follow him onto the gravel.

Cameron's phone starts ringing and, for a second, Lucy wonders if he's getting picked up at this stop.

But the world's not that kind.

It's put her on a bus with Cameron Webber after all.

'Hey, sorry,' Cameron begins, snapping her into the moment, 'can I squeeze out past you for a sec?'

A thousand words bubble on the edge of her tongue. She swallows, trying to think of a comeback — something ruthless — that will make everyone on the bus cheer and carry her on their shoulders down the aisle. Maybe it'll be so fierce that his cheeks will burn strawberry red, his palms will sweat so much they stain his jeans and his voice will stammer as he apologises to her for everything he did.

'Sorry,' he tries again, still holding the buzzing phone, 'can I get past or …?'

Lucy pauses, chest puffed and tight. 'Yeah.'

Fudged that, Faris.

Lucy moves her knees to the left, opening up a small gap for him to get through. Her fingers stay intertwined, like she doesn't dare move them in case they brush the same air as him.

'Thanks,' he mumbles, pressing past her body, his thighs scraping past her bare knees. 'Sorry.'

Once he's gone, Lucy glares at the spare seat.

Three sorries.

None of them for the right thing.

7.58 p.m.

Her heart races as she remembers there are still six hours to go. Six hours breathing the same stuffy coach air as Cameron Webber. *Seriously, I know you can't read this message, but this is worse than when Tamiko got stuck in the lift with the dude with rank BO, I swear,* Lucy types, her stomach feeling as tightly wound as steel wool. *Nate, haven't you sorted out the crappy reception at Maya's place by now? There's gotta be a way.* She stares at the empty seat, panicking at the thought of Cameron's return. *Please, Nate-boy, I can't do this.*

8.01 p.m.

A few spots have opened up on the bus. The nearest seat is two rows ahead and across the aisle next to an old man who's snoring with drool trickling down his chin. He's whistling through his nose, but Lucy decides anything is better than being stuck next to Cameron Webber.

The bus rumbles back to life, which wakes up the old man.

Lucy makes her move. 'Hi, sir, can I sit here?'

The man's eyes widen behind his smudged glasses. 'I hope you can,' he says, baring his chipped, brown teeth. Lucy grimaces, already wishing for him to get off at the next stop.

'Er, thanks.' She rushes back to her seat to collect her stuff before Cameron returns from the bathroom, then slides in next to the old man.

'Drink?' he asks, holding up a silver flask.

Jesus.

'Er, no. No.'

Once the driver turns off the lights, Lucy tries to relax into the seat, no longer needing to worry about the distance between her knee and Cameron Webber's, or if Cameron Webber could hear her breathing as loud as she could hear him breathing, or if Cameron Webber had noticed she'd changed into a dress since he got on the bus.

8.06 p.m.

She fumbles for her phone.

Free at last.

8.55 p.m.

More people file off the bus at Wagga Wagga. Sadly not the old man, but enough seats open up for Lucy to get a spot by herself a few rows down. As she bundles her luggage into her arms for her third shift of the night, she notices Cameron's sneakers hanging out over the edge of the seat.

Maybe the driver is right.

Maybe she is brave for getting on the bus.

11.27 *p.m.*

'Food stop, my lethargic companions!' The driver calls out over the loudspeaker. 'Now I need you all back on the bus in thirty minutes. I'm leaving any dawdlers in Albury to hitchhike across the border.'

Passengers file off, one by one, each trudging under the streetlights into the roadhouse restaurant. Lucy plods through the cold air with the pack, her legs erupting with goosebumps. Once inside, she orders a hot dog and slides into a booth at the far end of the restaurant, swiping at the sauce then sucking it off her fingertip.

''Ello again, petal.'

Lucy looks up.

Oh no.

The old man takes a swig at his flask. 'Eating a hot dog, are you?'

'Ah … not unless it eats me first.'

'Funny one, you are.' He snorts out loud. 'What's your name? Got yourself a boyfriend?'

She bites her lip. 'Ah … yeah, I do,' she says, ignoring the first question and lying in response to the second one.

''Course you do. Girl like you.'

Picking at her hot dog, Lucy spots Cameron waiting to collect his food by the counter, fists stuffed deep into his hoodie. The old man follows her gaze and sees Cameron in line. 'That fellow?' He wheezes, breath smelling like it could clean rusty metal. 'Him?'

She doesn't reply.

The old man takes another sip and stumbles off, elbowing a shocked Cameron on the way out. 'Treat her right, buddy,' he says, pointing at Lucy back at the booth. 'She's a funny one, but not a bad looker.'

Cameron waits until the old man has stumbled through the sliding doors, then he heads for Lucy's booth, half-eaten sausage roll in hand. Wiping tomato sauce from his mouth, he slides in opposite her.

'Hi.'

She doesn't reply.

'Okay, so you do know who I am?'

Lucy swallows. 'Yeah. Cameron Webber.'

He nods. 'Full name and everything. When I said hi before it seemed like you didn't recognise me.'

She pauses. 'Guess I had a hairball.'

'Excuse me?'

'Oh, you don't speak "bushpig" anymore?'

'What?'

'Or do you only understand people whose throats you *haven't* had your tongue stuck down?'

Cameron shakes his head. 'Lucy, I —'

'No,' she blurts out. 'You can't just slide into my booth and start talking to me.'

'Okay … what's … what's up?'

'Seriously?' Lucy says, heart racing. 'Don't do that. Don't act nice, like nothing happened that day. When I met you, I thought you were nice, but … but you were nothing more than a Mitch in disguise. You were awful, you all were. You made life hell.' Her eyes drill into his. 'Now get out of my booth.'

'I know you're upset, but —'

'I'm not upset.' She leans forward, her elbows smacking the table. 'I'm pissed off. There's a difference.'

'Then give me a chance to explain.'

'*You* cracked the hairball joke, didn't you?' Lucy says in mock confusion. 'And … and I'm speaking English, right?'

'Ah … yeah? What do you mean?'

She rolls her eyes. 'Just get out of my booth … please.' Her voice falters. 'You know what, I'll go.'

Lucy storms out of the restaurant, leaving behind a stunned Cameron and a cold hot dog on the table.

12.03 a.m.

Her thumbs tremble as she types.

> *Done.*
> *Told him what I thought.*
> *Slayed.*

12.04 a.m.

Kinda thought it'd feel better than this.

12.05 a.m.

Lucy watches as Cameron walks to an empty seat right up the front. His head is down as he types on his phone, hitting the keys hard with the pads of his thumbs. She imagines him texting Mitch: *Bushpig's here, hairball's imminent, 3/10.*

12.06 a.m.

Maybe it takes time for the good vibes to kick in, she types to the group. *Like medicine.*

12.08 a.m.

Lucy swaps to the opposite side of the bus; far away from the old man, but mainly to avoid seeing Cameron's fingers tapping on his armrest.

12.09 a.m.

Still waiting.

12.13 a.m.

This is the worst trip. Ever.

12.15 a.m.

Lucy's phone beeps.

Battery's nearly done.

Chewing on her inner cheek, she hurries through a new message to The Olivia Bensons — *Only biscuits can fix this* — but her phone dies before she presses 'send'. Closing her eyes, Lucy falls asleep to the sound of the couple behind her bickering about whether to spend their honeymoon on Hamilton Island or in Fiji.

CAMERON

1.02 a.m.

The Stones' 'You Can't Always Get What You Want' thumps in Cameron's ears as he nibbles on the jagged edge of his thumbnail.

An overnight coach.

Lucy Faris.

Endless texts and calls.

The bus lurches along the highway as acidic bile burns up his throat, his stomach churning at the taste.

And now motion sickness.

The fun continues, he thinks, replaying the moment Lucy drilled him back at the roadhouse restaurant. Her words were laced with a disgust he'd never seen in her before — like she loathed the taste of their conversation on her lips. Like she wanted to wash her mouth out with a bar of soap after speaking to him.

Like she hated him.

Lucy freaking Faris.

The chances.

Unbelievable.

'Oi, driver, I think something's burning back here!' a deep voice booms through the silence, snapping him to attention. Cameron looks around the back of his seat, feeling everyone's panic swelling like a tidal wave. The smell hasn't reached him in the front row, but he watches as passengers unbuckle their seatbelts and cram into the aisle, grabbing bags and arms and shoulders and pillows, and inch forward step by step, like they've forgotten that there's nowhere else to go.

Didn't he know it.

'It's getting hot back here, like an oven!' a woman in a beanie shouts, as a small boy clings to the back of her jacket.

Cameron spots Lucy in the middle of the bulging line, squashed between a young couple fighting about their hen's and buck's parties. He notices as Lucy checks then rechecks over her shoulder at the chaos at the back of the bus, before smirking to herself as the girl shrieks at her fiancé, 'Stop being such a groomzilla, babe! Mum's bought the penis straws for the party, and she's not returning them. They were half-price. I told you that!'

Cameron watches Lucy cover her lips, trying to disguise her amusement as the couple launch into another round.

'It's starting to stink!' The same deep voice shouts again. 'Pull over or something! There are kids on the bus, man.'

The driver clears his throat into the loudspeaker as the passengers jostle for space in the aisle. 'Just looking for a spot to pull up here on the left, folks. The old girl's probably just overheated — please, let's all remain calm.' He draws in a sharp breath and exhales, not realising his microphone is still on.

As the bus screeches to a stop on the side of the highway, everyone shoves and pushes to the front of the aisle. Cameron lets in passenger after passenger, biting his tongue when no-one bothers to thank him.

'Quickly please, everyone, let's go!' the driver says, mustering people off the bus. 'Grab what you can and stick together, please, just wait over there, out of the way. We're all friends, or at least we're gonna be after this.'

Cameron steps onto the gravel with a crunch, the icy air burning his nose and cheeks. 'Where are we?' he asks the driver, shoving his fists deeper into his hoodie pockets.

'I can tell you where we *ain't*, big fella,' the driver says, still frantically directing people to stand by the wire fence surrounding endless acres of paddock, 'and that's Melbourne, so keep moving so I can get a new bus called out, yeah?'

Cameron nods.

The driver claps in frustration when he sees the group starting to spread like ants along the grass flanking the highway.

'Miss, did you hear me?' he barks at a woman shuffling backwards to take a selfie with the bus. 'No wandering into the dark unless you fancy spending the night alone — although the cows *are* friendly around these parts. Now move away from the highway and into a group, people! The emergency lights are on for a reason.' He claps again. 'Miss, I said into a group! Into a group! It's as if you all want to be flattened like pancakes.'

Cameron gets lost in the mix of beanies and jumpers and flashing mobile phone lights, but he's only looking for her.

He spots Lucy on the other side of the huddle; her lips are hardened into a faint line as she stares at the cars whooshing past, lighting up the highway.

She's not looking for him.

Cameron lets his body get jostled to the edge of the crowd.

1.11 a.m.

Despite the driver's orders, everyone's melted into sections.

A nervous pack stands on the gravel, whispering and dissecting every move or word the driver utters as he paces back and forth while speaking on his phone, demanding a new bus is sent out because the old one is overheated and 'buggered to buggery'. Others sit on the damp grass, relaxed and chatting, while a handful suck on cigarettes by the fence behind them.

Cameron keeps one foot on the grass and another on the gravel — and both eyes on Lucy, who's staying close to the driver. She's still bare-legged but has pulled her hoodie sleeves down over her hands and crossed her arms around herself. Shivering and shaking, she steps from side to side to a beat all her own.

Cameron's phone buzzes in his pocket.

Nan.

First the texts, now the calls.

'Hey again,' he answers, wandering away from the group. 'Everything all right? ... Oh, okay. Go back to sleep, Nan, it was just another bad dream. I promise ... Promise. Okay, bye, love you ... No, it's after one ... Yes, one in the morning, you've been asleep so it was just a nightmare. You're safe … Love you, too … Yes, Nan, it's me … Tiny. I said, it's Tiny, Nan … You've got my number, it's saved in your phone, remember? You just rang it so … Love you, too … Yes, it's Cameron … I said, it's Cameron.'

She's hung up.

Sighing, he stuffs his phone back in his jeans pocket.

'Righto, folks,' the driver shouts, standing on his tiptoes and rubbing his palms together. 'I've sorted a bus, but it'll be at least forty-five minutes,' he shouts. Everyone groans. 'May I suggest hugging the person closest to you to stay warm? Actually … don't.' He chuckles. 'Everyone, keep your hands where I can see 'em.'

'Er, sir,' Lucy asks him in a soft voice, but loud enough for Cameron to hear. 'Do you have a quick second?'

'For you, Eight, I've got a long second. What's on your mind?'

'My trackies. I must've dropped them on the way out and … can I go and get them?'

'From the bus? Nope.'

'What? *Why?* You have to let me back on so —'

'Can't risk it. You don't want me to have to tell your parents you were fried like a dim-sim in that lemon, do you, Eight?' He unbuttons his coat and passes it to her. 'Here, take this.'

'But then you'll be cold.'

'I'm a tough nut,' he says with a laugh. 'On your way. I've got a bus with a temperature to curse for busting me good run.'

Lucy's mouth splits into an enormous grin and Cameron wishes he'd thought of offering her his jacket earlier.

1.20 a.m.

Cameron kicks at a patch of dirt next to the fence, glaring at the moon shimmering white in the sky. The silence creates empty moments to sink into, but he fights being dragged down into them as they smother his mind one by one. Lucy's penetrating glare across the restaurant table. The way she stormed off back to the bus. When she called him awful. He's already lost count of how many times he's replayed the spray from her. With a shake of his head, Cameron gives in to it all at once.

'When I met you, I thought you were nice … but you were nothing more than a Mitch in disguise.'

Stuff it.

1.22 a.m.

She's sitting on the grass now, the driver's jacket wrapped around her legs. Cameron watches from a distance as she shoos away the old man with the flask, no longer bothering to be polite. Her gaze has found Cameron's a few times through the crowd, piercing into him for a second, maybe two, but then she looks away whenever their eyes meet.

Not that he blames her.

He remembers the day she calls *that day*.

Mitch's ratings. Their mob surrounding her. The way her bottom lip shook when she realised he wasn't going to stand up for her, and the stabbing in his stomach that started the moment he'd spat out those awful words — words he didn't even mean. Words that came from an ugly, insecure place inside him that he never wanted to tap into again. Because he liked Lucy — he liked the way she plaited her hair to show off her smooth olive skin. And how she laughed when her friends teased her: eyes open, mouth open, hands clutching her stomach as though she might explode. He even liked the way she swam laps at the pool until the same time every day, and how she'd guide overwhelmed Year 7 kids to class when they were running late after their internal compasses had conked out.

He knew all of that, and she knew some of that, but she didn't know any of what had happened to him before that moment.

How Cameron didn't have any real mates because his parents were in the army and they moved every year or two, and he couldn't handle another school where everyone left him to sit alone at recess and lunch. He was always too sporty, not sporty enough, too big, too shy, too cocky on the field, not confident off it. He was never what everyone else wanted.

Just never enough.

Lucy also didn't know this was the first time that anyone, let alone the popular guys, had welcomed him into their space.

It took less than a day for Cameron to realise Mitch, Matt, Davey and Lee weren't his kind of mates. Lee was all right when he was away from the others; turned out he didn't agree with much of what the group did or said, but all their mums were friends and he was happy to be dragged through school with them. Better than being a nobody, he once told Cameron. Mitch and the boys were Cameron's safety shield. His armour. With them, he felt invisible, protected, strong.

Then Lucy saw him. Really saw him.

And damn, he saw her, too.

At the pool.

In the halls.

That night at the party when she'd cracked jokes until his eyes were wet from laughing then pressed herself against him, fizzing up every part of his body. She also never knew that she was the first girl he'd kissed.

Cameron kicks at the dirt again.

No wonder Lucy never forgave him for *that day*.

Every scowl from her after that moment stung him all over. He'd barely had the confidence to speak to her when she liked him, let alone when her looks were heavy or sharp, so he didn't apologise. He couldn't. That night he'd drafted a text, scribbled a letter, started a Facebook message, but he didn't follow through with any of them.

She deserved more. He just didn't know how to give it to her.

Cameron remembered the following day — the day after she calls that day — even better. Revved up on guilt, he'd told Mitch off in front of the other guys, told him to stop being a dickhead, told him to stop taking things too far, told him to rip down the posters. Mitch's eyebrows had narrowed; he was apparently not used to anyone biting. But then he laughed, a low snigger, and said: 'Yeah, yeah, I will, it's all just jokes, bro, yeah?'

Cameron didn't realise he'd burned any last traces of invisibility.

Mitch's text message had told him to blow off periods five and six for a cheeky game of backyard cricket at his joint, which was around the corner from school. So he did. Sport was the only space where Cameron felt like he fit; rules were in place so he knew what to say and how to act. He trudged to Mitch's, tossing a tennis ball that he'd found in the gutter between his palms as the sun belted down on his face. Cameron let himself into Mitch's backyard through the rusty side gate like he'd seen the other guys do, then, figuring he was early, squatted down on a yellowed patch of lawn alongside a row of withered lemon trees.

He'd only made it easier for Mitch to jump him.

Cameron writhed until he broke free from Mitch's grip, his school shirt torn open, and sprinted for the gate. But Mitch dived at Cameron's ankles, fingers wrapping around them, tripping him over. Mitch shouted as he wrestled his way onto Cameron's flattened back, digging muddy knees and elbows into his shoulders, spine and legs. A thick grunt slipped out as Cameron shoved Mitch off him. 'What the hell?' he said, catching his breath. 'Back off.'

That was when Mitch pulled out an open pocketknife, his blade glinting in the light peeping through the lemon trees.

Cameron swore at the sight of it. He waited for Mitch to crack up laughing, announce it was all a convoluted prank gone wrong, then put the knife away. But Mitch leaned in closer, jaw clenched, knife waving in front of Cameron's face. 'Think you're so freaking tough, don't ya, sasquatch.'

'Put it away.' Cameron edged backwards, chest rising with each huff of breath, nails caked with dirt.

'Scared or something?' Mitch continued. 'Thought ya had balls, bro.'

'Piss off.'

Mitch's arm shot forward so fast that Cameron didn't have time to move away. He sucked in a breath. The knife was now only centimetres from his neck.

'Don't mess with me again,' Mitch said. 'Don't even look at me. You're nobody. And you've got nobody.'

Cameron's dad got the truth out of him later that night after his mum found the dirt-stained clothes stuffed down beside the laundry hamper.

When Mitch was expelled, the teachers promised to keep Cameron's name out of it to avoid any further trouble, and they did. Rumours spread but nothing stuck. However, Cameron still shrank further into himself because Mitch was right about one thing: he had nobody left at the school.

It was almost enough to relieve the guilt he felt about what he'd done to Lucy.

A month later, Cameron's dad announced they were moving to Queensland for his new job and, for once, Cameron didn't fight him on it.

He could be invisible again.

1.38 a.m.

His phone rings again, so he strides along the gravel away from the group.

'Hey, Nan … No, you rang me … It's Cam … Yeah, Tiny … Go back to sleep 'cause it's late and you need … I love you, too … I said, I love you, too, Nan.'

1.43 a.m.

The new bus is still twenty minutes away.

Cameron takes it as a sign, not that he's ever cared about signs, and strides across the grass to plonk down next to Lucy before he changes his mind.

'Yeah?' she asks, twirling an earphone in her hand.

'Hi. Just … well …' He hesitates, unsure where to go from here. 'Whatcha listening to?'

'Nothing. Phone's dead.'

'Oh. That sucks.'

She shrugs.

'So …' He tries again, heart racing. 'I was thinking and … could we talk for a bit? Privately?'

'We'in the middle of nowhere. Not sure how much more private you want to get, Cameron Webber.' There was a time when he would've loved the sound of his name on her tongue, but not the way she's grating it out now. Once again she says it like the words are poisonous, like she can't bear the sensation of them touching the insides of her mouth. 'Spit it out.'

'Okay.' His lips are dry. 'I guess what I wanna say is ...' Now that he's here, next to her, he doesn't know what can fix it. If he can fix it. 'Lucy,' he tries again, 'this is kinda weird for me.'

She scoffs. 'For *you*?'

'God,' he blurts out, voice hardening. 'Didn't you ever do something stupid at school? Something shit? Something you're not proud of?'

'I'm still in school.' Pause. 'You're not?'

He shakes his head. 'Chippy.'

'What?'

'Carpentry apprentice. Getting there, anyway,' he corrects himself, tone softening again. 'So ... so you've never gone into survival mode? Where you do something, anything, to get through?'

'*Do something?*'

'Yeah. Or ignore something, maybe something you shouldn't have ignored.'

'Maybe. I hope not.' She shakes her head. 'What did someone like *you* have to survive anyway?'

'You're kidding, right?'

'You dominated every sport, the jerks adopted you, the girls all loved you —'

'No way.'

'Don't fish for compliments.'

Cameron picks at the grass. 'It might've looked like I had stuff sorted, but ... nah. Not even.'

She scoffs again. He thought she might. 'You sat with those guys. Same footy team and everything. And you were with them that day — you made it worse. You're the reason Davey pretended to cough up hairballs when he'd get me alone in between class.'

'Shit ... I'm sorry,' he stammers. 'I am. That's messed up.'

'Come on, give yourself credit.'

'I didn't even mean it, that's the thing, I thought you were great.' *Still do.*

Lucy cuddles her knees to her chest. 'Yeah, well ... not that it matters anymore, right?'

'But ... I really am sorry. For all of it. And I know it's not an excuse, but I'm no Mitch.'

She groans. 'Denial, thy name is Cameron.'

'Listen, they let me think I was one of them, for a bit, and I was a tool to believe it — to even want it.'

'Won't argue with that.' Lucy purses her lips together.

'You don't think people can learn from their stuff-ups?'

'Do I think *Mitch* feels sorry for all the bad stuff he did? No way. Look, you've said sorry, I accept it, whatever. Now you won't have to wet yourself if you see me at the ten-year school reunion. Just leave me alone.' She pulls the jacket tighter around her thighs. 'You don't get how hard the rest of us had it back then. That's all.' She shrugs. 'How could you though?'

'But I could 'cause ...' he begins, palms sweating as he wonders if he can get through it without bolting into the darkness. ''Cause, well ...'

Lucy narrows her eyebrows until a deep slit appears between them.

''Cause Mitch pulled a knife on me.'

'*What?*' Lucy turns to face him. 'No … wait, *what?*'

Cameron exhales, yanking at the grass again. So much for telling the truth making people feel lighter.

'Oh my … Jesus.' Her eyes are wide. 'What happened? Are you okay, Cam?' She called him Cam. To anyone else that might be nothing, but right now it's everything to him. 'I mean, I know it was years ago … but … are you okay?' She pauses. 'Sorry, silly question.'

She's talking to him again. 'I'm okay. Thanks.'

'Okay. Okay, good.' Lucy nods. 'I'm … Mitch is more unhinged than I realised.'

Cameron doesn't reply so silence fills the air.

Moments pass, maybe a few seconds, maybe a minute, before she asks him for the time. He checks his phone — 1.58 a.m. She mutters a soft *thanks*, then rests her chin on the top of her knees, slightly rocking her body to keep warm. As Lucy looks to the stars sprinkled across the blackened night, Cameron wonders how this will all feel in the daylight of Saturday. Before he has a chance to work it out, the replacement bus arrives, flicking up gravel before screeching to a halt on the side of the highway.

LUCY

2.07 a.m.

Cameron dumps his backpack on the front seat of the new bus, so Lucy takes the one on the opposite side of the aisle.

'This all right?' she asks.

He nods. 'Sure.'

As he settles into his spot, a lopsided smile escapes out of the corner of his mouth, like he hopes she won't notice.

She notices.

2.16 a.m.

Their bus rattles along the highway, not loud enough to disguise the sound of Lucy's stomach growling. She cringes and wraps her arm around her middle, peeping across the aisle at Cameron, who's nodding along to the music in his earphones while texting on his phone.

Lucy sucks on the inside of her cheek, fingertips prickling at the thought of messaging The Olivia Bensons a blow-by-blow account of the last two hours, and she berates herself for not snatching the charger out of her suitcase before stuffing it under the bus. She smirks at the thought of her friends reading through her roller-coaster of messages when they're back to reception and decent Wi-Fi in the morning. There's no way they'll get anything done at band practice now; they'll be on the phone to her all day.

Another stomach growl.

Lucy rifles through her backpack for her packet of biscuits, remembering how Cameron's cheeks had darkened to burgundy when he'd told her the truth. Shame had been imprinted on every centimetre of his face; for the series of events he triggered for her, to the humiliation over what happened between him and Mitch.

But the 'I hate Cameron Webber' switch flipped for her three years ago and she can't change it back in an instant just because their lives overlapped one serendipitous morning between Canberra and Melbourne.

Lucy stuffs a choc-chip cookie in her mouth, licking the crumbs from her bottom lip.

2.22 a.m.

She peeks across the aisle again. This time, he spots her.

Her breath catches, but she fights her natural instinct to look away.

'Biscuit?' she whispers, holding out the packet across the aisle. When all else fails, offer food. That was the Faris way.

Cameron's eyes sparkle. 'Sure,' he says, stretching over to pluck one out of the plastic.

'Take two. If you want.'

He pauses, then grabs another one, sending crumbs all over the bus floor between them. 'Thanks. Thanks heaps.'

'Midnight bus picnic, had to be done,' Lucy says. They salute each other with their biscuits and settle back into their seats without saying another word.

2.31 a.m.

'Psst, Cam. 'Nother one?'

He doesn't hear her across the aisle with his earphones in.

''Nother one, Cam?' she tries again.

'Inside voices please,' the driver announces, causing Lucy to start in her seat. 'And, Eight … pass me one of those.'

'Yes, sir,' she hisses, trying not to laugh as she hands him a biscuit, then slides in next to Cameron before she chickens out. He looks up, eyes wide. She can't tell if he's surprised or terrified. Maybe both. She's already forgotten why she plopped down next to him.

Guilt.

Boredom.

Loneliness.

Delirium.

'Er, hey,' she says, offering him the packet. 'More sugar?'

'Sure.' He takes a biscuit. 'Thanks.' He gestures to his phone. 'Wanna listen? Kill some time?'

'That's cool, you'll be bored without it.'

'With me, I mean.'

'Oh. Sure.'

Holding her breath, Lucy wiggles in a little closer, not letting herself close enough for their shoulders or arms to touch, and pops in the earphone. The familiar bass and drums of Queen and Bowie's 'Under Pressure' pulsate in her eardrum.

'*Tune.*' She elbows Cameron in the arm. 'You're into Bowie? And Queen? *You?*'

'You gonna pay me out for liking old people's music or something?'

'No, they're kings,' she whispers into the dark. 'It's just a surprise.' A good one.

Cameron's playlist clicks over to KISS's *Rock And Roll All Nite*, which thumps through her body the way it always does at band practice.

'Love this one,' he says, right thumb drumming to the beat on his jeans.

Lucy's feet tap out of sight.

CAMERON
2.54 a.m.

She's fallen asleep on the edge of Cameron's shoulder. Her ponytail falls down across his chest, her breaths are long and deep. He hasn't dared to move. When Lucy sighs in her sleep, he reminds himself to exhale. That it may all be a dream.

LUCY
2.57 a.m.

Cameron's phone rings in his pocket and Lucy snaps awake and upright, realising she's nodded off on his shoulder.

'Oh, sorry … sorry,' she says, bleary-eyed, opening up the space between them as he fumbles to answer his phone.

'It's cool.' He's rosy-cheeked. 'It's fine. Just gotta get this.'

Lucy sinks into the back of her seat, hoping she didn't drool on his hoodie.

3.02 a.m.

Lucy watches Cameron sigh as he hangs up the phone and stuffs it back in his pocket.

'Everything okay?'

'Yeah, it's my nan,' he says. 'She rings sometimes, especially after I visit.'

'You're close, huh?'

'Yeah. She hates her nursing home. Don't blame her, really …' His voice trails off as he rummages in his backpack. 'Anyway,' he adds, retrieving a red pen, removing the lid and scribbling loopy swirls down his wrist. 'The parentals reckon they'll be in Canberra to be closer to her by the end of the year.'

'That's great.'

'I don't buy it.' His voice is harder now. 'Dad just got a promotion and Mum's loving Adelaide, so … we'll see.'

'Adelaide?'

'For Dad's work. They go all over.' He shrugs. 'I used to, but my uncle put me up when they left and Melbourne's good.' He pauses. 'Good for now anyway. Stuff trying to predict the future.'

'If only.' Lucy nibbles on her biscuit. 'Well, my sisters live in Melbourne — it's why I was on that stupid broken bus.'

'Twins, right? Few years above us?'

He remembers. She'd told him about them on the night of Soo-Yin's party. 'Simone and Ana. That's them.' Lucy inhales through her nose, unable to hold in the next part any longer. 'Cam … about you and Mitch.'

'We're back to thinking about that?'

'Sorry, yeah … I never stopped,' she admits. 'What I don't get is, why? I thought you and Mitch were mates.'

'Nah. Not really.' He squeezes out a tight smile. 'Not at all, I guess.'

Lucy tucks one leg under herself and swivels to face him. He doesn't maintain eye contact. '*Cam.*'

'It's nothin', really, I guess I just finally stepped up about … about stuff.'

'Stuff?'

'Yeah. About how he gave it to everyone … gave it to you,' he adds. 'He didn't like that.'

'Wait … you said something about me? To him?'

He nods.

'Cam, you shouldn't —' She cuts herself off. 'Look what he did to you! With Mitch, there are no winners. Yeah, I wanted him to stop treating us all like pieces of meat, but I didn't want anyone else to get hurt. I mean, a knife. *A knife!* He could've really hurt you.'

'Nah. He was showing off.'

'Don't play this down.'

'I'm not.'

He is but he won't admit it. Lucy hangs her head, letting his words settle between them.

'Back then, all I wanted was to show that I wasn't …' Cameron pauses, nibbling on his nail as he searches for the right words. 'Stuff it, all I wanted was for *you* to know I wasn't one of them, but I'm no good with words. Then my plan to hash it out with Mitch didn't exactly go to plan.' He shakes his head. 'Anyway, after what I did, standing up to him was nothing.'

'No,' Lucy says, voice sharp as it slices the air. 'It was something.' Cameron's cheeks flush. 'It was.'

3.07 a.m.

The driver flicks on the lights and radio.

'Folks, some good news: we're now pulling into Melbourne's Southern Cross Station. Thanks for ya patience and sorry about the interruption earlier. A quick reminder to please check under the seats and in the front seat pocket for any belongings. Hope it's been an enjoyable ride, and I look forward to seeing ya on our coaches again soon.'

Lucy looks out past Cameron through the window into the terminal. A small crowd of shivering people wrapped in scarves and puffy jackets wait by the side of the bus.

'So,' Cameron says, staring through the glass as passengers seated in the rows behind them fuss with their luggage, 'guess this is it, then.'

Lucy nods.

3.10 a.m.

Their knees rest against each other.

Neither of them budges.

'We did good,' Lucy says. 'Three states, one night. Well, two states and one territory.'

'It's gotta be a record.'

'Can't say I'm excited about my trip back, though.' She sighs. 'My bum's already killing me.'

Cameron grins. 'Flying next time, for sure.'

'Correct.'

'So, ah … so there might be a next time for you? To Melbourne? I mean, I know your sisters live here so …' His voice is quiet again despite the loud commotion around them.

'Oh. Yeah. Well …' Lucy's mouth struggles to keep up with the thoughts thrashing around in her mind. 'Maybe, but the next few months are pretty crammed: exams and training and band practice and eighteenths — and don't even get me started on how much the school captain delegates when she can't be arsed to do her share of the workload and …' Her voice peters out and an embarrassed laugh erupts from her lips.

Cameron spirals his earphones around his fingers. 'But maybe one day, huh?'

'Yeah.' Lucy nods again. 'Maybe.'

Last Night at the Mount Solemn Observatory

DANIELLE BINKS

The first word I ever learned was *King*, for my brother.

Fingertips and thumb to the top of my head in a circle, like a crown.

Most babies learn survival signs first — *drink, food, up* and *hurt* — words that get them what they want.

Mum says I always wanted King — *hook her finger and tap her nose* — she liked to say, 'Bowie, you're never happier than when you're being his little sister.'

For the longest time I thought our parents had chosen our names for the signs they made, rather than sound or meaning. Because there's something about the action of signing King's name — like I'm pulling the very thought of him out of my head — that suited my big brother.

And this is how he appears tonight — shadows one minute, then King in all his gangly glory under the buttery spill of a streetlight the next. Dressed in his weekend uniform of white Bonds T-shirt, black jeans and runners, with his skateboard idling under one foot, making the lowest of growls as he rolls it back and forth over bitumen.

He's waiting for someone — or, someones — when a glob of torchlight suddenly appears on the street, just a few metres in front of him, and outside the pool of lamplight. He doesn't notice it at first, until it's joined by a second and then a third light that goes racing up his body to flash in his eyes — once, twice, three times — until he squints, turns his head, and makes a circle with his thumb and forefinger to say, *Stop doing that*, waving in the direction the lights are coming from — the darkened end of our street.

I stay crouched by my window, where I've been since hearing King leave — the familiar sound of his feet hitting the floor, a creak on the staircase and the little bang of the back door. Mum and Dad are trained deep sleepers at the back of the house, but I can hear it all through the wall we share, and from my bedroom window I have a perfect view of the street down below.

Then just as quickly as they appeared, he's following, right foot on the board, left pushing off the road, sailing him through the night and after those three lights.

Off on some adventure on his last night in Orianna.

And before I've even fully decided, I'm already pulling on jeans and a T-shirt, reaching for a pair of thongs. Because all I'm thinking is *no guts, no glory*, and of squeezing fists over your heart, as that's where the guts are.

So I pad down the stairs, out the back screen door and run round to the junkyard side of our house to retrieve my waiting Malvern Star bike — ready to follow the roar of his skateboard.

According to the puppy-of-the-month calendar hanging on our pantry door, we're four days into the January Jack Russells, and

King doesn't plan to return until some undecided date in the dachshunds of December. He's drawn a big red question mark over all the little squares, which freaked Mum out.

She told him she's putting her foot down — then she did, literally — and made him promise that he'll at least be home by Christmas. She even bought this honest-to-goodness pink porcelain piggybank to start collecting all our five-dollar notes in, hoping that we'll have enough saved by the end of the year to help him buy a plane ticket home.

Not that King knows what his point of origin will be by then — Chile, Barcelona, Romania, Malaysia — they're all on his list, along with a hundred other places that are anywhere but here.

And Dad just keeps reminding him that it's okay to come back, *arching his hand for home*, and doing this shoulder-squeeze thing: — squeeze — *You can come home anytime you want* — squeeze — *nothing to be embarrassed about if it's sooner than you thought* — squeeze — *your room will be just as you left it* — squeeze.

But King has been planning this escape since he was my age, fourteen.

That was the year we moved to Orianna, and he bought a world map the size of our dining-room table and cork-boarded it to his bedroom wall. He collected brochures from the only travel agent in town, tore out the endpapers of airline route maps and started push-pinning places and plotting routes with string, like a detective on one of those American crime shows.

I think we may even be into a whole new kitten calendar year before we see him again, and before I get a chance to tell him how I feel.

They're a way ahead of me, their torchlights dancing in the distance and winking around corners. Down Andromeda Lane, veering off Hubble Street, which intersects with Pollux Avenue, and Eridanus Esplanade, until I know for certain that they're heading for the main street of town, which is called Orion.

I ride far enough behind that I can just make out their four inky figures — two on skateboards, two on bikes — as I watch them ride over Pigott's Bridge at the entrance to town. But by the time I get there I have to back-pedal and brake at the mouth of the main street, because they're nowhere to be seen.

Disappeared.

And Orianna looks sickly tonight, bathed in sodium streetlights.

Our town was founded for a gold rush, so everything is two-storey and imposing Victorian with balcony filigree. When we first moved here, I thought all the buildings had toothy grins, but right now they're more like sharp-toothed smiles hiding hauntings.

I hop off my Malvern and walk the bike down the wide, empty middle of the main street until I'm far enough into town that I can hear the low hum coming from The Parallax Pub on the corner.

It's a warm, still night — now that I'm off my bike I can feel the sweat collecting in my jeans, right behind my denim-clad knees. As if I couldn't tell already that there's no breeze anywhere, I need only look at the *Tree of Life* — this beautiful, kinetic sculpture planted in a patch of grass beside the old sandstone bank, now post office. It's by this guy called Phil Price, and it has a tall, silver trunk and these impossible branches with flat discs at the end that spin like mad when the wind is up. But tonight they're crooked and quiet, silently pointing me to where the music is humming.

It's playing from the pub's ancient jukebox, and above the constant rumble of conversation I can only tell that it's a song about flame trees.

As I approach The Parallax, I see men and women sitting on the pretty garden benches lined up outside, or leaning against the white wooden pillars of the archways, drinks in hand. And on one of the benches sit three people I recognise — two bikes propped against the sandstone wall beside them, and probably two skateboards tucked under the bench — it's Ravi, Em and Adelaide.

They're collapsed the way they were at school all those years, didn't matter if it was the grassy lower oval, common-room floor, or if a teacher was crazy enough to let them sit together at a desk, they always spread like margarine.

Tonight is no different; Em's legs are in Adelaide's lap and she's sitting up to talk to her, their faces so close together that Ravi has to lean round the back to hear, one hand on Em's shoulder for balance. All they need to be complete is King, who just then comes out of the pub holding four green glass bottles by the neck, one for each of them. They all thank him — *fingertips touching chins* — and then Ravi gets up and gives the bench to the girls, so he can stand with King in an archway, clink bottles and gaze out at the main street.

Which is when they see me, standing beside my Malvern, and blinking up at them in the glare of pub lights.

Ravi arrived in town in Year 10. His mum had just left and his dad couldn't cope, so he sent Ravi to live with his aunt and uncle, who run the Orianna licensed post office. Em's their kid, and the only one of Ravi's cousins who's the same age as him — they both work in the mail room out back, though Em works counter now that Year 12 is over and she's going to be more involved in the family business.

Ravi was always mad back then. There was a spree of smashed car windows in the weeks after he first arrived, and we drove past him once on the back road of town, Dorado, wearing an orange fluoro vest and picking up litter with a bunch of kids from about four other municipalities. As we drove past, he gave us a jaunty salute with his trash spike.

We'd been living in Orianna for three years by then. Dad had taken over running the shop since Pop died, Mum liked her job with the council, and I had Laura and Kylie to hang out with at school. But the move was hardest on King, 'cause he had the most to leave behind. His specialist school and the friends he'd known since kindergarten, and Mum's side of the family where he was third-generation. To come to Orianna where the teachers just kept saying how hard it was for them, and classmates who had grown up in each other's pockets, who even after three years had no interest in learning a whole new language just for him, turned his world upside down and inside out.

So I guess he and Ravi had a lot in common.

Ravi smashed windows and King mapped his escape.

Looking back, I think friendship was inevitable.

I wasn't there when King broke Ravi's nose. Em was however, and Adelaide, though none of them were friends with her at the time. But by recess I'd heard the whole story, probably with a few embellishments thrown in — like, I'm pretty sure Ravi didn't respond with a Guile high kick.

They were in PE, playing footy, and Ravi apparently said, 'Kick it to me!' because nobody had told him to forget King on the field.

'Kick it to me! Kick it to me!' just like that Uncle Tobys ad. And because he didn't, Ravi pushed King at half-time and King punched back. Just let fly so fast that Ravi was on his arse, with his hands still in mid-air, grabbing at King's shoulder that wasn't there.

Then it was *on*. Apparently.

I know that Ravi and King needed more than sickbay medical attention, and his uncle, Mr Singh, drove the boys to a bulk-billing place where Mum met up with them and he and Mum got along like a house on fire — commiserating over raising testosterone — and Mum invited the family over for dinner with a side of forced apology.

That night, King and Ravi folded their tall frames onto our sofa lounge and sat facing each other.

'Sorry, I didn't know you were,' Ravi paused and quirked his eyebrows at King, 'you know, Deaf or *whatever*,' he said.

King had been watching his face intently, and I could tell Ravi felt embarrassed by the scrutiny.

Sorry is a *clawed hand, palm facing you, shaken across your mouth.* And as King apologised I watched Ravi's own hand curl into a claw, mimicking the sign.

'Like this?' he asked, head down to look at his hand.

I was sitting next to Ravi on the couch, so I reached all the way up to tap the underside of his jaw. 'Look up, he needs to see your face,' and Ravi obeyed, looked King in the eyes — well, *eye*, since one was swollen shut — and apologised again.

That time, he meant it.

Bowie? What are you doing here?

King hands his bottle to Ravi and marches towards me, grabs my elbow so I'm forced to release the handlebars and let my bike clatter to the road.

Do Mum and Dad know you're here? Were you following us?

Em and Adelaide are standing with Ravi in the archway now, watching King and me have this awkward, one-handed conversation, when Kel steps out and I nod in her direction for King's benefit.

Kel owns The Parallax with her husband, Aidan. King's only worked here since last year, when he turned eighteen, as a busboy, cleaner and then helping Aidan out on the grill.

'Everything all right out here?' she asks, and Ravi shrugs his shoulders and sticks his thumb out sideways, cranks it in a circle to interpret for King.

'Fine, thank you, Kel!' I say, giving the universal thumbs-up sign and smile, and then I shrug my shoulder until King finally lets go.

'Okay, and who's driving tonight?' she asks, turning to the others.

Adelaide puts up her hand, and Kel gives her a set of car keys. 'You break it you buy it,' she says, followed by, 'So please, break it!' and I know it must be the old silver Holden Commodore wagon, the one that Aidan's been trying to sell since forever. It's practically another sculpture along with the *Tree of Life*, a fixture on the main street every weekday that it's parked at the back of the pub with a FOR SALE sign in the front windshield. Aidan let

King borrow it a few times while he worked here, and apparently one last time for tonight.

'You tell your brother to look after himself, you hear?' Kel says, and I roll my eyes once she's turned away, sign *Take care* to King and then crouch down to right my bike.

Aidan actually learned a few signs, but Kel was like most everyone else who first tried shouting at various volumes, and then only really interacted with King when family or friends were around to interpret. It bugs the crap out of me, and Ravi, too, judging by the gesture he's giving Kel's back, but King just seems used to it now.

Em, Ravi and Adelaide grab their bikes and the skateboards, wheeling them down to stand beside me and King.

Go home, he says to me.

I shake my head. *No.*

King's gestures get bigger. *GO HOME!*

No.

BOWIE!

My name is *one hand zigzagging downwards*, and I've never been brave enough to ask if that suits me, in case it does. Right now King cuts out my name like his hand is a knife, and for just a second I think how much I'm going to miss this — the very picture of sibling rivalry — and a second is all I need to crack a smile and then start laughing so hard that it hurts.

King throws up his hands, takes his bottle from Ravi, and by the time he's knocked it back my laughter has started to trickle out. I kick out my bike stand so I can have my hands free to touch my chin and curl my fingers. *Please.* Again and again, and again — *Please, please, please.* And I can see Em at least, is about to cave.

We're not doing anything. King shrugs.

I want to hang out with you tonight!

He looks up and down the empty street, as if to say, *This is it — this is all there is!* Then he takes a long pull from an imaginary glass, gesturing at the pub behind us and reminding me that I'm not old enough to drink.

We're attracting a few onlookers now — all those people sitting on the pretty park benches are leaning forward in their seats, or turning their bodies to watch me as I take an imaginary wheel and ask him what the car is for, then?

Now he's frustrated, swiping at his blond fringe, which keeps falling over his eyes. He huffs and comes back round to *BOWIE! GO HOME!* all over again.

Adelaide eventually breaks us up by stepping in between King and me and nodding her head at the small crowd gawking behind us. Ravi turns around, too, and pretends to be trapped in a glass box — *mime*, he's saying — and the people think he's enough of an idiot that they look away. King slaps him upside the head.

Ravi comes back to me, crosses his heart for honesty and fingerspells *L-A-K-E C-L-A-I-R-E*, then makes a circle with his thumb and forefinger that he slides slowly, teasingly, down his body while jiggling his eyebrows at me.

They're going to get *naked* at Lake Claire?

'Skinny-dipping?' I ask.

Ravi gives me a solemn nod and a shrug. ''Fraid so, kiddo.'

But Em can barely contain her disgust, and she's next to slap Ravi's head, then sign zipping up her pants — telling him to keep it in there, as she points at his offending crotch.

It's Adelaide again who throws up her hands. *Why do you want to come tonight?* she asks me, and King rolls his eyes.

I don't know if I can put it into words just yet, this feeling like something's ending and I have to be close to it.

Instead, I squeeze my hand to my head and say, *I want to be part of King's last-night memories. He's my brother; I don't know when I'll see him again!* And I channel our puppy-of-the-month calendar — those liquid eyes gazing out of the September Staffordshires.

King rolls his again. *I don't want to hang out with my kid sister on my last night in town!*

Ravi agrees, and starts sliding his circled thumb and forefinger down his body, until Em hits him again.

King says, *I don't want you here!*

You are such a jerk! I sign in quick, sharp bursts.

Adelaide tries to step in, but we're not finished yet.

And you're a little shit! he says, hooking his fingers.

Until Adelaide has to shake her hands and step between us. 'Okay, okay, okay,' and conscious of the gawkers who are still within earshot, she doesn't speak as she signs to the group. *We're not letting Bowie ride home by herself, and if she does go home she'll wake the whole house up and then we'll get held up explaining that we didn't knowingly lead your fourteen-year-old sister to the pub …*

King scowls at me.

… Because we'll run out of time, and the mood will be ruined anyway. So she comes with us!

King raises his hands, about to disagree, but Adelaide firmly says, *No.*

I knew Adelaide would be on my side — she was my friend first, after all. If you consider a friend someone you pay ten dollars two days a week to teach you maths for two hours after school. Which I do.

Adelaide makes a steering wheel and points at herself, to say, *I'm driving! I'm deciding!*

And with that we chain the bikes, walk round to the dead-end street at the back of The Parallax and pour into the old Holden Commodore.

Adelaide drives with Em riding shotgun, and me sandwiched in the back between Ravi and King.

We go over Pigott's Bridge again, but this time we hang a left and follow the signs to Lake Claire. I'm worried for a second until Adelaide catches my eye in the rear-view mirror, shakes her head and gives me the smallest of smiles.

The way is illuminated by a sliver of blue moonlight, and the car's neon beams cutting through the night. But between Orianna and Lake Claire, there's not a whole lot to see except rolling foothills in the distance, big patches of drought-dry land and pylons standing sentry.

I read somewhere that Iceland makes giants of its pylons. Twisting and bending the electrical poles and wires of the steel-framed towers so they look like men and women walking over land, like they're carrying the currents above their heads. I love that idea, Icelandic pylons inspired by *The BFG*, but I don't know if they've started making them or if it's just an idea someone had, to turn something functional into something fantastical.

There's no air-conditioning in Aidan's wagon, so everyone rolls down the windows and Em sticks out her hand to stroke the wind rushing past. Adelaide does it, too, keeping one hand on the wheel, and from the middle back seat it looks like they're flying us forward.

'Where are we going?' I sign and ask, but Ravi and King are looking stubbornly out their windows, while Em and Adelaide crack up laughing in the front.

Em turns around to say, 'It'll be good, I promise.'

And I believe her.

The moment Ravi and King became friends, Em followed. She's the eldest of three sisters, and even when Ravi wasn't living with them he and Em stayed in constant contact through emails and texts. I don't really remember who she hung out with before Ravi and King — she was just another face in the crowd, really.

Adelaide Jones was different.

Tonight she's wearing a T-shirt that says, 'To-do list: 1. Invent Universe 2. Make Apple Pie'. She has another one with the words, 'Know Yourself, Before the Cosmos Can Know Itself'. And she once explained to me that her favourite with 'Girl Code' followed by a black-and-white photo of a woman standing beside a taller stack of papers, is something to do with going to the moon. She makes them all herself; designs them on her computer, buys cheap cotton T-shirts and gets them printed at Officeworks.

She's made one for King as a going-away present; written in the tiniest of fonts is this Gwen Harwood poem he liked when they studied her in Year 12. And underneath the poem are these sketches Adelaide drew of hands held up, spread out, and little curved lines springing off the fingers to make them look like movement, clapping in excitement.

They are King's hands; I know because Adelaide mapped them for a whole summer last year, sitting at our kitchen table or lying on a blanket down by Lake Claire — the last one I didn't see myself, but know from the photos Blu-tacked to King's wardrobe. Adelaide complained that they're the hardest part of anyone to get right, so she needed practice — she said hands are like mountains up close, with all these infinitesimal ridges, and you have to be a cartographer to get them right.

I can't say exactly when the four of them became friends, I can only guess it was around the time the rumours started, when they were at the end of Year 10. That was when Adelaide stopped hanging with her old crowd — the footballers and weekend riders — and after a party where people said she got too drunk to say stop.

King knew Adelaide — everyone did, because of who she hung out with — but also because she was tutoring me. And when she stopped hanging with the people meant to be her friends, King started walking her home after our sessions. Then I began teaching her signs in between sines, cosines and tangents. Until one day they were Ravi, Em, Adelaide and King — fundamentally and completely quadrilateral — and the rest, as they say, is geometry.

Claire is a corrie lake, and once the wagon is curving round the road at the edge of her without stopping I get an idea of where we could be going.

After the gold ran out, people turned to the skies above Orianna, and the galaxies, too. She became an astronomy town, and home to the Goodricke telescope that mapped the Delta Cephei star. Orianna was remapped, too, and the streets named in honour of their astronomical responsibility.

The telescope itself was named for this guy John Goodricke, who hypothesised regular variability and is still the youngest ever recipient of the Copley Medal — given when he was just nineteen. He was also Deaf, a fact that Mum and Dad tried to spin into a good omen when we moved to Orianna.

They tore the stupid thing down, King said, *so what does that tell you?*

It's true. Goodricke was the fifth largest telescope in the world in the nineteenth century, and the largest in the southern hemisphere. But that all changed with the Second World War — when they tore down the telescope and used its lens for rifle scopes.

These days the old observation dome just sits like a fallen moon atop Mount Solemn — and it's where Adelaide is steering us to, up the wide road leading to the abandoned observatory. Up, up, up to where I've never been.

And already Orianna is just a smudge of light on the horizon, getting smaller and smudgier the higher we go, at a steady thirty-degree angle that Aidan's wagon seems determined to climb. Until we're there, parking in the old designated spot for scientists and tourists.

Adelaide turns off the ignition and we all just sit for a moment, staring at the fat, dome moon the size of a house, still so brilliantly white that it casts its own light.

Then Ravi opens his door and the spell is broken, so we all tumble out.

Of course they've all been here before. It's one of the first things kids in Orianna do when they get their licence, or access to a car.

The observatory is too far out from town to get here any other way — I know because me, Laura and Kylie tried to ride it once on our pushbikes. We didn't even get as far as Lake Claire before the uneven road killed our backsides, and we knew we'd never make it home in time before nightfall. As we rode home, Laura said she thought her dad would drive us up the mountain if we asked — but there was something about parental supervision to an abandoned place that sucked all the point out of it; we knew that much, even in Year 5.

Now I'm here, looking at this steel balustrade that wraps around the lip of the mountain, and some rusted old signs showing shadow men leaning too far over and falling to their death. I do it anyway, hooking my feet onto the rung of the balustrade and heaving myself up, when I feel someone grab my T-shirt tightly and keep me steady. I turn round, and it's King.

Then a light flares from the corners of our eyes, and we both turn to Em who's flashing her torch, motioning us to come. We walk over to where Ravi and Adelaide are standing at a little steel door with a KEEP OUT sign hanging at a jaunty angle by one last rusted screw.

Ravi backs up, turns side on, takes deep breaths and starts shaking out his body, preparing to ram, when Em leans forward and pushes on the handle that swings the door open easily.

We all give Ravi a pat on the shoulder as we file in.

There's a short corridor and to our left a little spiral staircase going up somewhere, but we walk ahead and through another door that swings open just as easily — leads us into what must be the circular observation room. Then Em's torch beam swings around, joined by Ravi's and Adelaide's as they pull flashlights out of their back pockets to reveal how depressing the place is.

It looks like what I imagine the inside of a big concrete water tank would look like, with cement floors, tall cement sides, and the smell of concrete after rain. There are some cigarette butts on the floor, a few glass bottles scattered about … and rainbow-coloured graffiti covering every spare inch of the smooth concrete curved wall.

I tap Adelaide on the arm, asking for her flashlight, and walk up to a section that's mostly covered in names — 'Winsome '94', 'Jack + Alice', 'Class of 2005'. There are the usual graffiti bubble letters and jagged font, a few drawings I can't quite make out because people have written over them … there's nothing crude or rude, at least not where I'm looking. It seems like mostly everyone just wanted to leave a little bit of themselves; proof that they were here.

Adelaide comes up behind me, touches my elbow and moves me over a few spaces to a spot closer to the door we just walked through — she takes the torch and points the light on 'Ravi + Em + Adelaide + King' that's scrawled in big bubble font I recognise from Ravi's juvenile-delinquent days. She looks at me and smiles, then motions behind us, so I turn back around and notice a large cement block in the centre of the room where the Goodricke telescope must have once been mounted, plus a rusted cogwheel still there with a chain, and a hand-crank.

Ravi and King move in perfect synchronicity to that crank, which they both start heaving and pushing at — and they've clearly done this a million times before, because they find a rhythm and pretty soon a slice of shutter is slowly lowering in the dome's roof … a little window to the sky that perfectly frames the waxing crescent moon. And all we need is that weak moonlight, to fill the dome and see the truly spectacular sight.

Ravi steps back, looks up, and throws out his arms like, *TA-DA!*

Behind me I can feel Adelaide move to stand beside King, then watch as Em tucks herself under one of Ravi's arms that's still thrown out in triumph, so he curls it around her shoulders while they both look up.

And I suddenly feel like Pinocchio after he's been swallowed; dome roof with curved steel beams like a whale's ribs, the moon and Milky Way right there at the yawning shutter of its mouth.

I try to picture this place with the Goodricke telescope still inside, because for the life of me I can't understand tearing something like that down when there's still so much to see. And I don't even realise that I'm saying this out loud, until King waves at Ravi to shine his light on me, and once I'm cast I say it again, and sign at the same time so they can all hear me.

Adelaide waves, and Ravi throws his light onto her. 'There are abandoned observatories all over, just like Mount Solemn,' she says and signs. She fingerspells *E* for east and moves her hand to the right as she tells us that somewhere close to here, in a paddock in the middle of nowhere, there's a large array of satellite dishes that were planted in the 1980s, only to have a newly elected government decide that funding should dry up a few years later.

I remember reading about those satellites in science class, that they sent out a message when the radios were first erected; a message of numbers and DNA elements, song notes, the double helix, and a picture of humanity all strung together in binary and sent out, to 25,000 light years away.

It's crazy to think that those metal ears of radio telescopes are stuck in the ground now, and aimed skywards but rusted brown.

And the funny thing is that their messages are still bouncing around up there — messages that were sent over 25,000 light years away will take 25,000 years to reach their destination (or 24,900-and-something years now). Our teacher, Ms Sims, said it was more of a symbolic gesture, a just-in-case we-come-in-peace that was never really intended to get anywhere. But I remember thinking how sad it'd be if someone up there waited long enough, got the message, and then replied. Sent back an answer to a question without knowing there was radio silence even before it had reached them. Put that way, the universe seems so lonely — with all these messages bouncing light years away to life forms unknown, when all the senders are long since gone. And maybe that's all stars are — messages that have already burned up by the time they arrive.

Em waves and Adelaide lights her up. 'Lucky you're seeing this place tonight, Bowie, when everyone else has left for S-C-H-O-O-L-I-E-S,' she mimics Ravi's *TA-DA* with a smile on her face. 'Sometimes on a weekend this place is too packed with kids.'

Ravi clears his throat and Adelaide gives him light. 'Or those toolie dudes who come up here trying to hook up with high school girls.'

Em elbows him in the stomach. 'Is that going to be you, Rav? Now that you've graduated?'

Ravi steps away from Em's elbow. 'No, not anymore. And I can't believe —' he starts, then remembers and tucks his torch under an arm, motions Em to light him up. 'I can't believe we're not going to get another chance to be here again.'

Em swings her light to King, who says, *You can still come here without me.*

'And me,' Adelaide says, then for my benefit, 'I've decided on the city campus, so I'm going to board.'

Ravi says, 'It wouldn't be the same.'

And it's hard enough being an outsider, without having to watch something end that you've always wanted to be a part of.

I click my fingers and Ravi swings back to me. 'So, this is it? You're all just *leaving*?' I push out my hand.

Em says, 'I'm not,' then nods to Ravi, 'but his old man's got a job waiting for him ...'

'I haven't agreed yet!' Ravi says.

I'm shaking my head so King comes to me, puts a hand on my arm, but I shrug him off. Because I'm suddenly so tired, thinking about that big question mark over all the little squares of December, and being able to hear King snore through our bedroom wall, and how when I was little I used to think that I could pull the very thought of him out of my head, because he was just always supposed to *be here*.

I turn around, watch their globs of torchlight dance around the cement walls as I walk out the door, but this time I turn right — go up the little spiral staircase, and hold tight onto the rusted rails that take me to a trap-door roof that opens with little effort.

There's a platform wrapped around the circumference of the dome, just wide enough for one person to walk single-file. There's another balustrade like the one round the mountain, and I lower myself so I sit with my legs pushed through the rust-flaked rails.

Orianna is in the distance, with the Milky Way fading to light overhead.

A few minutes pass and I hear the main entry door open and slam shut, turn my head and watch King walk a little way out, looking for me. When he doesn't turn around, I fling the thong from my right foot, so it lands just in front of him. When he turns and looks up, I make my fingers march for *staircase*.

He crab-walks along the platform and lowers himself next to me, sticks his legs through the rails like I've done, then hands me my thong.

The sky keeps lightening.

You okay?

I try to wave him away, but it's too hard to wave and wipe tears from my eyes at the same time.

Sorry, he claws.

What for?

He shrugs.

I swipe a sorry across my mouth, and King raises an eyebrow at me.

I shouldn't have come tonight.

He bumps my shoulder, and then again, until I crack a smile for him. I take a deep breath. *I'm just really going to miss you.*

I'll be back.

Yes — but not soon, right?

King stays still, and I take that as a no.

I make a gun with my pointer finger. *Mum will shoot you when you don't come back for Christmas.*

King flattens and tips a hand to say, *Maybe*, then he raises both. *Sometimes I forget why I wanted to leave in the first place.* He leans so his back is against the dome. *Because I worry about Mum and Dad worrying about me, and you missing me, and Adelaide falling in love with someone else or Ravi getting in trouble because I'm not around to stop him being an idiot, and I don't like the idea of all of us leaving Em here by herself.* He holds his hands steady for a moment, before saying, *But mostly I'm scared that I'll like the idea of going more than being gone.*

The sky has been breaking open while he's been saying these things, and it's just gone *beautiful.* But however I describe it will be wrong, a list of colours running and leaking into each other. So instead I'll hold it to my lips, and feel it all the way to my fingertips.

You hated it when we first moved here, and for the longest time, I sign, *and then I thought things got better. Because you have these friends that I'd kill for, and you always seemed to know exactly where you wanted to go.* I shake my head. *But I've seen you start to accept the bad things about being here, like that people won't even try to get to know you, because they won't reach farther than they have to.*

I can hear the others in the observation room down below, their echoing voices getting louder as they make their way through the corridor.

I want you to come back, I tell him, *but I don't think this place will ever be your home again.*

King takes my hand, squeezes it as we watch Ravi, Em and Adelaide file out to meet the sunlight. And I can't imagine what King must be thinking while he's looking at them, except that maybe they were the only people in this town worth knowing — mostly because they made an effort to know him right back.

And before we have to climb down from this dome, and meet his friends so they can all say goodbye to our tiny speck of a town in the distance. Before we all pile back into the old Holden Commodore, and drive King home for the last time. Before my brother gets on a plane and takes a trip he's been planning since he was my age, with no end in sight.

Before all that — I tap him on the shoulder and tell him, *There are giants in Iceland.*

What?

They make them out of the pylons.

He smiles and raises an eyebrow. *Is that true?*

I don't know — I flatten and fist my hand — *Find out for me,*
I say.

Competition Entry #349

JACLYN MORIARTY

To enter, tell us in twenty-five words or less why YOU deserve to win an exclusive time-travel package consisting of five (5) ten-minute Time Journeys, return flights to Sydney from your nearest capital city, accommodation at the Novotel on Darling Harbour, and transfers to and from the Time Travel Agency™.

Okay, first of all, I want to say that twenty-five words are nowhere near enough. I intend to use a lot more. You should forgive me for this because look how many words *you* use to describe this competition! There are, like, fifty or something!

Not like fifty. Exactly fifty. I just counted. That's a minute of my life I'll never get back. UNLESS I GO BACK IN TIME! To get the minute back!

Which is why I deserve to win this competition.

And that concludes my entry.

Ha-ha.

No. I haven't even started on the reason I deserve to win. It's a sound and noble reason with educational overtones. Also, as you will eventually see, choosing me will benefit you guys as well. It's what I like to call a win-win.

I made that expression up, by the way: win-win.

Ha-ha, no, I didn't. But that's the kind of thing my dad does all the time: he takes a cliché and acts like he invented it. 'You know what I just realised,' he says, in a voice like he can't quite believe where this sentence is heading, but he's pretty sure we'll all drop to the floor and cry out with amazement when we hear. 'I just realised that *every cloud has a silver lining.*'

Then Mum goes, 'Yeah, there's a poet named John Milton, had that exact same thought about four hundred years ago?'

It never embarrasses Dad. He just steps up his amazement. 'No way! What are the chances? Milton and I, eh? Two peas in a pod. Hey, did you hear that, everyone? *Two peas in a pod!* Whoa! What a metaphor! So vivid!'

Another thing I would like to say, before I get started, is that I will not need return flights to Sydney, thanks, as I am already IN Sydney. However, it seems fair, as the winner, that I get some flights. Otherwise, you guys will be like, 'SCORE! We save money on flights! Let's have an office party with the leftover cash and buy all the cakes and the beer!' Not cool, guys. Not cool.

You can give me flights to a capital city of my own choice instead. Melbourne seems nice in the TV ads. So elegant and swishy, with mood lighting. Or Honolulu would work? You don't specify that it has to be a capital city in Australia. There are plenty of capitals out there. New York? Paris? Anyway, we can sort that out when I win. We can iron out the details.

Finally, I live on Wynton Road in Neutral Bay, which means I am a four-minute walk to the Time Travel Agency™. So it would make zero sense for me to stay in Darling Harbour and get 'transferred' back to where I started. But before you start fist-bumping ('Score! We save cash on her hotel! Office party, here we come after all!'), please note that I'll stay at the Novotel another time. I'll take some friends from school and we'll make a night of it.

(Cheer up. I'll bake you a cake for your office party.)

That was a pretty big introduction. Interestingly, I always get my school essays returned with huge, red circles around the opening paragraphs and scrawled across the margin: *Get to the point!*

On the plus side, I have built up suspense. By now you must be desperate to know the reason *I* deserve to win your time-travel package.

To answer that question, let me take you back in time.

Ha-ha.

But no, seriously, that's exactly what I'm going to do.

We're going to this morning. So. Not far.

It was a mild and cloudy morning.

It was the morning Taylor Morgan came to school with the quadratic formula tattooed on her arm. ('Totes indestructible cheat plan. They can't make me wash it off 'cause it *can't* be washed off,' she said. 'They could make you cover it?' I reasoned. 'Holy crap. Didn't think of that. Oh well, I know it now. Intense pain association, right?')

And, finally, it was the morning my Year 9 history class went on an excursion to the Time Travel Agency™. Each of us took five (5) ten-minute Time Journeys.

'*Whoa!*' is what you are saying right now. 'You've already *been* on Time Journeys? And you want to win more?! No *chance!*'

And you're about to shred my competition entry. Forgetting that I offered to bake you a cake.

Stay away from the shredder until you've heard my story! There is a point, and I intend to reach it.

Back to this morning.

We knew we were going on the excursion, of course. It wasn't like Ms Watson said, 'Surprise! Today, we time travel! Am I the best teacher ever or what?' and we all *whooped* and gave her flowers.

No, as you will recall, the Time Travel Agency™ offered all the local high schools free trial packages to 'celebrate' its opening in our neighbourhood. Our school was the only one to take up the offer. Some parents complained that this was a 'disgraceful waste of school time', but most laughed, made us promise to take photos and signed the permission slips.

So all Ms Watson said this morning was, 'Best behaviour on the walk over, please.' But she didn't sound that invested.

No offence, but many jokes were made about time travel on the walk. Ms Watson pretended not to hear, or maybe she was distracted. She was really bothered by how short a 'window of time' the lights stayed green at crossings, and by the way the class 'straggled' so that we kept missing the 'windows', and by the way we kept tripping from the path onto the road because we were laughing so hard at the jokes being made at the expense of your agency.

'Honestly, what is it that keeps you people *alive* in your day-to-day *lives*?' Ms Watson asked. Nobody answered her. It was too complex a scientific and philosophical question.

We arrived at the agency at 10 a.m.

Now, I will say that I like your shopfront. Some might have gone for a big, blazing sign like, **The Time Travel Agency!** with fireworks exploding from each letter. Like, to indicate the excitement of *movement through time*! Others might have used a historical font, 𝕮𝖍𝖊 𝕮𝖎𝖒𝖊 𝕮𝖗𝖆𝖛𝖊𝖑 𝕬𝖌𝖊𝖓𝖈𝖞, with pictures of carriages and gentlemen in top hats.

But you just have that white screen and the tiny, neat: TIME TRAVEL AGENCY. PLEASE ENTER, alongside a stack of pamphlets setting out your price list.

There are maybe twenty of us in the class, and we were all suddenly silent, staring at this shopfront.

Still, there is something about the idea of a time-travel agency sitting on Military Road between a sushi place and a 7-Eleven, cars and buses crawling by, half-heartedly honking their horns, that splits right through a moment of doubt like this. By the time Ms Watson pushed open the door we were laughing again.

You've got a great colour scheme in your reception area. Black and orange, and all dim and moody, like Melbourne. Striking! Surprising after the understated shopfront, too.

A woman in black-framed spectacles stepped out from behind the reception desk and welcomed us. She had a hip look and a warm smile and we stared at her, interested to find that this sort of woman would agree to work in time travel.

'Kara,' she said and Kara Ripley said, 'Yes?' in a trembling and astonished voice. But it turned out the receptionist's name was Kara. She was just introducing herself. Our Kara was, like, 'OMG, I thought you must have travelled back in time to find out my name in an alternate universe and that this was, like the twenty-fifth time we'd got here, and we're in a *loop* where you'll just keep finding out *all our names!*'

The receptionist looked at her for a long moment and then she said, 'No.'

After that she asked us to follow her into a briefing room with a podium, and she gave us a quick summary of the Time

Travel Agency™. How it was started by the cosmologist, Professor Eliza Raskdfjsa, when she discovered the key to time bending, and how Neutral Bay was the flagship store, but eventually the professor hoped to have agencies all over the world, and how her mission was to make time travel an affordable, comfortable option for everyone.

We already knew all this because of the articles in the *Herald* and the *Telegraph* and all the talk on Twitter and Tumblr, etcetera, and here I might gently remind you that this coverage has universally mocked and savaged Professor Raskdfjsa, the agency and time travel itself.

Put simply, nobody believes in it.

Anyhow, next, Kara-the-receptionist warned us about 'time lag'. 'You may experience mild dizziness and confusion,' she said. 'Don't be alarmed. They fade. We've found that the symptoms are minimised if a single time destination is visited in any twenty-four-hour period, and if that visit is split into ten-minute increments with short breaks to rehydrate.' The agency only offered journeys to the past, not the future, she said, and we would each get our own time booth, and —

'Why not the future?' Ari Dadash asked.

'Because this is a *history* class,' Ms Watson scolded him. 'Not science fiction. Don't interrupt.'

'In fact, the agency doesn't *offer* trips to the future,' Kara said. 'The future hasn't happened yet. Nowhere to go.'

'If you can travel *backwards* in time,' Lila Saraya declared, 'you can travel forward. Basic physics.'

Kara smiled at her. 'A lot of our ideas about time travel come from movies,' she said. 'For example, I bet you think you'll be able to *change* the past while you're visiting? You will not.'

'Did you hear that, everybody?' Ms Watson put in. 'No messing around with the past! You will interfere with the space–time continuum!'

At the podium, Kara scratched her ear. 'Mess around with the past as much as you like, actually. The space–time continuum is rock-solid. My point is that your actions *can't* affect it. No matter what you do back then, the present will stay the same.'

A voice spoke up. A soft, low voice. The sort of voice that makes feathers slide up and down your spine, and fireflies zing around your stomach. Take note of this voice. It belongs to Noah Brackman.

'This is a big part of why people doubt your agency,' Noah said (in his voice). 'If nothing changes, you haven't really *been* there, have you? I mean, at most, it's all in your subconscious?'

There was a brief, startled silence. Noah had just changed the rules. None of us actually *believed* in time travel (except maybe Kara Ripley), but that was something we joked and smirked about between our*selves*, not brought up with the *agency employees*!

Ms Watson was frowning. 'Noah,' she said. 'These people have kindly offered us a free trial of their program! If they have the technology to provide you with an immersive historical experience, we will *play along*.'

Kara smiled again but in a sad, weary way. She turned to Noah. 'Of course you can't change the past,' she said. 'It's already happened.'

Then she pointed at the door behind us. 'Booths are down the corridor to the left. Time destinations have been locked in: all within your teacher's preferred frame. England in the seventeenth century. Right, Ms Watson?'

'Ha. Trolled,' Farrell Kafji said. 'Wrong century. We're doing the *sixteen* hundreds.'

We all explained to him how centuries work while Ms Watson sighed at the ceiling.

'Wait,' said Taylor Morgan. 'Is this *safe*? I mean, will we get the plague?' She held up her new tattoo. 'I don't want this getting infected.'

So maybe Taylor Morgan believed in time travel, too.

'Perfectly safe,' Kara said. 'We've had people stabbed on their journey! They *feel* it, but in the present, nothing has happened to them, so they come back fine.'

'That,' said Noah, 'is another reason.'

Kara seemed not to hear him. 'Everyone get settled in a booth. I'll seal the doors and send you on your way. Happy travels!'

Now, I've been pretty honest with you in this entry so far. You probably appreciate that. So I may as well continue with the honesty.

You know how I laughingly mentioned that Kara Ripley and Taylor Morgan maybe believed in time travel?

Well, so did I.

Not completely, you understand. It was more that my mind was like a peach. The fruit part was going: *Ha-ha, total scam! Oh well, have fun anyway*, while the stone in the middle whispered: *Wait, this could be real.*

I had no basis for that stone's whisper. I just *wanted* it to be real. Time travel! So cool! Plus, I like the pictures of Professor Raskdfjsa in the papers. Her face, her clothes, her eyebrows, her bangles — everything about her, basically, is a shrug.

Print whatever you like about me, she seems to be saying. *I know the truth. Shrug.*

So when I got into that booth, I was trembling. England in the seventeenth century? It would be noisy! Smelly. I might get kicked in the face by a horse!

That was my main concern, really. Landing in the path of a horse and getting kicked in the face. Sure, I might come back intact, but in the moment, a broken nose would hurt.

Also, the plague seemed like it might have more serious implications than an infected tattoo.

I'd like to compliment you on your booths. Slick whites and chromes, but so comfortable. There was a monitor with keyboard and headphones, a bottle of water in a holder, a muesli bar leaning up against this. Also, surprisingly, a pink post-it note with a scribbled number on it, and a set of keys on a Pokémon keyring.

I sat in the reclining leather chair, put on the headphones, and admired the font on the screen. Here is what it said:

Destination: Woolsthorpe, Lincolnshire, England, 10 January 1643, 8.35 p —

A cursor blinked after the 'p'.

It wasn't finished.

I leaned forward, touched the keyboard, and typed 'm'. So now, as you will have guessed, it said:

Woolsthorpe, Lincolnshire, England, 10 January 1643, 8.35 p.m.

I thought about that. 8.35 p.m. January. In England? That was winter. It would be freezing, and dark!

With respect, Ms Watson, you're an idiot (I thought to myself, respectfully).

I leaned forward and typed again. So now it said:

Woolsthorpe, Lincolnshire, England, 10 June 1643, 2.35 p.m.

'Stand by,' said the voice of Kara through a loudspeaker, 'doors *closing*.'

Hiss went the doors, and I heard the *hiss* echo up and down the corridor.

My heart really wanted my attention. It was like a little puppy scrambling all over my chest.

I looked down at my clothes. We'd been told to wear 'casual' rather than our uniforms. I was wearing jeans! A T-shirt that said, *Save it for the Subterraneans*, which I'd stolen from my brother's closet! Very hip and enigmatic, sure, much like Melbourne, but how would it look to the good folk of Woolsthorpe, Lincolnshire?

They'd totally stare at me! And maybe throw rocks?

Also, what if I got trapped in the past? Why had nobody addressed *that* issue? At the very least we should have been provided with a stack of seventeenth-century currency and a help line!

'In one minute,' piped Kara through the loudspeaker, 'your journey will commence. If you have any concerns, please press the *red* button marked HELP.'

I reached for the red button.

My hand paused.

I looked at the screen. At the keyboard. Back at my hand.

'*Time destinations have been locked in*,' Kara had said. Not in my booth, they hadn't been. I just changed it. I considered the pink post-it note and the Pokémon keyring. They had a left-behind feeling about them. Someone was interrupted, I realised, before they'd finished here.

My heart stopped jumping around. It sat still, blinking at me. So did the cursor on the screen.

'Twenty seconds till departure.'

I leaned forward, deleted, typed at high speed —

'Departing! Now!'

The booth lit up and blasted sideways: *32 Wynton Road, Neutral Bay, NSW, Australia, 23 May 2016, 4.25 p.m.*

And that's where I went.

To my own home.

On a Monday afternoon, two weeks ago.

I landed just inside the front door. My dog, Babstock, lying on the carpet, seemed surprised and amused to see me. He got straight up, pressed his nose to my stomach, wagged his tail a bit, and lay back down. *You know your way around*, he seemed to say.

I headed to the stairs.

Whoa, is what you're saying right now. (You should stop saying that.) And you're thinking I'm a right wuss. *Scared of a little kick in the face from a horse! Scared of a touch of the plague!* And so on.

Let me be perfectly clear. Yes, I was scared, but that's not why I changed the destination.

I changed it because *23 May 2016, 4.25 p.m.* is a date and time that has been seared into my skull, inked into my consciousness, *spring-loaded* into my brain ever since it first took place.

Here is why.

Noah Brackman kissed me that day.

It was my first kiss.

And he hasn't spoken a word to me since.

⁂

In the last two weeks, every waking and many sleeping moments have been *consumed* by my *fierce and fiery* desire to go back in time and find out what the heck I did wrong.

I could use stronger language than 'heck' there, but I don't want to get disqualified.

Anyhow, here I was at home.

I walked up the stairs. From the kitchen, I could hear the sound of my parents arguing. 'Cerulean blue!' my mother shouted, just as I reached the top step. 'Candy-apple red!' my dad retaliated in a roar. (They run a graphic design business together.)

Along the corridor, I passed my sister's room. Someone was crying in there. My sister's voice was talking to the crying person in a quick, sensible tone. She's always very practical about emotional anguish, my sister.

I passed my brother's room. Music was playing. There was a crashing sound, and someone swore.

I reached my own room. I'm the youngest so I get the small one down the end.

The door was ajar. I went to push it open further — and stopped.

Someone had just laughed.

The someone was *me*.

I was in my room *laughing*.

I stood in the corridor, hyperventilating as quietly as I could, and listened to my own laughter.

And there it was.

The answer.

Right there.

I couldn't believe I had solved the riddle so quickly. No *wonder* Noah hadn't spoken to me since that day!

My laugh was ridiculous.

Hee-hee ha-ha, up high, down low, then a sort of trail of raspy ha-ha-has. I recognised it, of course, as that is exactly how

I always laugh. But ordinarily, when you hear your own laugh, you're busy finding something funny! You take no notice of the sound! Now, however, visiting from my own future and standing outside my room, I could be objective. And objectively speaking I sounded like a falling cockatoo. The cockatoo's wings have failed it. The cockatoo is high-pitched panicking, resigned moaning, then hitting the ground with a squawky *thud-thud-thud*.

I couldn't believe my parents hadn't sent me to some kind of Laughter Rehabilitation Centre years before. I couldn't believe my brother and sister hadn't sat me down and said, 'This laugh of yours? It has to stop.'

I leaned against the wall.

Noah was speaking in there. In his voice. I heard myself laugh again. Noah's voice. My laugh. Noah's voice. My laugh.

He was saying funny things. I couldn't hear exactly what they were, but I remembered now: we'd been working on a chemistry assignment together, and just before he kissed me, he'd been hilarious about our chemistry teacher. Why? Why keep being funny, Noah? He must have known the direct consequence of humour would be more laughter!

Mysterious.

Although, now that I thought about it, maybe it suggested that he *didn't* have a problem with my laugh?

Plus the kiss hadn't happened yet. It was about to happen.

Logic would suggest that if you were appalled by somebody's laugh and wanted no more to do with her, you'd say, 'Gotta go, sorry,' as opposed to kissing her.

The bathroom is opposite my bedroom. I crept over there, *creaked* open the door, unhooked the mirror from above the vanity and carried it back into the hallway.

At that moment, my brother's door opened. Sebastian stepped out into the hallway along with a blast of music. He turned, still grinning at something in his own world, and saw me.

I was holding the bathroom mirror at a high angle, pointing it at my open door. He raised an eyebrow, interested. Then he looked at me more closely.

'That's my shirt,' he said. I could only just hear him over the music from his room.

'No, it's not,' I replied automatically. But it was, of course. *Save it for the Subterraneans*. 'It's okay,' I said instead. 'I'm not actually wearing it today. That happens in two weeks.'

He considered this, raising his other eyebrow to join the first. Then he nodded, apparently satisfied, spun around and ran down the stairs.

I played with the mirror angle.

It worked. I could see into my room.

And there we were.

Me and Noah.

We were sitting on my bed.

Me-of-the-past was facing the window, so I could only see the back of my head and a bit of my profile. My hair looked fine. In its regular ponytail and quite shiny. So it wasn't that. He hadn't stopped speaking to me because of a failure of hair style/quality.

Now, as I watched, Noah's hand curled around the back of my head. He leaned towards me. Past-me took the cue. I mean, I didn't just sit there and make it difficult for him. I didn't rush it either. Hurtle myself forward with lively enthusiasm, and send him flying off the bed so that he crashed against my desk and got concussion. No. I leaned forward at his exact, careful speed, and then we were kissing.

I don't know if you've ever watched your own first kiss taking place in real life, but I have to say it is a situation that makes you feel many complex emotions. Especially if it's Noah Brackman doing the kissing. Noah with the eyes that disappear when he smiles. Noah with the thoughtful way of moving around life, thinking about things, and now and then commenting on those things, in his voice.

I tried to be a scientific observer.

I noted that: (1) I placed my hand on his shoulder, to give myself balance. I admired myself for this. It seemed a smooth and natural move. (2) Noah's eyes stayed closed for the whole kiss. They didn't fly open and widen in alarm and horror at anything I was doing. (3) When the kiss finished, we both sat back and smiled at each other. (I could tell that I was smiling from my profile.) (4) Neither of us said anything. (5) We kept smiling for ages! (Longer than the kiss, actually.) (6) Then Noah looked behind me at the clock on my bedside table and said, 'I am unbelievably late for work.' (He works at his dad's plant nursery.) (7) He stood up, and (8) I also stood, ready to walk out with him.

At this point, out in the corridor, I panicked, of course — and then, there I was, back in the booth.

That's how it happened. No rush of lights or zoom this time. Just: oh look, here's the booth.

'Welcome back, everyone,' said Kara's smooth voice over the speakers. 'You have thirty seconds before your next journey. Please use the time to rehydrate. If you feel light-headed or dizzy, we urge you to eat the muesli bar.'

I opened the lid of the water bottle and drank.

'Ten seconds until departure.'

I only had time to have two specific thoughts — *I don't think that I did ANYTHING wrong in that kiss!* and *This would not be nearly enough time to eat a muesli bar* — when the booth lit up and blasted sideways again.

Once again, Babstock was surprised and pleased to see me, welcomed me politely, and lay back down.

Once again, my parents were arguing in the kitchen while I walked up the stairs. I walked a little more slowly this time so my mum shouted, 'Cerulean blue!' and my dad, 'Candy-apple red!' at the third step from the top, rather than the top.

Once again, there was crying in my sister's room, and loud music in my brother's. The *crash!* from my brother's room, and the sound of swearing.

I stopped outside my own room and there I was laughing in there. My laugh had not improved. I went right into the bathroom and unhooked the mirror. In the hall, I looked at my brother's closed door. Any moment it would open. Sebastian would see me with the mirror. He'd raise an eyebrow and say, 'That's my shirt.'

I should avoid that.

I ducked into the bathroom, out of sight.

Sound of door bursting open, blast of music. Footsteps along the corridor, and down the stairs.

I stepped out again.

The mirror seemed heavier than last time. I hoisted it up, and it swivelled and tilted. Now it faced *across* the corridor instead. Straight into my brother's room.

Max Stephenson was in there, sitting at Sebastian's desk. I recognised his swoopy, swirly hair. (I assume he asks his hairdresser to make his head look like cappuccino foam, please.) Max has been a casual buddy of Sebastian's for years, but he's really stepped things up to super-friendship this year. Dropping by almost every day and saying, 'Dude!' My brother seems cheerful about this development. 'Dude!' he says right back. The rest of our family exchange many doubtful glances.

I don't mean to boast here, but my brother is a mild genius. He's also super-efficient and super-conscientious, and these elements, in combination, mean he blasts into first place in every subject that he takes. He's in Year 12 now, which means that life is suddenly looming from behind the HSC exams (he explained to us the other night).

A lot of time, when Max Stephenson comes by, the second thing he says after 'Dude!' is something like this: 'Logarithms! What the f***, eh?'

To which my brother replies, surprised, 'Really? I like them! You want me to show you?'

Followed by a free tutoring session.

This explains my family's doubtful glances.

So I did not beam with delight to see Max Stephenson in my brother's room. He was hunched forward, studying the computer monitor, hand on the mouse. I moved the mirror around a bit, so I could scan the bedroom. It's always a treat to see how neat, filed and colour coordinated a life can be. The only glitch today was the smashed glass lying on the floorboards, right by Max's sneaker. A puddle of Coke stretched from the shards towards the rug.

That explained the crash and the swearing I'd heard. Sebastian must have run downstairs to get a cloth.

I looked up at Max with disapproval. It seemed likely to me that he had knocked the glass over. Sebastian is careful with his surroundings.

A document was open on the computer screen in there. *Extension English Assessment Task: In* The Great Gatsby, *F. Scott Fitzgerald explores the life of the imagination, and the imagined life. Discuss.*

Discuss. Those are the cheapest questions. Teachers can't think of something to *ask*, so they fall back on the vague and helpless: *Discuss.*

My brother didn't seem to have had an issue with it. Max was scrolling down the screen now, and one paragraph after another was appearing at high speed. Now Max reached into his pocket, with his left hand. He took out a USB — one of those novelty ones, in the shape of a little red car — and jammed it into the computer.

After that it was hard to see what happened. You will recall I was watching all of this through a heavy mirror that kept tipping and losing its focus. But I caught a flash of files flying across the screen. The 'trash bin' icon. And then Max was pulling out the USB again, and dropping it in his pocket; iTunes flipped onto the screen.

I didn't think. I strode right over to my brother's bedroom door and shouted, 'Hey!'

I had to shout. The music was still blasting.

Max spun around in his seat. His eyes were startled. He tried to hide this startlement with a smile. 'Hey yourself.'

'What are you doing with that USB?' I shouted.

Now the smile broke into pieces, like that glass.

'Just copying some music!' he said.

'*Music?*' I pounced, with huge amounts of wither and scorn, which, it turned out, were wasted because now I was back in the booth.

'Welcome back,' Kara's voice said. 'You have thirty seconds before your next journey.'

Once again, she instructed us to rehydrate, and suggested we eat the muesli bar if we needed it. In fact, I *did* feel light-headed and dizzy now, but I was pretty sure this was fury at Max Stephenson, rather than time-travel discombobulation. I thought of the trash-can icon on the screen. He hadn't just *copied* my brother's essay, he'd also *deleted* it.

'Ten seconds until departure,' and I was in my own front hallway. I gave Babstock a fierce yet cursory hug, pelted up the steps, two at a time ('Cerulean blue!' 'Candy-apple red!'), skidded along the corridor, and reached my brother's door.

I stopped.

My hand was raised, ready to turn the handle and throw open the door.

But of course, nothing had happened yet. Max, at this point, was innocent.

Crash! from behind the door, and swearing.

I pursed my lips. If I hadn't hesitated, I might have saved that glass.

My brother was about to fly out of the room. I sidestepped along the corridor towards the stairs.

But if I *had* saved the glass, I would *not* have saved the glass. *Of course you can't change the past,* Kara had said in the briefing room, *it's already happened.*

The glass *broke.* It was *broken.* In the real world of the present, it *is* broken.

That seemed terribly sad to me, and also quite wise.

My brother's door flew open, and here he came with the music and the grin. 'Hey,' he said to me, friendly, but I wasn't holding a bathroom mirror in the air, so he had no reason to pause, stare and notice his shirt. He carried on by, and down the stairs.

Now was my chance.

Catch Max Stephenson in the act!

But, again, I stopped. *It's already happened.* Max Stephenson has *already* stolen my brother's essay. It happened two weeks ago. He'd probably handed it in as his own by now. My brother would have discovered it was gone, and written another one.

The glass was already broken.

Instead of pushing open my brother's door, I pulled it closed, dimming the music, and sat down on the floor. I needed to think through my new wisdom. So far, I wasn't sure exactly what was wise about it.

I was sure that it was sad.

Somebody was crying somewhere, as if they agreed with me on that.

Of course, I remembered. There was somebody crying in my sister's room. Her door was half-open and I was opposite it now, leaning against the wall, so I could hear quite clearly: the sound of a girl crying. There was some rustling and rattling going on. 'Here,' said my sister, Harper, in her efficient voice, 'take this.' I decided she was offering the person a tissue.

'Thank you,' mumbled the girl. I didn't recognise the voice. The girl blew her nose. So I was right about the tissue.

'There will be *other* auditions,' Harper said. 'And at *other* auditions, you will *not* have a twinge in your shoulder that impedes your boogaloo!'

I slapped a hand over my mouth to stop myself snorting. Boogaloo. Funny. But insensitive to laugh.

'You think?' murmured the girl, sniffing.

'I don't *think*, I *know*!' declared my sister. 'You *rock* the Humpty Hump. And as for the Kriss Kross? And the Twist-o-flex?'

Okay, it was hip-hop. I recognised those terms. Harper is the athlete in the family: she rows, does Tae Kwon Do and dances hip-hop at a professional level. This girl must be in her troupe. And she must have just messed up an audition.

I still didn't know who she was, but I did know she wore a really powerful perfume. It was one of those high, sweet smells, like freesias and watermelon, with insect-repellent undertones, and it kept wafting out of the open door and into my face. (My sister is not a perfume sort of a person.)

'Here,' Harper said briskly. 'These are the keys to my locker at the studio.' More rustling. Jangling. 'There's a CD in there that Malik burned for me. The set list will —'

But I didn't know what the set list would do, because here I was back in the booth.

⁂

'Welcome back!' said Kara, more upbeat this time.

Yeah, yeah, I thought. Have a drink. Eat the muesli bar. I drank, reached for the muesli bar, and flew sideways.

The front hallway again.

I felt despondent this time. 'Hey, Babstock,' I said, and sat down beside him. He seemed pleased to have me.

If you couldn't change the past, what was the point of coming here? What was the point of *life*?

My parents were arguing in the kitchen. I could hear them quite clearly now.

'Seriously, that was mad,' Mum said.

'What are you talking about?' Dad complained. 'He knew it was a joke! Anyway, I can't help it, I do it automatically.'

'He signed off on the artwork, right? Before you went mad?'

'As long as we change the logo to cherry pink.'

'He's nuts,' Mum said.

Cherry pink, I thought. Yum. (I have lip gloss in that flavour.)

'I know, right?' Dad said. 'But I agree with him that yellow is wrong for the Ely logo. Should be candy-apple red.'

'No way. Cerulean blue.'

'Candy-apple red,' my father said firmly.

'Cerulean blue!' my mother shouted.

'Candy-apple red!' my dad roared in reply.

That escalated quickly, I mused to myself. But that's always the way with my parents: flighty, tempestuous, artistic types, the pair of them.

Beside me, Babstock sighed. 'I know, right?' I said to him.

It seemed a good idea, sighing. I tried it, too. *Sigh*. It was just the thing.

Upstairs, I knew, I was laughing at Noah's jokes and kissing him. Max Stephenson was smashing a glass and stealing my brother's essay. A strange girl was weeping about a failed boogaloo.

And there was nothing I could do about any of it.

I played with Babstock's ears while my parents carried on bellowing, 'Cerulean blue!' and 'Candy-apple red!' at each other.

My brother ran down the stairs.

'Hey,' he said, seeing me there and, 'Yo!' to Babstock, then, 'Isn't that my shirt?' to me, but in a distracted way. He disappeared into the kitchen. There was a brief pause in the battle of colours, while Sebastian chatted and moved about in there, then he hurried by me again, a cloth in his hand, back up the stairs.

My parents picked up their profound philosophical debate immediately, 'Cerulean blue!' 'Candy-apple red!' but Mum tripped up and shrieked, 'Cerulean-apple red!' and they both burst into laughter —

And I was in the booth.

※

'Welcome,' said Kara's voice.

Then, disconcertingly, she changed the script. 'You are about to take your fifth and final journey. Here at the Time Travel Agency™, we trust that you have enjoyed your travels today. Be sure to share your experiences on your favourite social media platforms. Departing in ten, nine, eight ...'

I straightened my shoulders.

The booth flashed white and skidded sideways.

'Yes, Babstock,' I said. 'It's me. Surprise!'

It was unfair of me to be snarky with him. He didn't know this was a loop. Only, I was feeling a little tetchy. I blamed Kara-the-receptionist. She hadn't reminded me to *rehydrate* and now I was thirsty. (Knowing that this was my own fault rather than Kara's, only increased my irritation.) But it was more than that.

Your fifth and final journey, she had said.

Last chance, is what she meant.

Last chance to *achieve nothing you mean, Kara,* I thought spitefully.

Oh, blah. May as well give it one last go.

I stomped up the stairs.

'Cerulean blue!' I mouthed along with Mum's shout, and 'Candy-apple red!' with Dad. I rolled my eyes at them, like a proper teenager.

My sister's room and the crying girl. My brother's room and the *crash!* followed by the same old swearing.

Could you not at least vary your curses? I withered at the door.

I turned into the bathroom, waited while Sebastian's door flew open and his footsteps disappeared down the stairs, then I unhooked the mirror and stepped back into the hall.

Outside my own room again, I hefted the mirror high. *Ha-ha hee-hee.* Yes, me-of-the-past, chortle away in there. Soon you will have *nothing* to laugh about for *soon* that boy will tear your heart to shreds!

Noah continued being funny, and I continued being amused. His voice, my laugh, his voice, my laugh.

Yes, yes, I know this bit.

But then I stopped. I adjusted the mirror slightly so that the image was all Noah's face.

There! I was right! His eyes had just skittered sideways. He was looking across the room, at my bookshelf. They skittered right back to me so he could be humorous again.

Obligingly, I laughed.

And there! Now his whole *head* had turned away. I was saying something *myself* now, at the same time as laughing, and he had turned his head to *look out of the window.* He swung his head around quickly. Okay, again, *there!* His eyes were on the *light fittings now!*

All this was happening in quick, darting flashes, you understand. Only a girl watching very closely from the hallway with a mirror in her arms would have noticed. But to me, such a girl, it was very clear.

Understanding crept up behind me and got a good grip on my throat.

In the room, Noah was leaning in, me-of-the-past was leaning in, and the kiss was about to happen. I turned away just in time. I couldn't watch again. It would be an intrusion. *Let her have her moment*, I thought, referring tenderly to the me-of-the-past. *This one, single moment of joy in a life that from henceforth will be desperate with tragedy.*

I looked again. The kiss was done. We were at the part where we smiled at each other.

And it was still happening. Noah's eyes kept wandering the room in quick little bursts. If you can wander in bursts. Well, I know you can because that's what Noah was doing. I lowered the mirror a bit and saw that he was also doing this weird thing where he tapped his fingers against his elbow. Then he actually pinched the elbow. I lowered it further and there! His foot was tapping madly!

'I am unbelievably late for work,' he said, and I lifted the mirror quickly, catching his eyes over my shoulder now, on my clock radio.

He stood up, me-of-the-past stood up, and there I was in the booth again.

'Welcome back,' Kara said. 'Take some time to compose yourself. Re-entering the present can be disconcerting, so —'

Blah, blah. I don't know what she said next. I was lost in my own forlorn wisdom.

The glass was already broken.

Now I understood what it meant.

It wasn't anything I had done wrong. It wasn't the kiss.

The whole time he'd been in my room, his mind had been on other things. He didn't want to be there. *Noah had never been interested in me in the first place.*

Kara-the-receptionist hurried into my booth as I was standing to leave.

'There they are!' she said, scooping up the post-it note and keys. It was strangely intimate hearing her voice in real life, instead of over the speaker. 'Good trip?' she asked, but she swept out before I answered. She did not glance at the screen, so she did not come face-to-face with the grim consequences of her own carelessness.

Everyone was subdued as we returned to school, except for Farrell Kafji, who complained loudly that he had landed in the middle of a seventeenth-century field. 'And fields then are exactly like fields right now!' he shouted. 'I could've gone down to Forsyth Park if I wanted to see a field!' By the last visit, he said, he had actually *sprinted* across the field, trying to find his way to something interesting, but there were only more fields.

All he ever saw was a cow.

Other people murmured quiet little tales to each other about seeing productions of *Romeo and Juliet* at the Globe, or having rats run over their feet, or lighting tallow candles, or having met 'any number of coxcombs', or arriving just in time to see King Charles the First lose his head.

'The graphics were excellent,' somebody said. 'And the effects? Wow. Beyond gruesome.' 'State-of-the-art,' others agreed soberly. 'What is it, four-D holograms or what?'

So we were sticking with the sceptical. It was all high-tech theatrics.

I stayed silent. Noah was near the front of the group, and I hung way at the back.

At home tonight, my parents wanted to know about today's school excursion to the Time Travel Agency™. I made up a story about having seen things far too traumatising to discuss (which was true enough, and which impressed them both very much).

Dad and I were making tacos for dinner, and Mum was working on her laptop at the kitchen table. Somebody else, meanwhile, was pounding on the front door.

'Yo?' called a voice.

My mother rolled her eyes. 'Come in, Max!' she shouted. 'It's open!'

Max Stephenson, accompanied by his swoopy hair, strolled into the kitchen. He dumped his schoolbag on the floor.

Sebastian must have heard because his footsteps thudded on the stairs and here he was, in the kitchen.

'Dude,' said Max.

'Dude,' Seb agreed, but without his usual relish. He was frowning to himself. His frown roamed the room. 'That's my shirt,' he said to me.

'No it's not,' I replied automatically and then, also automatically, 'Oh well, it *is* your shirt, but I'm wearing it two weeks in the fut—'

Then I remembered that actually this *was* the future. And here I was, grating cheese and wearing it.

But my brother had lost interest. He was leaning against the bench, flipping through taco shells. 'I've lost my essay,' he said.

'It's not in the taco shells,' I said. 'Leave them alone.'

'It'll turn up,' Mum said. She always says that. It's both comforting and infuriating.

'Will it?' my brother asked hopefully.

Dad was at the stove, a spatula in hand. 'Where did you last see it?'

'On my computer. Yeah, no, I didn't have a backup, don't ask that question. Ask this one. How can three thousand five hundred words on *The Great Gatsby* just disappear?'

I stopped grating.

'Whoa,' said Max Stephenson, swinging himself into a chair at the table. 'That's due tomorrow!'

Now I turned around slowly.

Of course Sebastian had finished an essay two weeks before the due date. That was exactly his style.

'Isn't that what happened to Gatsby himself?' Mum pointed out. 'He disappeared?'

'Into thin air,' Dad agreed and then he whispered to himself, '*into thin air.*' He fluttered his fingers in the air, trying out the concept. 'Did you hear that, guys? *Into thin air.* So evocative. Takes your breath away, really.'

'Anyway,' Mum said. 'It makes sense for an essay on *Gatsby* to disappear, is my point, because that's exactly what the man himself did.'

'You two can be a little ridiculous at times,' my brother pointed out. Our parents turned back to their work, chastened.

'Just write a new one,' Max suggested. 'I was going to get the lowdown on calculus from you tonight, but no sweat. Your essay's more important.'

My heart was thrumming.

'Actually,' I said to Sebastian, 'Max has a copy of your essay for you.'

The room blinked. That's how it seemed anyway. Quick, startled glances from everyone.

'He has?' Sebastian asked.

Max's face was busy with expressions of confusion and innocence. 'Uh, what?' He decided a little laughter was called for. 'Sorry, dude. Why would I?'

'Good question,' I said smoothly. 'And yet you do. Remember? Two weeks ago? You copied the essay onto your USB? From Sebastian's computer?'

'I *what*?'

'You *what*?' my parents and brother echoed.

'The USB that's like a little red car?' I prompted him. Here, I took a bold step towards Max's schoolbag and swept it up into my arms. 'I'll check for you!'

People were too confused to point out my violation of privacy and etiquette.

I took a guess, opened the front-pocket zip, rummaged around and there it was.

The little red car.

'That's a USB?' Dad asked. 'No way!'

'I love it,' Mum agreed.

I tossed it to my brother. 'See if your essay's on here,' I instructed him.

Sebastian scratched his forehead. 'Why would it be —'

'*Just go check*,' I said, and he shrugged, tossing the little red car on his palm. Then he swivelled and ran up the stairs.

While he was gone, Max kept up a low, meandering chuckle.

'That's getting on my nerves,' Mum told him politely, so he stopped.

'It's here!' my brother bellowed from upstairs. 'It's here!'

There was a pause while my parents and I raised our eyebrows at each other, very high, and Max attempted to imitate our surprise.

Seb's footsteps thundered back down the stairs. 'Dude,' he said to Max. 'You legend! I owe you,' and he handed him the USB.

Now my parents and I swung wide-eyed glances at each other, but our glances were interrupted by the *whoosh* of the door.

My sister marched in. Hands on her hips, she surveyed us all.

'Uh-oh,' Dad said. 'What have we done now?'

'I need to leave in —' Harper paused and studied our kitchen clock. It's a sailboat clock: us kids gave it to my parents for their anniversary a few years ago, and the numbers are scattered everywhere. The idea is that they've been blown off course by a gust of good sailing wind. Clever, but very tricky to tell the time. 'I need to leave in *five* minutes,' Harper decided eventually. 'And I *cannot find my keys*.'

'They'll turn up,' Mum declared.

'In the next five minutes?' my sister demanded.

'Oh, that I cannot promise,' Mum said. She sorted through the papers that were piled around her. At this point, I was trying to set the table, and Mum and I were having a kind of silent battle over how much territory her paperwork could occupy.

'Maybe Max has got your keys,' Dad suggested mildly. 'He had Sebastian's essay. Check his bag.'

Max made a gurgling sound that I believe was supposed to be a laugh. He was looking pretty pale.

'You could just take Dad's car,' Sebastian offered.

'Could she?' Dad said, surprised.

'It's not my car keys, it's my locker key,' Harper said. 'For the dance studio. I haven't used it for weeks, but there are choreography notes I need tonight.'

Up to this point, I admit, I had not been paying much attention to the discussion. The key point for me was that Harper was going out, and therefore not staying for dinner. I was recalculating place settings and taco allocations. But now I straightened up.

'Your locker key for the dance studio?'

'Yes.'

'You gave that to a friend,' I said. 'Two weeks ago.'

'Nonsense,' said Harper. Honestly, she used the word *nonsense*. It's her style. 'I'd never give away my locker key.'

Here I had a moment's doubt. Harper has a real certainty about her. But I'd been right about the stolen essay.

'It was a friend who wears a lot of perfume,' I remembered. 'Really sweet perfume. Like freesias and watermelon.'

'Oh, that's Isabelle,' Mum said. 'She was here visiting you a couple of weeks ago, Harper. I remember I said to her, *What IS that perfume, Isabelle?* as a gentle way of suggesting that it was awful. But she took it as a compliment.'

Harper's hands had fallen from her hips. She folded them. 'Isabelle *was* here,' she said. 'But why would I ...?' She blinked quickly.

'She was upset about an audition,' I prompted. 'Something went wrong with her boogaloo.' I giggled. So did the family. Max just breathed quietly.

'She *was* upset!' Harper cried. 'I *did* give her my locker key! I told her to take a CD from it! She should have given it back! Well *done*,' she said to me. 'Thank you!' She is always very fair in her distribution of praise and gratitude.

Then she spun around, called, 'Bye! Don't call us! We'll call you!', shot the air with imaginary cowboy guns and ran from the room. (That's a family thing. Years ago, my parents went to pitch to a potential client and they both thought it went great until the end, when the guy said, 'Don't call us! We'll call you!' and shot the air with imaginary cowboy guns. My parents came home howling with laughter, and ever since that's become a sort of signature farewell with us. Even Max Stephenson has stopped startling at it.)

At this point, speaking of Max Stephenson, the boy himself pushed back his chair. His forehead looked a bit damp.

'You know,' he said. 'I think maybe I won't stay for dinner tonight.'

I started recalculating taco allocations again, but Mum was muttering to herself. She was tapping frantically at keys and zipping the mouse everywhere. 'Where's the confirmation?' she said. 'Where are the emails?'

'Something else lost?' Dad asked cheerfully. 'Max will have it for sure.'

Mum looked up, frowning deeply. 'The Ely Films programs?' she said. 'I can't see any confirmation here and they need them for that big premiere on Friday.'

'A thousand copies,' Dad agreed, returning to the lettuce. 'Don't worry about it. You sent the artwork to the printers a fortnight ago. They'll all be done and dusted. *Done and dusted.* Now that's a —'

'What?' said Mum. '*Who* sent the artwork to the printers?'

'You did.'

'Um,' said Max Stephenson. 'I'll just be off.'

'Yes,' Mum shot at him acidly. 'I expect you have a *Gatsby* essay to write for tomorrow. Sit down.' She swung to Dad. '*I* didn't send the Ely artwork to the printers, *you* did.'

Max sank into his seat. Beside him, my brother blinked.

Dad, meanwhile, was swaying slightly. He bit his lip. 'You thought I sent the artwork?'

'You didn't?'

'I thought *you* did.'

They stared at each other.

'It's Monday,' Mum whispered.

'And they need the program for ...'

'The *world premiere* is Friday,' Mum repeated. 'The *stars* of the film are flying in for it. Sydney's *A-list* celebrities will be there. Australia's!'

'We can still do it,' Dad said, suddenly pumped. 'AJs print overnight so as long as we get it to them by their cut-off tonight, they'll have it for tomorrow — spot UV and celloglaze Tuesday, Wednesday to dry, collate and stitch on Thursday, delivery Thursday afternoon.'

'Right.' Mum nodded, looking excited. 'And AJs' cut-off is six p.m., so we have ...'

They both swung around and studied the sailboat clock. Seconds ticked by.

'*Three minutes*,' they concluded at the same time.

'Isn't there a clock on your computer?' Max mused.

They ignored him. 'Quick,' Dad rushed to Mum's side. Her hands were moving around the keyboard at a high-speed tremble.

'Where is it? Where's the artwork? Okay, here it is!'

I looked over their shoulders. The screen filled with a blaze of colour and bubble font. A yellow tiger scowled from centre-top.

'Okay, he's approved the artwork, right? Except for the colour of the tiger. It's their new logo. They're launching it at the premiere. So just fix the colour, stick it in an email and send!'

Dad was jittering like a teabag. Mum's fingers flew. On the screen, the yellow tiger turned blue.

'Done,' Mum said. 'The tiger is now cerulean blue. So I just —'

'Candy-apple red,' Dad said firmly. 'He wanted candy-apple red.'

'No.' Mum shook her head, still typing. 'It was cerulean blue.'

'Candy-apple red!'

'Cerulean blue!'

Seb, Max and I looked back and forth between them and the clock, with great interest.

'Stop!' Dad said. 'We don't have time to argue!'

'You're right. Let's call him and check.' Mum reached for her phone, then stopped. 'We can't!' she said. 'He's in New York, remember? He flies back tomorrow.'

'So we call him in New York!'

'It's four a.m. in New York.'

'He's an early riser!'

'How can you possibly know that!' Mum demanded.

Sebastian looked at his own phone. 'You have forty-five seconds,' he said.

'Is six p.m. an absolute deadline?' Max wondered. 'There's no wiggle room?'

'Yes!' Mum and Dad snapped at once. 'No *wiggle room.*'

'I'm *sure* it was cerulean blue, he wanted,' Mum said. 'I'm sending it like this.'

'I *swear* it was candy-apple red!' Dad reached for the mouse. Mum slapped his hand away.

My heart began a low, slow hammer.

'It was neither,' I said quietly. 'Your client wanted cherry pink.'

Mum and Dad were now wrestling each other for the mouse.

'Cerulean blue!'

'Candy-apple red!'

'Cerulean blue!'

I placed my hands firmly on their shoulders.

'Look at me,' I said in a voice like a calm school principal. They looked at me. '*It was cherry pink.*'

They glanced at each other. They glanced at me.

Mum reached for the mouse. The scowling tiger turned pink.

The cursor flew across the screen. Email. Attachment. Send.

'Six o'clock,' my brother declared.

There was a long pause.

Ding, said Mum's computer.

'Confirmation,' she said. 'They got the order.'

She put her head down on the table.

Dad pulled out a chair and slumped into it. 'And we're sure it's cherry pink?' he asked me quietly.

Mum straightened up again. 'This is the *world* premiere.' She looked a bit dazed. 'If the logo on the screen doesn't match the logo on the program, I just ...' She turned her dazed expression on me. '*Are* you sure?'

I nodded.

My parents glanced at each other now, like, *why* did we just trust her?

Of course, I wasn't sure at all. My heart was skidding around like my brother that time on new rollerblades.

I *did* know I'd heard Mum say that the client wanted cherry pink, right before they started arguing. I'd thought of my lip gloss when she said it.

But I'd heard it in a booth at the Time Travel Agency™.

And everybody knows the Time Travel Agency™ is a scam.

Sure, I'd been right about my brother's essay and my sister's locker key, but maybe those were wild coincidences? And if I *had* been wrong about those two things? No big deal. I'd only have lost some dignity.

Whereas, if I was wrong about this, my parents could lose their biggest client. Their reputation. Their business.

Dum-de-dum, I hummed to myself. I always hum when I'm nervous.

'She's humming,' Mum said.

'She hums when she's nervous,' Dad agreed.

'What have we done?' Mum whispered.

A telephone rang.

It was Dad's. He pulled it out of his pocket and looked at the screen. 'It's him,' he said. 'Told you he was an early riser.'

We all watched as he put the phone to his ear.

'Ely!' he said. 'Must be the middle of the night in New York!'

There was a pause. Dad nodded along.

'Jetlag, right? It's a killer … Yes, yes. You're all set … Yep. We changed the logo colour just like you asked. Yep, to …' He paused, looked around at us, gave a huge, terrified wince. 'Cherry pink.'

There was a moment of intense suspense in which not a person in that kitchen breathed.

Then Dad's face broke into a mighty grin. 'You bet! And you were right! Cherry pink looks awesome!'

I sank down to the kitchen floor in relief.

'You bet! Have a great trip home!' Dad said. 'Bye! Don't call us! We'll call you!' And he shot the air with two imaginary cowboy guns.

We all cheered and applauded loudly. Then Dad checked that he'd actually hung up, and confirmed that he had, so we cheered again. They wanted to know *how* I'd known it was cherry pink and I just shrugged and said I'd overheard, which is true. So we ate our tacos, going over the whole thing many times, the way you do after a crisis has been averted.

Even Max joined in the celebrations and, after dinner was finished and the clearing up was done, he said quite happily, 'Better go home now.'

My brother looked across at him.

'Dude!' Max said.

'Dude,' Sebastian echoed. Then a number of extremely complicated expressions crossed my brother's face. My parents and I watched him. Despite Seb's mild genius with schoolwork, he can be a little slow at life. But he usually gets there in the end.

'I wonder,' Sebastian said softly, '*why* you had my essay on your USB.'

'Right?' Max tried, stumbling a little as he grabbed his bag. 'I wonder, too. Crazy!'

Sebastian gave him a long, hard look.

'See myself out, then?'

My brother nodded. 'You do that.'

We listened to Max's steps in the hall. The front door opened and closed. Sebastian drummed his fingers on the benchtop thoughtfully.

None of us spoke. He straightened up his shoulders, raised his eyebrows at us, tried for a small smile, and left the room.

(That's another family thing. We don't always spell out the obvious.)

However, I would now like to conclude this competition entry by spelling out the obvious to you.

Remember I said that choosing me for the prize would be a win–win?

Here is how it's a win for you.

You can *publish* this entry. (Please change the names though, to protect privacy.) I mean, look at it! *It proves that time travel is real!* This is *just* what you need to silence all the doubters! And make the Time Travel Agency™ legit!

The fact is, there is no question that I visited the past today. People say that there are two explanations for the 'illusion' of time travel that you guys offer. First, they say you use high-tech effects. But I changed my destination at the last minute! No way you could have rushed through the technology to reproduce my home and family within the half-second that I gave you!

And second, they say it's all in the subconscious: that people are just *imagining* their time travel.

Well, with the greatest respect to my subconscious, it is just not that sharp! No way it could have reproduced, with pinpoint accuracy, the events that occurred around my home while I was in my bedroom kissing a boy!

Generally, I have an extremely scatty, dreamy, absent-minded subconscious! It collects *absolutely* no details. It's probably not even listening *right now*! Which is why I can get away with insulting it like this.

So. The only explanation for the events I have outlined here is *time travel*.

Congratulations. To you and to Professor Raskdfjsa. (*Shrug*, she will say in reply.)

You have done it. You have invented time travel.

And this competition entry is the proof.

As for me and why I need to win?

Well, when we returned to school after the excursion today, Ms Watson said that, next week, we will have to do presentations on our journeys to the seventeenth century. For obvious reasons, I am not in a position to do such a presentation. Therefore, could I win the competition quite quickly please, and come back to the Time Travel Agency™ in the next couple of days so I can actually visit the seventeenth century and get my presentation sorted?

Sure, I could do some research and invent the whole thing. But would that be fair to my history class?

No.

And thus I bring this competition entry to a close. As promised, I have offered you a sound and noble reason with educational overtones. And I have taken considerable time to do it.

It is now 11.35 p.m. and I've been writing this since dinner. Mum and Dad are arguing in the stairway right now. I smile wisely, listening to them. Certain things, I think, cannot be changed. They simply are. This is the great, sad lesson I have learned today.

Farewell, my past. You, I cannot change.

Farewell, Noah Brackman and your voice.

I don't know why he kissed me. Maybe he couldn't figure out how to get out of my room after we'd finished the chemistry assignment? And that seemed the only way?

Anyway, although I have learned a terrible lesson, and most likely will never trust anybody again, I'll be okay! And it's good news that my brother knows the truth about his false friend, and my sister has her locker key, and my parents did not lose their business!

They are shouting quite loudly outside my door right now, my parents. 'But again!' my mother is saying. 'You did it *again*, that's the thing. I keep *telling* you not to do it!'

'I do it automatically!' Dad said. 'He knew it was a joke!'

'You *cannot* say to our biggest client, *Don't call us! We'll call you!* Clients *can* call you! Anytime they want! *That's* what you say to clients! *Call us anytime!*'

Ha.

That's what they're arguing about. The way Dad finished his phone call with the client and shot the air with the guns and so on. Well, what are you going to do? You can't really blame Dad. It's a family thing, like I said. We all do it to each other so often that sometimes we forget and do it to people outside the family. My friends at school have asked me to please not do it to them as they find it pretty weird and disconcerting. The point is, that —

Oh.

Do you know what I just —

The strangest thing just —

Okay, wait, I just —

I'm having trouble getting my head clear here.

But the strangest thing just happened. A memory came swooping across my brain. It was like a sheet flying off a clothesline in the wind and splashing over your face.

Here is the memory.

I am running down the stairs with Noah Brackman.

He has just kissed me.

We haven't said anything to each other. Just smiled at each other.

He's running late for work.

We stop at the door. I'm still smiling.

'Well, bye,' Noah says.

'Don't call us! We'll call you!' I say to Noah. And I shoot the air with cowboy guns.

Noah blinks.

He smiles again, nods slowly, then runs down my front steps.

Idiot, I think to myself, looking up at my hands in the air. And I go inside again, mortified about having played cowboys.

But I didn't just shoot the air.

I also said to Noah, *Don't call us! We'll call you.*

How exactly did that sound to him?

No. I'm being ridiculous, right? Reaching for slivers of hope? Like, maybe he hasn't spoken to me because I *told* him not to call me?

I've visited the scene of the kiss! I *saw* the way he acted! His eyes flew everywhere. He fidgeted. He wanted to get out of there!

Like I said before, he was never interested in the first place.

Unless.

Well, this sounds —

I mean, I was pretty nervous myself. That's why I did the weird, 'Don't call us!' shooting thing. I didn't have a clue what to say to a boy who had just kissed me. I was all atremble.

What if Noah was nervous, too?

And now that I think back, those darting eyes and fidgeting hands, they could have been nerves? And the way he looks around thoughtfully all the time? He could be *shy. He could be waiting for me to call him!*

    The reason he hasn't spoken to me could be that he thinks I'M NOT INTERESTED IN HIM!

    Wait.

    Just wait here a moment.

Okay, I'm back.

    I just sent a text to Noah. *Hiya, when can I see you again?*

    I can't believe I just did that.

    I honestly cannot believe it.

    I have just made myself ridiculous.

    I blame you, Time Travel Agency™.

    That is the most humiliating thing I have ever done. He is probably looking at it right now and shaking his head with contempt. He is deleting it. He is shuddering at the idea —

    Hang on.

    Okay. He just replied.

    I'm going to look.

    This is what he said: *Thought you were never going to call. Tomorrow arvo? Coffee? xxx*

    I believe I may be crying.

    Thank you, Time Travel Agency™. I will love you forever.

    (But I still need to win the five (5) free journeys. Thanks.)

    And *that* concludes my entry.

ABOUT THE AUTHORS

Danielle Binks is an editor, book blogger, literary agent, and youth literature advocate. The short story in *a #LoveOzYA* anthology is her first book publication, and marks her as an emerging voice in the Australian YA landscape.

Visit daniellebinks.com to find out more.

Amie Kaufman is the *New York Times* and internationally bestselling co-author of *Illuminae* and *These Broken Stars*. Her multiple award-winning books are slated for publication in over thirty countries, though none of them have made it to space yet. Amie did get to work as a storytelling consultant with NASA, though, which was as awesome as it sounds.

Visit amiekaufman.com to find out more.

Melissa Keil has lived in Minnesota, London and the Middle East, and now resides in her hometown of Melbourne. Her YA novels, *Life in Outer Space* and *The Incredible Adventures of Cinnamon Girl* have both been shortlisted for the CBCA Book of the Year and the Gold Inky awards.

Visit melissakeil.com to find out more.

Will Kostakis is the award-winning author of *The First Third* and *The Sidekicks*, but his real claims to fame are a Twitter spat with Guy Sebastian, and that time a member of Destiny's Child said his name.

Visit willkostakis.com to find out more.

Ellie Marney is a teacher and author of the Every series (*Every Breath, Every Word, Every Move*), a highly-awarded YA crime trilogy. She advocates for and promotes Australian YA literature through #LoveOzYA, hosts an online book club — #LoveOzYA book club — and is a Stella Prize Schools Ambassador. She lives near Castlemaine, Victoria, with her partner and four sons.

Visit elliemarney.com to find out more.

Jaclyn Moriarty grew up in Sydney, lived in the US, the UK and Canada, and now lives in Sydney again. She is the prize-winning, best-selling author of the Ashbury-Brookfield books (including *Feeling Sorry for Celia* and *Finding Cassie Crazy*) and the Colours of Madeleine trilogy (*A Corner of White, The Cracks in the Kingdom* and *A Tangle of Gold*).

Visit jaclynmoriarty.com to find out more.

Michael Pryor has published more than thirty novels and fifty something short stories. He is one of the co-publishers of *Aurealis*, a premier Fantasy and SF magazine. He has been shortlisted for the Aurealis Award seven times, and seven of his books have been CBCA Notable books.

Visit michaelpryor.com.au to find out more.

Alice Pung is a Melbourne author whose award-winning books include *Unpolished Gem*, *Her Father's Daughter* and *Laurinda*. She also wrote the Marly books for the Our Australian Girl series, and edited *Growing Up Asian in Australia* and *My First Lesson*.

Visit alicepung.com to find out more.

Gabrielle Tozer is the award-winning author of contemporary YA novels *The Intern*, *Faking It* and *Remind Me How This Ends*. Her first picture book, *Peas and Quiet* (illustrated by Sue deGennaro), hits shelves in 2017.

Visit gabrielletozer.com to find out more.

Lili Wilkinson is the award-winning author of ten YA novels, including *Pink*, *Green Valentine* and *The Boundless Sublime*. After studying Creative Arts at the University of Melbourne, Lili established the insideadog.com.au website, the Inky Awards and the Inkys Creative Reading Prize at the Centre for Youth Literature, State Library of Victoria. She has a PhD in Creative Writing, and lives in Melbourne with her husband, son, dog and three chickens.

Visit liliwilkinson.com.au to find out more.